THE SAINT AND THE SHADOWMAN

A.B. FINLAYSON

PARLIAMENT HOUSE PRESS

"Babe, I want to dedicate this book to Uncle Mike. Do I just write 'For Uncle Mike,' or do I write something longer, like how he's always been there for me, and believed in me, and how I might never have learned to read if he hadn't given me Misery by Stephen King when I was ten, and I honestly don't know how to thank him? Is that cool? Do you mind if it's not about you this time?"

"Sure, you know I'm his favourite anyway."

AUTHOR'S NOTE

This story takes place in the City of York (the old one, not the new one) and is a complete work of fiction. Names, characters, and incidents are either products of the author's overactive imagination or are used fictitiously...except for the names of my friends which I sprinkled in for a laugh. All of the places mentioned are very much real (and you can visit most of them) but the people are not. Any resemblance to real people is entirely coincidental. Although, as disclaimers go, it gets a little tricky with the ghosts. Most of *them* are real. That is, they are based on the real legends and myths contained within the walls of my favourite city.

The map at the front of this book was created by my friend, James Lockwood, for little more than a bottle of scotch. He's a legend.

As an animal lover I feel I should warn you that danger is present to animals in this story. Some demons take the form of dogs, and a few birds, squirrels, and a fox come to harm, as do a couple of cats. Although I can confidently assert the cats each have many lives left.

And finally, a word to the A.I. tech bros - not a stitch of A.I. touched this book so keep your grubby little hands to yourselves. I absolutely DO NOT give permission for my work to be used by any form of artificial 'intelligence'. Seriously, just write. You might find you like it.

The
The Museum Gardens
Th

Mad Alice Lane
Shambles
The Golden Fleece
Clifford's Tower
le Hill

PROLOGUE

They say bad things come in threes. They don't. Not really. We just tend to look for patterns and meaning to make our lives seem a little less shit. It's far easier to accept a bad run of luck if you can order a beer, lean on the bar with a sigh, and utter some meaningless cliché.

What can tha do when thi boots let watter?

Not a lot.

Bad things don't come in threes and neither do the good (third time's a charm is just as arbitrary). Not too long ago, it was considered bad juju to light three cigarettes from one match. That's not an omen; that's common sense. By the time the first two have been lit and the match passed along, the third is bound to burn a thumb. But the act of putting a number on something as strange as the concept of luck is a way for us to pretend we have a modicum of control. Maybe we say bad things come in threes as a way to cheat the system because at the very least we know that after two all the bad shit will soon be over.

It is the rule of three.

Stories are predicated on this theory.

The departure of a hero from their normal world is step one. Their initiation into some great mystery or challenge is step two.

Their return to the status quo a changed person is step three. One, two, three, and they all lived happily ever after.

Bollocks. We've been here before.

How do you return to the status quo when the change that happened to you is a sudden ability to speak to the dead?

How do you go about living a normal life when you know the bogeyman isn't just real but could be a ten-foot bastard with boar's tusks and enough strength to bring down a helicopter?

How do you go about paying the bills, buying groceries, going on dates, and taking your dog for a walk when your dog is the reincarnation of a dead office worker who likes chasing squirrels and talks during Netflix?

Forget bad things coming in threes, that's a whole lot of crazy wrapped up in one big package, and the psychiatrists are no help at all. Anxiety is an entirely different ball game when you know what's in the shadows. So, try as you might, you may as well drink. Just because you're paranoid doesn't mean they're not after you. Kurt Cobain said that. Smart man.

Either way you look at it, *this* story is the beginning of the end, or perhaps it is the end of the beginning. We'll have to wait and see. Trilogies are tricky beasts.

The question is, where do we start when we're already way past the beginning?

Most stories begin with the protagonist, but starting out slumped between two wheelie bins in the middle of a dank, piss-stained alley is probably not how a hero would like to be introduced.

So, let's not. Let's do it another way.

This story starts with a scruffy dog.

Because everyone likes scruffy dogs.

PART I
THE LONGEST NIGHT

CHAPTER 1

Steve walked warily down the street sticking to the shadows and avoiding the more built-up areas, which, in a city like York, was a tricky thing to do. York was one of those quintessentially British towns that was never meant to be as big as it became. Buildings sat upon buildings which sat above sewers that used to be streets. Over centuries, it was built up, built on, knocked down, and knocked through so many times that even the alleys have alleys.

What used to be servant's quarters were now luxury apartments, and buildings that once housed nobility were home to coffee shops, pound shops, and bakeries. In an area so small, ringed by a medieval stone wall so thick, the city teemed with life. Tourists and locals, students and workers, stag-dos, hen parties, and everything in between thronged the streets and jostled for position in the many pubs, clubs, cafés, and bars.

York was a city full of history. But often, on a hot Saturday such as this, when the skies are clear, the sun was shining, and the beer was flowing, York was a city full of drunks.

Steve was looking for one. A specific one. A needle in a haystack you might say, or a gin straw on the floor of a recently emptied racecourse. But Steve was looking for his best friend and had a pretty good idea where to find him...probably in the exact same spot he found him last week. It shouldn't be too hard, but with this being the longest day of the year—and a particularly hot one—the streets were a hazardous place for a wee dog.

Let's be clear from the outset, Steve *is* a dog. A small, scruffy, black and tan Yorkshire Terrier with big brown eyes and a tail that acts as a barometer for happiness, but he wasn't always a dog. Not so long ago, he wandered the city as a ghost. And before that... well, before that, he was a depressed office worker who let it all get to him. Now, he can barely remember what all the fuss was about.

Being a dog was much simpler and much more straightforward than being human. Dogs are joyful by nature and have the sort of courage most people can only dream of. For example, the old Steve would never have ventured into the city on a busy summer Saturday, but right now, his best friend needed him and so the choice was an obvious one.

The only problem...was people.

Who's a cute boy then? Oh, are you lost, little man? Come here, sweety!

Telling them to fuck off didn't work—only Arthur and the creatures from the other side could hear him—so running away was all he had. Although Steve *had* found that hiding behind the many beggars and homeless people allowed him to become damn near invisible. He wondered why as he paused beside a sleeping man outside a pound shop on Low Petergate.

Patiently, Steve waited. He waited for a gap in the crowd. A space wide enough for him to dart across the narrow street and into the doorway-sized tunnel called Lund's Court, formerly Mad Alice Lane.

~

High suns cast deep shadows, and the figure of a man stood in the shade of one at the top of the towering Gothic cathedral known as York Minster. It was the very heart of the city, a giant stone jewel set in the middle of searching streets and snickelways. They snaked like arteries through red-roofed buildings, parks, and trees—all leading to the same destination.

The sun baked the Minster gold, but the man was dressed all in black, a shade so deep and dark that it was not so much fabric as cloth cut from the world itself. He wore a hat pulled over his eyes, and his mouth was a thin line across a pale face. At his feet there was a book and a blade, the accoutrements of his employment.

The man had not moved for some time, and the stone grotesques had inched away from him over the tower roof. They were scared, and so they should be—the Shadowmen were fearful and single-minded.

Not quite human and not quite...not, the Shadowmen were something else, something in between. What they were was obedient. They existed with a singular purpose—to make things right.

They were the middle management of Death, and they *always* did as they were told. Although lately, this one had been thinking.

The Shadowman on the Minster roof stared at the book and tried not to notice the way it moved and trembled on the warm stones, almost as though something inside was struggling to get out.

He knew the feeling.

In his hand he clasped a fragment of ancient pottery, the pattern long since faded and worn away. He turned it over and over between pale, skeletal fingers. There was a word carved on one side. Just one... in a language long since forgotten by anyone but him.

Words had power.

Especially when they were names.

Steve darted through the moving forest of legs and vanished into the coolness of the alley. It was amazing how a few short steps away from the crowded city centre could transport you to a different world. Hardly anyone actually walked down Mad Alice

Lane despite the sheer number of photographs taken at the entrance. Whether they believed the stories or they just didn't like the cologne of stale piss and rotten cigarettes wasn't clear, but the narrow alley was a sanctuary amidst the bustle of a warm Saturday morning.

It didn't last long.

A door burst open and two men in chef whites threw bulging black bags into a skip, forcing Steve to dart behind a leaning tower of milk crates while the sound of a busy kitchen filled the small space. The door slammed shut just as suddenly, snapped off the noise, and left him in the strange solitude of the shaded snickelway.

Mad Alice Lane connected two of York's busiest streets, but the hum of the crowd fell into a low rumble as Steve made his way into the red brick-lined alley. The noises faded even more the deeper he went, though the smells did not.

For a creature with a nose as sensitive as his, Steve was not happy about this, but he carried on because there was one smell that filtered through to him above all the others. It was the smell of cigarettes, alcohol, and oddly enough, soap. His friend might've been on the proverbial struggle-street, but at least he hadn't let his personal hygiene slip too far into the gutter.

And here was Arthur.

Dark hair, dark eyes, unshaven. Not strikingly handsome, but at the very least he was interesting looking. In another time and place, Arthur might've been described as having a scruffy charm, but right now, here on the floor of the alley, he was just a mess. It was hard to cultivate a 'just got out of bed' aesthetic when you don't go to bed in the first place.

Arthur was fast asleep and snoring in the shadows between two wheelie bins. If you weren't looking for him, you'd walk right on by—the invisibility cloak of the down-and-out. Steve regarded his friend with a tilted head and an inside-out ear. This wasn't how he had expected their life in York to go, not by a long shot, but he knew it wasn't how Arthur expected things to turn out either. His friend would be appalled at this latest slump. Not just because he had passed out in an alley, but because it wasn't the first time.

Arthur wasn't overly arrogant or vain—he might even laugh this off in a few days—but Steve knew that inside, in the deep place that mattered to everyone, his best friend would be utterly ashamed.

The small dog barked loudly, and Arthur stirred. He yawned, stretched, and opened his eyes slowly.

"Where?" he began, but his eyes answered the unfinished question, and the headache filled in the blanks. "Fucksake," he grumbled and stretched his legs, the pins and needles of sleeping on concrete advertising their presence with all the subtlety of a second-hand car salesman.

Steve jumped forward and lifted his paws onto Arthur's thigh. He sniffed.

"You look like shit," the dog said.

"I feel like shit."

Arthur fumbled in the pocket of his suit jacket for his cigarettes, but the pack was empty. He scrunched it in his fist and threw it at the wall.

"Excuse me!" came a voice. This time it wasn't the dog.

Arthur blinked and looked up. The shadows in the alley were deep, but the sun was already high, and there were few places for anyone—or anything—to hide. He blinked again, and the ethereal form of Ann Barber swam into view.

To the rest of the world, she was Mad Alice. To Arthur and Steve, she was Ann. And the cigarette packet had flown right through her aproned bosom.

"Pick that up and put it in the bin," she admonished with a shake of her head. Ann Barber was almost transparent, and Arthur felt a sharp stab in the side of his head as he tried to concentrate and keep her in focus.

"Sorry," he mumbled.

Ann drifted closer, vanishing momentarily as she passed through a shaft of sharp sunlight and then reappeared right in front of his face.

A little old lady with curly hair, a long apron, and an even longer reputation, Ann Barber reminded Arthur of his granny. Only his granny wasn't a ghost who peeled pieces of flesh from her face to throw at passing tourists, but then, with a name like Mad Alice, keeping up appearances was part of the deal.

Reputations were important.

Ann reached out with a cold memory of a hand to pat Arthur gently on the cheek. "I keep telling you, lovely boy. You need to be spending your nights with the living, not the dead."

"He tried that a few weeks ago," Steve said with a grin, and Arthur shoved him away.

"Shush, you!" he groaned. "We don't talk about that!"

"Talk about what?" Ann asked, noting the embarrassed flush that crawled up Arthur's neck and across his face. The functions of the body were absolutely fascinating to the dead. Most of them still went through the motion of breathing, gasping, even crying, but was all a memory, a shade of what it meant to be alive. It was very easy to forget about things such as blushing when you lived a monochromatic existence without a central nervous system.

"Nothing," Arthur repeated, climbing to his feet, and groaning as the hangover scratched long fingers down the inside of his skull. He leaned against the wall and cracked his neck. "I...made a mistake."

"A good one, I hope."

"Hmm."

"Keep your little secrets then," Ann said with a smile, "but it won't do you any harm to spend the night with a warm young woman rather than passing out drunk down here with Mad Alice. *Alice, Alice, Alice,*" she sang, her voice drifting away. "*A-lease, A-lice, Mad Alice. She lost her mind, it's hard to find, the old lady scared our Alice!*"

The song died into an echo, and Ann vanished.

Ghosts did that.

Arthur and Steve barely blinked.

"What time is it?" Arthur asked when they realised she wasn't coming back.

Steve looked at him for a moment, then raised his paw and tilted his head. "Hang on," he said. "Let me check."

He looked at his paw and then at Arthur with one perfectly raised eyebrow.

"Smart arse," the man grumbled.

Steve barked.

The Shadowman glanced at the sky and shielded his eyes against the glare of the sun. As a creature of the dark places, he had almost forgotten how the heat felt as it pressed against him —oppressive and yet strangely seductive.

He had a nagging thought that momentous undertakings such as this shouldn't be taking place on so beautiful a day. There wasn't so much as a cloud in the sky. There should at least be a portentous storm. He looked to the horizon, but the world was pristine and shining in the summer sun.

North Yorkshire lay before him, a patchwork of clustered housing estates and rolling fields as far as he could see. Roads, rivers, and railways ran like arteries across the landscape, and he knew that it was beautiful. This was not something he had ever considered before. Not really. But the knowledge was there now. Doors had been opened, wheels had turned, and he wanted more. He closed his eyes against the glare of the brilliant blue sky and steeled himself to do what he knew must be done.

It was the only way.

The Shadowman had served his time, paid his dues a thousand times over. He never asked for this. Not once. He never had a choice and yet choice appeared to him to be the greatest factor of what it meant to be truly alive. The man called Arthur had taught him that when he spared his life. Before meeting Arthur, the Shadowman had never really considered that *his* was a life that *could* be spared.

Arthur showed him there was more than mere duty to a book and a blade.

The Shadowman stepped back into darkness as the birds raised a chorus high above the Minster. An ominous roll of thunder would have been nice, he thought, and then he vanished.

The cat that had been watching knew something was wrong, but it either didn't care at all or didn't care enough, which, for a cat, was basically the same thing. It stepped from behind the outcropping of stone it had been resting on (not hiding; cats never hide), and sauntered with indifference in the vague direction of the two objects the man had left on the ground.

The book appeared to be trembling, but it stopped when the cat sniffed it. In fact, everything paused. It was as though the world held its breath.

High above, two ravens hung like black dots in the piercing blue sky as the cat placed a paw on the cover and growled.

It was well known that cats were half in and half out of this world; they knew what was happening on both sides, though just because they knew didn't mean they felt inclined to pay any attention.

This cat stretched and then climbed onto the book where it scratched at the cover with kneading claws and settled down for a nap.

Thunder rumbled somewhere. But it wasn't here.

Arthur walked out of Mad Alice Lane and blinked in the bright light of the morning sun. It was already high in the sky, and the restaurants and bars along Swinegate had tables and chairs in the bustling street crammed with loud drinkers. Wide windows and French doors were thrown open to the world, and the smells and sounds of busy kitchens and bars floated through the warm air.

Arthur took his jacket off and rolled up the sleeves of his crumpled white shirt while Steve marked the bricks of the alley entrance as his. When the dog finished, he looked up at his friend.

"You really do look like shit," Steve said. "You've got eyes like piss-holes in the snow."

"I don't exactly feel tip-top."

"What now?"

"I need breakfast. Have you eaten?"

"Only what was left in the bowl."

Arthur knelt. Utterly ashamed. "Shit, I'm sorry, mate," he said. "That's really not cool. Come on, I'll buy us breakfast." He scooped Steve into his arms and they pushed into the crowd, ignoring the strange looks from people who only heard one side of the conversation.

The city swallowed the two friends in a mass of folk excited by the prospect of a full day drinking in the sun, but Arthur quickly grew quiet, lost in his own thoughts as he stopped on the corner of Back Swinegate, not quite sure where to go. Buffeted and pushed in all directions by the crowd, he felt momentarily rudderless as behind them the dark maw of Mad Alice Lane was swamped by tourists. The tall buildings were bathed in glorious golden sunshine, a mockery of how he felt inside.

It had been just here, on this very spot, that Arthur was first attacked by the Fetch. Nearly a year ago now, a dark shadow of malevolence straight from his nightmares (or a direct-to-DVD horror special) had chased him down this street and almost tore him apart.

This was where it all began.

There was the narrow tunnel leading to Barley Hall where he first spoke to Tom, one of the lost boys of York. Beyond that was Stonegate and Ye Olde Starre Inne, the former haunt of Lord Acaster and his cats. Everywhere Arthur turned there were ghosts. And ghosts of ghosts. York was full of them.

Nearly every street, church, and old building of the ancient city had a story of visitations or strange happenings that pulled in tourists from far and wide. But the other thing the city had plenty of was pubs. It was said that there were three hundred and sixty-five places to drink inside the walls of the small city, one for every day of the year, and maybe that made sense; it was a lot easier to see a ghost when you couldn't see straight, after all.

Alcohol was the cause of, and the solution to, all of Arthur's problems.

For him, the familiar streets had changed entirely just under a year ago when he started seeing ghosts as clearly as you or I see each other. To say it had taken some adjustment would be an understatement. Arthur was a logical man, a realist, and not someone prone to flights of fancy, but when the shadows spewed forth a dark doppelganger, evil witches unleashed boggarts and Jack-in-Irons on the world, ghostly Roman horses took ethereal shits in the street, and some strange Arthurian battle with a murderous hound of hell ensued, the bounds of logic and reason became a tad strained.

Hell, anyone would need a drink after that!

Arthur had tried the other route. He'd tried therapy. But telling trained professionals you can see dead people went about as well as you might expect.

He even told his parents…eventually…and they believed him. They had no choice, really, not after they were attacked by a barghest and a witch during Christmas dinner. And now his own mother could speak to ghosts and seemed to be having a wonderful time driving around the country, communicating between the living and the dead. But Arthur—Arthur was struggling. No matter which way he turned, he was haunted by ghosts and plagued by demons. These were phrases used by most people as metaphors but, for Arthur, they were quite literal. The spirits of the dead were drawn to him like moths to a flame, or, for those too far gone, they feared him and hid whenever he came near.

But ghosts weren't really the problem. No, not really. They were, after all, just people. Some were nice and some were dicks. If you were an arsehole in life, you were probably going to be an arsehole after you died. Not a whole lot changed after death. Arthur could deal with that.

It was all the other things that caused problems.

Spirits and sprites and creatures from the dark places. The

legends and myths that danced around the edges of reality and jumped across the gaps with no regard for the boundaries between fact and fiction.

If you *knew* ghosts were real...and hobgoblins were real and boggarts were real, and barghests were real, the most logical question became, what *else* was real?

You see, there was *another* other side.

An *after* after the after.

Perhaps even a heaven and a hell?

And, despite knowing about the bits in between, in this Arthur was just like everyone else...ignorant and alone.

Wherever he turned, he saw things other people did not. He heard voices other people could not. The sound of children's laughter was beautiful...unless you were in bed at 3:00 a.m. and didn't have kids.

Arthur had far more people around him than most, but he was entirely alone.

Steve licked his face.

Well, apart from Steve.

Steve was a good dog.

"Cute!"

Arthur looked up and caught the eye of a short woman with bright red hair as she pushed past him in the throng of people, a smile lighting her face. Their eyes locked for a moment, and she was gone, lost in the crowd as it flowed like a river into Swinegate.

Arthur was left with a sense of green eyes, red hair, pale freckled cheeks, and a simple grey T-shirt.

And dimples.

"Ooh, you just got bitten!" Steve said.

Arthur laughed.

"What?"

"You got bitten! You got a bite. You know...a nibble."

Arthur looked down at the strange little Yorkshire Terrier and smiled. It was the first genuine smile Steve had seen on his friend's face in quite a while, and his tongue fell out in excitement. He yapped happily.

"A nibble, huh?" Arthur said.

"Yep. She was into you, mate."

"More likely you," Arthur said, stepping into the flow of people and heading deeper into Back Swinegate where the crowds were slightly less dense.

"Yeah, probably. But there's not a lot I can do about it, so I guess you'll have to take one for the team."

Arthur laughed again and felt Steve's tail wiggle under his arm.

"She's gone now, mate. I'll never see her again."

"Shame. She was cute."

"Yeah, she was."

They turned the corner into Little Stonegate and threaded their way through the crowd and the dazzling silver tables and chairs that sparkled in the sun. Arthur glanced over his shoulder, looking for a glimpse of red hair, but there was none. Just a moving sea of people drifting in and out of restaurants, bars, and shops.

"Feels good, doesn't it?" Steve said.

"What does?"

"Looking at the living and not the dead."

"Yeah, you're right."

"Perhaps Mad Alice was onto something?"

"Don't call her that. Her name is Ann." Arthur caught the raised eyebrow from yet another passerby who heard him talking to his dog. "We've got to stop talking like this in public," he hissed.

Steve barked loudly and enthusiastically, drawing looks from all over the street.

"Dickhead," Arthur said with a grin.

"Tosser," Steve replied, his lips curled back and his teeth showing between shaggy brown and black hair. His tail beat furiously on Arthur's side. "You know," he said slowly, "if you don't find the girl with the red hair, you could always call—"

"Shut it!" Arthur cut him off, knowing exactly what his friend was about to say. Steve might not have had the tell-tale facial expressions of a human, but sometimes you just knew when someone was smirking.

"I'm just saying—"

"No!"

"But—"

"We don't talk about it."

"She was—"

"No! Bad dog!"

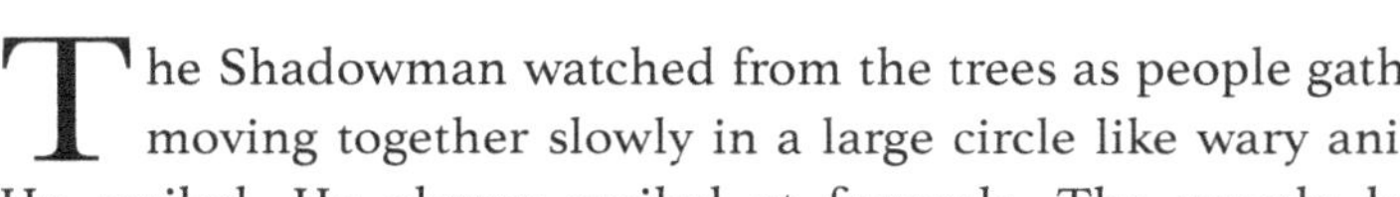

The Shadowman watched from the trees as people gathered, moving together slowly in a large circle like wary animals. He smiled. He always smiled at funerals. The people looked like him.

Sometimes if it was dark, or if the clouds gathered close around the mourners, he would walk among them, little more than a shadow. Sensed but never seen. He realised now what he liked about it. It was the camaraderie, the feeling of being part of something. He could imagine himself being one of them.

His...brothers...weren't exactly the social sort. And it wasn't as though there was an annual convention or office picnic to look forward to. Just eternity, moving people from one place to the next, opening doors and closing them, drawing lines through lists. His work meant he often crossed paths with others like him, but they were rarely keen to stop and have a natter.

The Shadowman stepped away from the shade of the oak and joined the stragglers who filtered awkwardly around the edges— those too scared, too upset, or too nervous to get too close to that ominous hole in the ground.

Everyone wore dark glasses and dark suits, and the Shadowman slipped between them as he worked his way to the front. Music played and filled the sombre morning with calling guitars and drums. He tuned into the lyrics as the singer began. He'd spent millennia observing, and he had never really listened to a song. He thought it was about time.

Smile, childhood memories, and the bright blue skies.

Interesting. He looked up and tilted his hat backward, allowing the sun to warm his face. It felt good. He wanted more. He had not wanted anything for as long as he could remember, but lately he had been…feeling. It was unusual and complicated. But today was an auspicious day, and he was almost sure he knew what he was doing.

Almost.

People around him sobbed loudly as a coffin was brought through the crowd, and he turned to watch, a smile creasing his face as his fingers worked on the pottery shard in his hand. The singer talked about being a child and hiding, waiting for the thunder and rain to pass.

As he stepped toward the hole, he considered once more that thunder would be far more appropriate than the glorious sunshine that instantly evaporated tears from cheeks.

Not his cheeks, of course. Never his. Not yet, anyway.

He watched as the coffin was gently released by six crying men, and the machinery took over, the straps taking the weight and lowering the person to their final resting place. He knew that was bollocks, of course. There wasn't a *person* in there. They were long gone. It was just meat. But meat could be useful if you knew what to do with it. He stepped forward, completely unseen even in the crowd, and held his hand over the hole.

There was a moment of hesitation.

Just a moment as he stood beside a kneeling man in a leather jacket. A man who sobbed beside the grave, unable to leave, unable to let go, watching the box vanish into the dark.

But it was only a moment.

The Shadowman opened his fist and the pottery fell, bouncing off the wood and vanishing into the shadow of the soil.

It was done.

Arthur felt a lot better with a warm Gregg's steak bake and a can of Coke inside him, though he couldn't shake the intense feeling of shame at falling asleep and waking up in an alley, not to mention his neglect of Steve, who was now tucking into his second large sausage roll with disconcerting enthusiasm for such a small dog.

They sat side by side on a wooden bench against St. Samson's Church on the aptly named Church Street and let the sun warm their bodies. The world seemed much nicer in the sunshine, but then, York was one of those cities that wore all the seasons well, and it was hard not to feel lifted by the carnival atmosphere of a busy day. The over-exuberant sound effects of Steve eating a too hot pastry roughly the size of his leg filtered through to Arthur, and he laughed at his small companion as he wrestled the sausage roll and growled at it. There had been some steep learning curves for the two friends in the last few months, and life hadn't exactly gone according to plan, but when did it ever? Arthur had struggled a lot more than he expected trying to fit back into the normal routine.

Normal was quite a thing to wrap your head around when you spent most of your evenings talking to dead people.

Work was good, though. Work was easy, and Arthur knew he should be grateful for that, but each day, as he headed into the basement map room of the city planning office, he couldn't shake the feeling that there was more to life than this, that there were far more important things he could, and *should*, be doing.

This was, of course, the exact same reaction shared by every single person in the history of the world who had ever worked for the council, but for Arthur, it was slightly unique. He did, in fact, know there was more to life than this.

Agent Mulder was right; the truth *was* out there.

The young man sighed and glanced at Steve, who growled at his food. Arthur couldn't even remember the last time they went for a proper walk down by the river. Most days they just sauntered around the grassy banks below the city walls on Lord Mayor's Walk with Steve running off into the undergrowth to take care of business while Arthur had a smoke. He carried the requisite bags with him, of course, but they were just for show. That had been part of the deal with Steve. It was all well and good clearing up after your pet, but when your dog could talk to you, scooping their warm shit into a thin plastic bag took on a whole new dimension.

Arthur looked at Steve and smiled, his mind made up. He owed him.

"Do you want to go for a walk today?" he asked.

Steve barked loudly and wagged his tail. He always barked when he was excited. Arthur wondered if one day the remains of his human life would fade away, and he'd just be a dog like any other. He hoped not. He liked having someone around who understood. He laughed as his friend's tongue bounced in juddering, excited pants, and so he cleared up the paper bags and got to his feet, brushing the crumbs from his legs. Steve jumped to the floor and ran around in a tight circle. Arthur laughed.

"Come on, mate. Let's go home, and I'll get changed. Then we can hang out by the river. It's a perfect day for it."

And it was a perfect day. Warm and clear without a cloud in the sky. A gentle breeze to soothe the heat the city bathed in. Nothing ominous or portentous about it at all. Just lovely, in fact.

The long summer day stretched endlessly in front as ravens drifted high above and cats sunned themselves on the rooftops of the city. The world was full of hope and possibility.

So that was nice.

The Shadowman watched as the first handful of soil was tearfully dropped onto the coffin. It fell like rain on the polished wood, and he smiled as the shard of pottery vanished beneath dirt and flowers. He would have liked to stay and watch how it all panned out, but for once, he had no time.

CHAPTER 2

Midsummer's Eve was the longest day of the year and marked the summer solstice in the northern hemisphere. It was the time when the sun seemed to slow in the sky and pause for a moment before making a stately descent into the latter half of the year. It had been celebrated in countless ways for centuries, long before events were ever organised by committee or invitations accidentally sent to everyone on Facebook.

The dazzling sun glistened from the statue of Emperor Constantine as he looked over the mass of tourists and smiled benignly for his millionth selfie beneath the Minster. The bells of St. Michael's rang out to mark the middle of the day, and as the sun intensified, the heat forced people to find shade and shelter in one of the many dark pubs, or—because this was England and the sun was a rare treat—they basked half-naked in beer gardens and parks, sweating profusely as their skin quickly cooked in the unremitting heat.

Constantine knew how they felt. Hundreds of years exposed to the elements had turned his bronze body blue, and he had lost track of how many kids called him Papa Smurf.

He had no idea what that meant. He was a statue.

The real emperor had been dead for a very long time, and there was no evidence to suggest he ever came back for a visit. Not that it mattered. They say a man never truly dies while his deeds are remembered, and this man's deeds shaped the entire world.

The giant church beside him was a testament to that.

At the height of summer, it was once said that the Oak King and the Holly King changed rule as the first half of the year ended and the latter half began. The spreading wave of Christianity—newly legalised by the emperor—stole this idea for itself, as it did with many other things. And so, Midsummer's Day became the Feast Day of St. John.

"I decrease as he increases," the Baptist supposedly said of his cousin, which was pretty much the same idea, but that's the thing with plagiarism: give it enough time, and no one remembered who said what first.

Some people, however, had long memories.

Some *countries* had long memories.

Yorkshire had a *very* long memory.

Just because the festival was usurped by the church didn't mean it was forgotten.

Midsummer's Eve was a time when the boundaries were thin, and the rules and bonds were weak. Evil sprites and the tricks of the fae became common as they ran rampant through the veil, and so it was important to form protections.

Hag stones, witch's bottles, horseshoes, and iron. Not to mention salt and daisy wheels.

But no one really believed in that sort of stuff anymore, did they? So, it would probably turn out alright.

Probably.

High above the emperor, the Shadowman returned. The cat knew he was there but chose to ignore the man and pretended to be asleep.

This, for once, would not serve the poor creature well.

The man in black stepped from the shadows and into the bright sunlight, kneeling in front of the book and the blade...and the cat. He tilted his head and regarded the small creature. He did not like them. He never had. Too nosy, too bossy, too arrogant.

Now, dogs. He liked dogs.

He looked to the sky and squinted. Time was ticking. He made a small hissing noise, but the cat ignored him. He said "shoo" but to no effect. He glanced to the sky again and cursed.

If it makes you feel better to imagine that his next actions were done with a heavy heart and no small amount of regret, then feel free—whatever makes things easier, but the Shadowman barely blinked as he grabbed the surprised creature by the back of the neck and tossed it over his shoulder.

Unfortunately for the cat, they were just that little bit too close to the edge of the tower.

As the poor creature tumbled and spun in the rapidly decreasing sky, it had time for one last thought.

Bastard.

"So, where are we going?" Steve asked Arthur as his friend dried himself on an already damp towel in front of the mirror. The small dog sat on the large bed, barely able to keep still. His tongue lolled as he panted, and his tail wagged in a blur. He made occasional jumps and turns just for the hell of it. Life was wonderful.

"Well, it's just after midday," Arthur said, looking up at the clock on the bedroom wall. He was really proud of the clock. Two lightsabres pointed upward on a stylised Millenium Falcon. It was something his ex, Wendy, would never have approved of. "We won't bother with the car. I reckon we go for a long walk down the river. Maybe grab a bite to eat later and go hang out at the gardens."

"Museum Gardens?" Steve asked with an excited bark.

"Sure," Arthur laughed, knowing full well how much his friend loved it there. As if to prove his point, Steve jumped off the bed and then bounced straight back up again, barking madly while turning in a tight circle.

"Calm down, bud!"

"Do you think there'll be squirrels?"

"There's always squirrels."

"Yes! Get in!"

Arthur pulled on a pair of jeans as Steve leaped to the floor and raced around the house. Blue jeans and a black T-shirt. Apart from the suits he wore for work, he'd pretty much worn the same clothes for as long as he could remember and saw no reason to change, even on a baking hot summer day. It probably had something to do with the number of times he'd watched *Wayne's World* as a kid.

Arthur sat on the edge of the bed to pull on his trainers, feeling infinitely better after the shower, though still tired and a little sore from the uncomfortable sleep on the floor of the alley. He shook his head as another flash of shame washed over him. *Imagine if Dad found out*, he thought. Sleeping in the street between two bins like a tramp. What a loser. What a drunk.

But that wasn't it. Not really. He just liked talking to Ann. She understood him. She listened. And when they got together, he lost track of time. Oh, sure, he'd had a few beers. It was Friday night after all, but as each of his workmates drifted off to late bars and clubs or paired up with one another, he invariably found himself heading off, alone, toward Mad Alice Lane.

Last night he got there a bit earlier than usual because Eileen had started buying him shots, and that never ended well. So, he and Ann spent hours together—setting the world to rights, as his mother would say.

Arthur sighed and lay back on the bed, groping with an outstretched hand for the cigarette packet hidden somewhere among a pile of books on the bedside table. There were books everywhere in Arthur's flat. A small desk in the corner was buried under a mountain, and even the floor was covered in neat stacks of journals and magazines. Every subject from magic and folklore, ghosts and Arthurian legends, to psychology, cognitive brain therapy, and the history of medicine—Arthur had it all.

He pulled a cigarette from the pack and placed it between his lips, pointing it straight up. Arthur clicked his fingers, and a purple flame burst to life on the end of his thumb. He lit the cigarette while staring at the ceiling and took a deep draw, dropping his hand to his side and letting the magic flicker and die. Before the ash grew much bigger, he sat up and looked for the ashtray. It sat on top of a colourful, battered copy of *The Colour of Magic* by Terry Pratchett, and Arthur thought once again how strange it was that fiction gave him answers other places could not. The closest he'd come to reading anything even remotely resembling his own experiences wasn't in scholarly tomes and academic papers, but rather between the bright, colourful covers of science fiction and fantasy novels.

He picked the book up and turned it over. One of his favourites. The browning, dog-eared pages were testament to how many times he had read it. He turned his palm upward and summoned a small ball of crackling flame with barely a thought.

It turned out the colour of magic was purple.

Arthur could summon flames that burned everything except his own flesh. He could make lights and cast fireballs. And he could draw ghosts to him like a candle in a graveyard. It was undeniably excellent, but also, somewhere deep down, Arthur couldn't help feeling that it all seemed a little *too obvious.*

The magic felt like an electric charge, like static, but he could change the size and structure of it at will. And that too seemed a little on the nose. But the more he practised, the easier it became, and by now it was basically second nature.

Steve said he might be a wizard, but Arthur couldn't wrap his head around that. Even with all the craziness of the last year, he was just an ordinary bloke who drank too much, smoked too much, and liked watching Netflix with his dog. And anyway, anyone who wandered around calling themselves a wizard was either really into D&D, an actor, or a bit of bellend.

Arthur watched as Steve raced past the open door of the

bedroom, wrestling a squeaky toy with his teeth. He smiled. The whole situation was so strange, and he had no real answers, but he wouldn't change this. Not Steve.

Steve was awesome.

"Come on, bud," he said, standing up and striding through to the kitchen, putting his wallet, phone, and cigarettes in his pockets. "Walkies."

Steve didn't even call him out on the condescending dog talk. He was too excited.

~

The two friends walked together onto the wide terrace of King's Staith beside the slow-moving water of the River Ouse. It was packed. The famous King's Arms pub had a queue lining the wall, and people sat shoulder to shoulder on the warm stone bank as the sun glistened off the surface of the river.

Red pleasure boats moved slowly up and down the water, and large ferries packed with tourists waved at the drinkers who waved back, shielding their eyes from the glare of the sun.

Birdsong lifted above the noise of the engines and the gentle splash of the river, and the laughter and murmur of hundreds of people enjoying too much beer in too much sun rippled over it all.

Arthur paused and lit a cigarette, letting the sun warm his face and the noise of the city wash over him. He loved it.

"I was going to suggest a beer," he said, kneeling down to Steve. "And a bag of pork scratchings," he added quickly as the little dog whined, "but I don't fancy that queue, so let's find somewhere else." Steve barked and jumped up to lick Arthur's face.

They ambled along the riverbank in no hurry to get anywhere. Steve darted in and out of the metal fence poles and raced over to scare a group of seagulls, yapping and leaping with excitement. The birds were twice the size of the small dog, but they obliged his enthusiasm by lifting lazily into the air and settling down again once he moved on.

The offices and old factories on the far side of the river seemed to rise directly from the water, and Arthur looked from dark window to dark window. It was a habit he had picked up in the last few months—checking in the dark places to see things other people might not see, but all was normal.

The sun beat against the bricks while the water lapped against the banks, pushed to the edges by the movement of the boats. It was just an ordinary day. The city was a hive of people and vehicles, growing quieter as they moved further away from the bustling centre. The buildings on their left turned from pubs and restaurants into a row of Edwardian townhouses, and once again the city seemed to fall into a different time.

Arthur could imagine Ann Barber walking this same path, or Sarah Brockelbank racing along looking for her missing keys. Both women lived hundreds of years earlier and yet Arthur could picture them in these streets as clearly as anyone else.

Although it was easier to imagine the past when you regularly see the dead.

Arthur realised his thoughts were drifting again and brought them back with an effort, snapping his eyes away from the dark windows and shadows. *If you go looking for trouble, you'll find it,* his mum said to him the last time they spoke. And, as ever, she was right.

The grass was green, the sky bright blue, the water as clear as it was ever going to get. A young woman cycled past in a summer dress singing quietly to herself, and couples walked arm in arm or sat together in the sun. The day seemed full of potential and bright possibility, and with Steve excitedly yapping at the seagulls, Arthur felt a shadow lift from him that he hadn't entirely been aware of in the first place.

Sure, life might be strange, and talking to the dead took a bit of a toll on the old mental faculties. But right now, in this moment, he was happy.

Although, because he was Arthur, this thought was immediately followed by another: how long would it last? Almost absent-mindedly, his fingers found their way to the worn piece of paper in his jeans pocket, and yet another part of his mind folded its arms and smirked at him. How long was it going to be before he did something to force the issue?

Not bloody long, knowing him.

There was something disconcerting about a newly covered grave. Some graveyards place turf over the top when they are finished, but most just let the grass grow naturally. There is a powerful solemnity in that bare rectangular patch of freshly disturbed ground. It speaks of the rawness of pain and the need for time to grow and to adapt.

It is also really, *really* disconcerting when the soil begins to move.

Mr. Gabriel thought he had seen everything the game had to throw at him. He had personally tended hundreds of graves with dignity and care for forty years, never once faltering in his duty or shying away from the more macabre elements of the job. He understood decomposition and soil subsistence and so had created a smooth mound to counteract the effect. But he realised now, as the earth moved, and grasping fingers reached for the sky, that he might not know everything.

A cool breeze touched his skin then vanished with the memory of a shiver.

Mr. Gabriel blinked at the sensation, then looked behind him. He blinked again, staring at the familiar figure lying on the grass, clutching its left arm. His mouth formed an *O* of shock and recognition.

Funny. He never felt a thing.

"Well," he said, his voice echoing in a strange manner, "thas a queer going on an' no mistake."

Ligh above the city, the birdsong changed. The melodic whistles and calls of starlings and thrushes was drowned out by the harsh caws of ravens. The summer birds retreated to the trees and fell silent, while above them the dark shapes swooped and circled.

Unfortunately, it was the dark shapes at the base of the trees the little birds should have been paying attention to. Small, searching hands reached through gaps that should not have existed and dragged many unsuspecting victims into the shadows.

A poetic, single feather may have floated gently to the ground to mark this mysterious passing. It may have. You can imagine it if you wish.

CHAPTER 3

"Where are we going?"

"For a pint."

The two friends walked along the far bank of the river, just over Skeldergate Bridge, heading back toward the city. Arthur rarely came this way, and Steve wondered what he was up to, although he had a pretty good idea. His friend kept reaching for his back pocket. It was an action the observant little dog knew well.

"Who's on the list?" he asked in a carefully measured voice. A group of teenagers cycled past, and Arthur stayed quiet.

"Sorry, mate," he said, as the group rode on, "couldn't speak in front of the kids."

"Where are we going?" Steve repeated.

"Just across the road here, come on."

Arthur jogged across the street and Steve followed. The little dog was having fun, that was true; he did love a walk, after all, but he recognised the look on Arthur's face and a seed of doubt crept in.

And anyway, he'd been promised squirrels.

Even running to keep up with Arthur—something he normally loved—Steve couldn't bring himself to wag his tail. And when they stopped outside a small pub tucked away in the middle of the sweltering street, the seed grew.

The building baked in the sunlight and looked completely out of place, nestled as it was among the offices and flats. A triangular roof reached to the sky, and the top half of the building was clad in black wood while the bottom was the same red brick as all the other buildings in the street, but that was where the similarity ended. Hanging baskets with bright purple flowers sweated in the heat, white latticed windows peered into the world, and the old-fashioned hanging sign refused to creak ominously as there wasn't a breath of wind to speak of.

Despite this lack of theatre, Steve sat on his tail and whined. He didn't like the look of it at all.

This was the type of inn that should've been isolated on a dusty moorland, enticing unwary travellers with the promise of food and comfort, a single light on the steepled wall acting as a beacon. But here it sat, snug among the offices, basking in the afternoon sun, the small door a dark portal to the promise of shade and refreshment within.

Arthur didn't hesitate.

He vanished inside the Cock and Bottle with a whistle, and Steve tucked his tail in and followed, grumbling under his breath.

It took a while for their eyes to adjust, but the inside of the pub was unexpectedly spacious, and some of Steve's misgivings fell away. A large open-plan room of exposed brickwork and thick wooden beams spread out before them. A sandstone fireplace sat dormant in one long wall, framed by more large wooden beams. Polished tables and seats with bright red cushions were everywhere, about half-full of happy punters, some watching sports on TV, others talking quietly, and a small group of teenagers playing the fruit machines.

Arthur ordered a pint of Deuchars IPA and a bag of pork scratchings from the bored-looking barman who tore his eyes away from one of the many big-screen TVs just long enough to hand the drink over and accept his money. The man went back to his re-run of a Manchester United game without a word and

Arthur turned to the bar, taking a welcome gulp of cool beer. The temperature here was much better. A soft breeze filtered in from some hidden air-conditioning and instantly cooled the skin.

Looking around, Arthur saw a vacant seat in front of the strange-looking fireplace. He nodded to Steve, and they walked across the room, weaving between tables and apologising for momentarily blocking the TV. The carpet changed to flagstone, and Arthur ducked under the large oak frame of the hearth. The dark posts and mantel were festooned with brass hangings and upturned horseshoes. It was an odd little place, Arthur thought as he took a seat, looking around. The two tables and the bench were almost inside the fireplace itself. The grate was in the wall, but they were *under* the frame, deep in the shadows beneath the low canopy. He imagined it was the best seat in the house during winter, but right now, people were more concerned with the TV screens or flashing fruit machines.

Arthur smiled. He could see everything from here. People-watching. He loved it. Under the table, Steve headbutted his shins, and Arthur opened the bag of pork scratchings, bending low to pass one to Steve.

"Go steady," he said in the singsong voice he used when talking to Steve in public. Just another dog doing dog things.

"What are we doing here?" Steve asked as he made short work of the salty snack. His tail wagged and he licked his lips. He loved pork scratchings.

"Having a pint," Arthur said in a whisper. There was no one in earshot, but it didn't do well to draw attention to the fact he was talking to his dog. They had done that far too many times in the last half a year. The reactions were always the same: amusement at first, then slight nervousness with a hint of 'shuffling away from the crazy man.'

"You know what I mean," Steve hissed.

Arthur looked at him and wordlessly handed over another pork scratching. Steve took the bribe. No regrets. Once devoured, he sat back and stared at his friend, but Arthur's eyes were already somewhere else, fixed on the other side of the low-ceilinged room.

Steve followed his gaze and sighed. He didn't need to ask again. The ghost that had just walked into the bar answered all the questions he had.

$\sim$

"Not by daylight nor by night. Not by weapons of steel or flight. Not in the sky nor on the earth, no death shall come from mortal birth." The Shadowman didn't even know he was speaking. The words just tumbled over his lips as though in a trance. They weren't necessarily in English either, but he had spent so long in Yorkshire the language came almost naturally to him, so the words danced and skipped around. He sat now, basking in the sun at the very top of the west tower of the Minster. His legs were crossed and he slowly rocked back and forth, staring at the book and the blade. He lifted his face to the open sky and let the sun warm his pallid skin. "Not by daylight," he whispered, "nor by night."

High above, the heavens moved, and the ravens tumbled and spun, fighting and twisting in a dark mass.

$\sim$

Steve knew it was a ghost for a number of reasons. The first was the smell. Slightly metallic—like tin or copper in the air. The second was the clothes. Even the most enthusiastic re-enactment society wouldn't wear something so flamboyant. The third was the fact that the exceptionally well-dressed man had entered the bar from the toilets without bothering to use any of the doors.

Despite years of firsthand experience with the afterlife, there was something about this particular man that caused Steve to pause and then jump onto the seat next to Arthur to get a closer look.

Arthur, for his part, took a slow sip of beer and watched intently over the glass. The figure across the room stood between two smartly dressed women enjoying a bottle of white wine at the bar. They both wore trouser suits and had their hair tied back, though due to the heat of the summer, their jackets rested on a vacant seat as they sat side by side in pristine shirts, laughing and joking.

The man stared lasciviously at their chests as they drank from frosted glasses, completely unaware of his presence. Arthur watched as he reached out, and the woman on the left shivered. He was too far away to hear what they were saying, but he saw the ghost laugh as the woman put her glass down and retrieved her jacket from the seat.

She stood and excused herself, pulling the jacket over her shoulders as she made her way to the toilets. The repugnant ghost followed, drifting through tables, people, and chairs before vanishing through the wall with a flourish.

Arthur fidgeted in his seat and patted Steve a little too hard. Steve growled. It was not directed at Arthur. But what could they do? It wasn't as though Arthur could burst into the ladies' room to warn the woman of a strange man in...the ladies' room. But the thought of the creepy ghost in there with the unsuspecting woman turned Arthur's stomach. If something was right, it didn't matter if you made a prat of yourself—it was still right.

He drained his pint and stood up. It wasn't like he drank in here often; if he got thrown out, he got thrown out. He'd just add it to the list.

Arthur looked at Steve, and the little dog nodded. They started across the pub just as the door burst open and the red-faced woman reappeared. She moved quickly to the bar and said something to her friend before turning on her heel and rushing out of the pub. The other woman looked confused but gathered her jacket and raced after, leaving their unfinished drinks where they were.

The ghost of the fat man appeared through a fruit machine and danced across the carpeted floor before he too vanished into the bright sunlight.

Arthur paused in the middle of the room and then started when the barman coughed.

"You all right, mate?"

"Erm, yeah," Arthur mumbled. "I, erm, I thought I knew that woman, but she left before I had chance to ask."

"Right."

"I'll have another pint, please," Arthur said to cover his awkwardness. He took the drink and collected his change before making his way back to the table, aware that the barman was watching him the whole time.

It was always like this. Always so bloody hard to keep the two worlds apart. Barmen watch suspicious people anyway, and there's nothing quite so suspicious as a man staring at something no one else can see, then talking to himself about it. He might as well go the whole hog and juggle fireballs.

He'd tried that once. It didn't go well. It ended up with a very upset Steve and a burn mark on the couch.

Arthur was about halfway down the next pint when the ghost reappeared through a different wall. The rotund man scratched at his crotch as he walked over to the bar, lifting the gut with one hand and rummaging with the other. Steve growled again, and Arthur felt a hot prickle of anger run up his neck. The ghost stopped in front of the barman and then leaned out to a cardboard tub of straws standing beside the till. With barely a pause, he flicked the box, and the straws spilled onto the floor. Arthur sat up straight, and Steve tilted his head to the side, one ear turning inside out with a pop. As far as they knew, the only ghosts who could interact in such a way were poltergeists, but the effort was so great, they ended up sacrificing any semblance of physical form in order to do so.

Both Arthur and Steve hated poltergeists. They were a bugger to deal with. Invisible, interfering bastards.

The barman swore, then slowly walked around the bar to retrieve the straws, one eye still on the match. As he bent down, the ghost turned to the two half-full wine glasses still on the bar and leaned over them. Arthur's eyes grew wide. The ghost appeared to be sniffing. That was new. As far as he was aware, ghosts had no sense of smell.

They shouldn't, realistically, have a sense of anything, but nothing in the last year had followed what Arthur might have considered to be "the rules." As far as he could tell, there weren't any. Oh, sure, the Shadowmen—whenever they appeared—bleated on and on about rules and the guidelines, often complaining that Arthur was breaking half of them, but there didn't appear to be a whole lot of consistency.

He looked closely at the ghost. The man was tall and portly with a large bulbous nose and hanging, jowly cheeks. His fat neck strained against the huge lace ruff fastened tight beneath his many chins. Folds of silk cascaded over each shoulder, and expensive furs stretched over his protruding gut. Arthur wondered once more how the image of a ghost was decided. He knew who this ghost was. The man had been handsome at one point—distractingly so according to the texts, famous for it in fact—but the spectre at the bar, seemingly trying to push his ethereal face through the glass and thrusting his tongue into the remaining wine, was anything but.

Damn the rules.

Arthur reached under the table and clicked his fingers.

Purple fire rose from his thumb, and the ghost's head instantly snapped in his direction. The man stared toward Arthur from behind the two wine glasses, though Arthur was careful not to meet his gaze. He wanted to see what the man would do first.

Steve growled as the ghost rose and drifted through the bar toward them, searching for whatever it was that arrested his attention. He came close to Arthur, almost touching the table. Arthur didn't react, he just picked up his glass, took a small drink, and put it down a little further away.

Beneath the table, the purple flame still flickered. He could sense the interest from the ghost, the confusion. Steve's growl changed pitch and then Arthur began to sing. Quietly. Just loud enough for the ghost to hear.

"Georgie Porgie Puddin and Pie. Kissed the girls and made them cry..."

He didn't get any further. The reaction was instant. The ghost stood up straight and glared at Arthur, who didn't look away. There was a brief flicker of confusion and surprise as their eyes locked, then the ghost's face twisted into a sneer, and shadows spilled into the room. They came from the dark places beneath tables and behind doors, leaching over the floors and walls like pools of water. Lights flickered and went out, the TV screens blinked into black, and amidst the rising complaints of the patrons, the ghost snarled at Arthur.

"I'll make you cry! You blasted scoundrel!"

He lashed out, but Arthur had been waiting for it. His own hand shot up from the table and caught the ghost by the wrist. Everything paused as the shock registered on the man's face and his mouth gaped open.

"George Villiers?" Arthur asked before the ghost could speak. The man nodded, dumbstruck, his eyes wide and staring as Arthur continued to look directly at him, the first clear and distinct eye contact in centuries.

"Take a seat and don't make a scene," Arthur said, then let go before anyone in the bar noticed the strange action, though he needn't have worried, as all eyes were on the barman, who was ineffectually trying to get the TVs to work.

The ghost of George Villiers, second Duke of Buckingham, stepped back, and with some difficulty, sat on the opposite side of the small table. The lights turned on, and the TVs came back to life. Around the walls, the various fruit machines once more became a riot of colour and noise, and a few customers grumbled and laughed, but soon, all was back to normal.

Well, as normal as a pub can be with a dead duke, a talking dog, and Arthur Crazy sharing a table.

The young man in the leather jacket and ripped jeans stood beneath the gargantuan Minster and stared at the famous Five Sisters Window of the west tower. His clothes, skin, and hair were covered in a fine layer of fresh dirt, which went a little way to mask the chemical smell that seemed to emanate from him, but people didn't come close enough to notice that. There was already something about him. Something different. Something off. The way he stared. The way he stood. The hint of makeup masking a pallid complexion.

Parents pulled their children back and gave him a wide berth, but the crowds that had gathered began to notice and take interest in the way that crowds do.

A circle formed as more and more curious onlookers wondered what the strange man was looking at. Phones snapped photos, and nervous giggles filtered through the crowd in the anticipation of another street performer.

Some wondered if it had anything to do with the cat. Police tape still fluttered in the gentle breeze as someone worked inside a small tent to clear away the remains of the poor dead animal, but the attention of the people had shifted now.

Suicidal cats were old news.

The man moved.

The crowds parted as he walked up the steps of the cathedral. He stopped for a moment beneath a statue of Adam and Eve, gripped the stone in cold hands, and began to climb.

High above, the Shadowman reached out and grasped hold of the black-handled knife. The blade glistened like oil in the dazzling sun. The noise and screams and cheers from far below came to him slowly, filtered and diluted by distance, but everything seemed to be slow now. His movements were dreamlike, as if he was pushing his limbs through treacle, and he felt the first thrill of hesitation, of doubt.

The Shadowman turned the blade over and back in his hand, knowing that this would be the last time he ever held it. He couldn't remember a time before the book and the blade, and he never used to think about a time after. He never expected there to *be* an after.

Time.

Time was everything. It was all that mattered.

"What manner of thing is this?" George Villiers asked. "How art thou to see me so brazenly during the day? To speak? To touch?"

Before Arthur could reply, the duke's eyes widened further and he sat back, drawing a lace handkerchief to his mouth. "Oh, what a prodigal I have been of that most valuable of possession, time. Hast thou come for me at long last?"

He looked Arthur up and down, and his nose twisted into a sneer. "But you?" he said, suddenly losing some of the airs and graces of his speech. "It can't be. I can't have waited all these long years for *you*."

"Charming," Arthur said, taking a slow drink. "I'm not what you think I am, but I can do what you think I can do." On the seat beside him, Steve scratched behind his ear as he worked this out. "If you want me to," Arthur continued, "I can set you free."

"Free!" snorted the giant man. "Free from what? From being able to do as one desires *when* one desires. Free..." He paused suddenly, and his mouth split into a wide smile. It was not pleasant. "Hold hard, sir! A moment! Thou speakest my name. Thou knowest who I am!" He sat back and practically glowed with self-importance. "Hundreds of years hence and men still speak my name," he declared. "A man whose name is still spoken lives forever. And not just that cursed nursery rhyme!" he added, banging his fist on the table.

Arthur was impressed by the contact as his nearly empty pint glass rattled and shook. He grasped hold of it and mimed rubbing his knee to the couple who had turned around at the noise. They turned back to their conversation, and Arthur looked at the duke. He hadn't come across many ghosts who knew how to touch things. He was thankful he caught the duke's arm when he tried to slap him.

"What do men say of me?" the duke demanded, leaning forward eagerly. Arthur smiled and pulled out his list. He'd been waiting for this; he'd done his homework.

The list was actually two A4 pieces of lined paper folded together with neat writing on both sides. Arthur had wanted a Moleskine diary, but they were so bloody expensive, so he just nicked some paper from the office and got to work. It was a list of names and places and other notes. Some had been crossed out. Some had been added to. Some were detailed and some were vague.

Arthur smoothed it out on the table and ran his finger down the names, tapping at *George Villiers. Cock and Bottle. Georgie Porgie. Ladies' bathroom.* Next to these brief notes was an excerpt from an internet search that Arthur had meticulously copied down. He read it out.

"Courteous, affable, generous, magnanimous...he is adored by the people."

"Ha!" the duke exclaimed. If he had feathers, he'd be preening. His smile nearly split his rotund face, the folds of his cheeks rippled and squished together.

Arthur continued with a slight smile. "On the other hand, he is an atheist, blasphemer, violent, cruel, and infamous for his licentiousness, in which he is so wrapped up that there is no sex, nor age, nor condition of persons who are spared from it."

He looked up.

The duke was speechless, staring, his neck straining against the ruff as he swallowed.

"Bastards!" he snarled suddenly. "Beggared by fools was I! Not a one among them fit to lace my boots!"

He sat back, dejected, folding in on himself and muttering.

"One lived a life of envy, but methinks I see the wanton hours flee, and now they pass, turn back to laugh at me."

Despite himself, Arthur felt a sudden wave of sympathy for the man and leaned forward in his seat. He reached out and touched the duke's bulbous hand. The fat man flinched but did not pull away.

"I can set you free," Arthur said. Purple sparks danced between his fingers, and the duke's eyes grew wide. "I can send you on to whatever comes next."

"And what comes next?"

"I have no idea," Arthur admitted.

He had decided long ago that he would never release a ghost against their will unless he absolutely had to. The way he saw it, becoming a ghost ripped a certain choice away from a person in the first place. The least he could do was let them choose what happened next.

Unfortunately, the magic that let him do so also let him see the true nature of the dead, and even though he was barely touching the duke, he could feel the desires and the debauchery leaching from the man like poison. He looked into his eyes and saw the glint of recognition and understanding. The magic went both ways. The duke leaned forward.

"What wouldst thou do if thou couldst get away with aught, lad?" he sneered. Arthur pulled his hand away, and the duke suddenly roared and punched his clenched fist on Arthur's fingers. There was a bang and a crunch. It hurt.

"Fucker!" Arthur gasped, yanking his hand back and gripping the fingers. The couple on the next table turned again to stare. He ignored them and looked at the grinning fat duke.

Georgie Porgie. Ladies' bathroom. That's what his notes said. The duke haunted the ladies' room...still a lecherous old perv after death. Years ago, an old landlady had felt icy hands on her body after she left the shower in the apartment upstairs. Arthur hadn't realised the ghost could make physical contact as well as this. He thought of the woman in the toilet just now and his eyes narrowed. This brought a whole new dimension to the standard ghost story.

To haunt is one thing—a ghost is a ghost, after all—but to touch...that was something else.

"So, you're free?" Arthur said, his voice cold. "Free to do what you want to do?"

"To have a good time," sneered the duke.

"And that's what you're going to do—have a good time?"

"Indeed."

"Touch whoever you want?"

"Why not?"

The duke sat back. Steve growled in reply, and Arthur stayed silent, unable to trust the volume of his own voice.

"Come now, boy," George Villiers said, running a ghostly tongue over his lips. "Thou hast power. One can see. Thou must have used it for thine own gain. What's a touch here or a look there? Where'st the harm? They were throwing themselves at me in life. It's not fair to deprive them of my attentions now."

Arthur shook his head but couldn't bring himself to reply.

"When thou canst do what one can do, boy," the duke said, leaning through the table toward Arthur. "When there are no repercussions for thine actions, when thou canst live as one sees fit, why wouldst thou give it up?"

"It's wrong," Arthur said.

"Balderdash! Right and wrong don't exist, child! There be no judgement! No God! There is only thou and thine and them. Thou"—he snarled, his fat lips cracked and yet glistened with moisture—"thou must have used these gifts for thine own ends. We are all selfish creatures."

"Never," Arthur said, and the ghost suddenly grabbed his hand and squeezed it in a grip that felt as real as any man. He pulled Arthur close to him, which, to the increasingly curious barman, was a definite warning sign.

"One sees a sword. One sees walls. One sees death." The duke let go suddenly. Arthur fell back into his chair, gasping for breath, heat radiating through his body. The hairs on the back of his neck stood like needles, but George wasn't done. "Thou hast used thine power selfishly, boy," he hissed. "And why not? A man who canst vanish through walls has no limitations. Thou canst do anything."

"Like hang out in the women's bathroom touching anyone who goes in there!" Arthur snapped.

"One only touches the pretty ones," the duke said.

"You're disgusting."

"*I'm* disgusting?!" spluttered the duke suddenly, choking and blustering. "Me! How dare you, you insolent whelp! I am a duke!"

"*Georgie Porgie...*" Arthur sang. He'd had enough, sometimes the rules needed to be broken. The duke raised a quivering finger. He was shaking with fury, but Arthur kept singing, "*Puddin and pie. Kissed the girls and made them cry. But when the girls came out to play, Georgie Porgie ran away!*"

"I run from nothing!" screamed the duke, standing up and kicking the table. A few heads turned toward them, and the barman said something, but Arthur didn't hear over the ranting duke. "I am a duke! I am the favourite of the King! How dare you presume to judge me! I got where I am today on my own skills, on my own wit. I was no lapdog. Unlike my father. I—"

"Everything alright here, mate?"

It was the barman. He was standing *inside* the duke. Arthur blinked and tried to focus, but the two men were sharing the same space, and if either of them felt it, it didn't show. The duke ranted and raved, ghostly spittle flying from his lips as the barman simply stood with his arms folded, trying to make himself seem a lot bigger than he actually was. His sleeves were rolled up to reveal a mass of faded tattoos like watercolour paints smudged across his skinny arms. Arthur tried to concentrate on him, but the duke was twice his size. His eyes began to itch with the effort.

"Sorry, what was that?"

"I said, is everything alright here?"

"Yeah. I mean, sure, why wouldn't it be?"

The barman stared at him and couldn't help but notice Arthur's eyes darting back and forth, seemingly confirming his suspicions that he was high on something. In truth, the duke was shouting about being able to do whatever he wanted and had moved closer to the older couple at the next table, his hands on the woman's shoulders.

"Leave her alone!" Arthur snapped.

The barman turned, the couple turned, and they all looked at Arthur. The old man grumbled something about the woman being his wife, and the barman stood straighter with his arms crossed and his shoulders back.

"I'll have no junkies in my pub, mate!" he said.

"I'm not on drugs!" Arthur said, but the fact that he kept

looking at something no one else could see didn't help his case. Neither did Steve, who had begun to bark, the noise loud and shrill in the confined space. People around them grumbled and complained, but the duke moved on to the group of teenagers at the fruit machine, drawing Arthur's attention away from the real world once more. Most of the kids looked barely old enough to drink, and they nearly all wore a matching array of grey tracksuit pants and branded T-shirts, though one of the girls stood out in a light summer dress covered in delicate yellow and orange flowers. The duke danced behind her, gyrating and thrusting. Arthur moved toward them as the fat man reached down, but the barman blocked his way.

"Where do you think you're going, pal?" he said. "The door's that way."

Arthur ignored him and pushed past. Steve was already halfway across the room, barking at full volume, but they were too late. The duke lifted the young woman's skirt and laughed as she screamed. Arthur stopped as the barman placed a hand on his shoulder. He whistled to Steve, who skidded to a halt, and the two scenes played out before them in painful contradiction. The young woman laughed and flushed red with embarrassment, smoothing her skirts down and turning to her boyfriend who had a wide grin on his face. Her girlfriends were laughing as well. What a strange accident—an odd gust of wind or a blast from the aircon, they thought. They were all giggles and smiles, but the duke was on his knees now, and Arthur felt a wave of revulsion flow through him. The power he tried so hard to keep in check surged in his gut, and his fingers tingled with an electric charge, the taste of tin strong in his mouth. He could fire magic at the disgusting old ghost and banish him forever. He could do it. There was nothing to stop him. No one to stop him. Arthur had the power to make him go away, but the barman was shouting, the old man was on his feet, a chair had been knocked over, and the real world came flooding back like a wave as the crowd at the fruit machine noticed him staring.

"Oy! Get your fucking eyes off my lass or I'll deck you!"

The boyfriend abandoned his game and strode toward Arthur,

full of beer and the kind of swagger that comes from having five or six friends at your back. The barman, who had begun to sweat, stepped between the two men. All eyes were on them now, the television screens and football forgotten. Arthur blinked, and it took him a moment to catch up. He shook his head.

"No, no, mate, I wasn't looking at your missus. I was looking at...my dog."

"You what?" the teenager sneered over the barman's shoulder.

Arthur hated this. He hated the confrontation. He hated the heat that grew like indigestion behind his heart, and the prickles that ran up his cheeks. He hated the feeling of nervousness he couldn't control. The fear. He also hated the fact that this kid was probably close to ten years younger than he was, maybe just a few years out of school and treating the real world like a playground. He stared at the shit beard and acne-scarred face, the mocking nose, and piercing blue eyes.

Arthur had faced demons. He'd fought witches and barghests and dark magic. He'd wielded swords, walked through walls, and cast fireballs from his hands. But a drunk scally in a dark pub with a tight grip on a bottle of Stella was a different story. He had never been a fighter. Not in this world, anyway. He swallowed drily.

"Look, mate," he said. "I wasn't looking at your missus, all right? Sorry if you thought that. Sorry," he added to the woman herself.

"Sorry?" sneered the teen, like he hadn't heard the word before. "What, are you some sort of poofter?"

Arthur's mouth formed the beginning of a reply, but his brain couldn't process that much stupidity to formulate a response. He knew immediately that this was going nowhere. The kid was on a roll, he had an audience, he had the upper hand, and he'd had a few beers on a warm day and no doubt felt invincible in front of a pretty girl. In short, he wasn't going to let it go.

Arthur turned away from him and whistled for Steve.

"Come on, boy," he said, "I think we should go."

Steve was still growling at the duke, and to everyone else, it must have seemed like he was growling at the girl.

"Yeah, you better!" said the teen, thrusting his chest out and pushing the barman who stumbled into Arthur. They bumped into a table, and glass shattered on the floor. There was a brief moment of silence, which, if this had been an American movie, would probably have been the calm before the storm of an all-in brawl. But this was North Yorkshire on a lovely summer day, so it was quickly filled by three or four sarcastic cheers and someone shouting "Taxi!"

Laughter broke the tension for a moment, and Arthur found himself face to face with the young man as the barman turned away.

"Come on then!" the teen snarled, lifting his hands, inviting Arthur to take the first shot.

Arthur didn't react, and the kid took it for cowardice, taunting and swearing at him. But Arthur was struggling with some dark temptation deep in his gut, the words of the duke rattling through his mind.

You have power. You can do what you want.

Even without the magic, he was pretty sure he could knock this little shit on his arse. He hadn't used magic when he fought the Fetch, after all. He'd punched a demon in the face, and it had been a bloody good punch. He'd used a sword when he fought the barghest, and that had been a bloody good swing. Arthur was strong. He didn't have to put up with this shit from cocky little fuckers who'd had too many shandies and wanted to show off in front of their friends. His fingers flexed and clenched. He glared at the kid. There was a flicker of something there in those blue eyes. Recognition, hesitation perhaps. A glimmer of nervousness.

It was enough for Arthur.

He took a step forward and raised a fist, but as he did, a number of things happened at once. The teen took a step back, the old man moved toward them, Steve barked loudly, and the ghost of George Villiers, Second Duke of Buckingham, stood up and slapped the young woman in the face. It was a hard slap, and she cried out, holding her cheek.

Arthur paused in shock, but Steve attacked, launching himself at the duke.

The young woman turned on an unsuspecting friend and shoved her two-handed in the chest. She, of course, had no idea why, and impulsively reacted by throwing a drink in the poor girl's face.

The teenager who had been squaring up to Arthur spun round as the girls grappled at each other, and the bar turned into the riotous mess of an American movie after all.

Everyone in the pub converged on the fruit machine like flies on shit, and Arthur headed toward the door where Steve had the duke bailed up in a corner. The fat man closed his eyes for a second, and a look of deep concentration crossed his face. Then, he stepped forward and kicked the little dog hard in the side of the body, sending him tumbling across the floor with a yelp. Steve scrambled to his feet and ran from the pub, the duke's laughter ringing out as he pinned his ears back and bolted.

"Don't you fucking touch my dog!" Arthur shouted, rushing forward and punching the man in the face. George Villiers' head snapped back, and his nose cracked. The man roared as he staggered, but his spluttering soon turned to laughter as Arthur saw the looks on the faces of the living who had just watched him punch absolutely nothing.

He stood at the entrance to the bar, bathed in sunlight and breathing hard. His hands prickled with sparks, and the hairs on his arms stood up as he tried to control the anger inside him. And everyone laughed. Everyone except for the old woman who looked at him with pity. That was worse.

The barman moved toward Arthur, but slowly, as if he didn't want to get too close.

"I think it's time you got out of my pub," he said.

"Yeah. You're a fucking nutter!" the tracksuit wanker added.

Arthur turned back to the duke, who was grinning and holding his nose between pinched fingers. "See, boy," he snapped. "Power!"

"This isn't over," Arthur said. And then he ran after Steve.

CHAPTER 4

There was an ancient tradition long forgotten in most parts of the world. It was a simple ritual used to raise the dead. A written magic designed for one purpose and one purpose only...to summon a vessel to do your bidding.

After all, the dead were far easier to boss around than the living. You just needed to find the right words.

The duke said no man was forgotten while his name was still spoken and he was not wrong, though this was a blessing and a curse. Because, as the saying suggests, names have great power.

The name scratched into the piece of pottery, now in the back pocket of a pair of dusty jeans halfway up York Minster, had perhaps more potential power than any name in living memory. The young man climbing the outer wall, his fingers gripping the masonry and crushing it with apparent ease in order to make handholds, had no control over what he was doing. He had no thoughts at all, such as we understand them. He was driven. Onwards, and in this specific case, upward, by the power of a name. It was very old magic. Magic that, perhaps, should have remained buried. But we do love to dig, don't we?

The Shadowman waited, fidgeting with the knife. The noises below were concerning. He chose this spot for a number of reasons, not least of which for the privacy afforded by being hundreds of feet above everyone else, but he had not considered the journey of his pursuer.

That was an oversight.

He heard sirens approach, and the noise of the crowd changed as the authorities appeared. Well, he was sure the *other* authorities would fix any mess that remained, but he would rather that come later.

After.

It did not, however, solve the problem of now.

A recently reanimated corpse climbing an ancient cathedral has a way of attracting attention.

The Shadowman was irritated with himself for not considering this, but then, he had never really planned anything before. There were bound to be errors, necessary adjustments to make. When you spend millennia moving through the shadows, you tended to forget about things such as walking and climbing...and daylight.

He looked at the sky. It shouldn't be much longer. Was there already a slight flicker toward the edge of the sun? He couldn't remember ever having this feeling before. What was it? Anticipation? Nervousness?

A piercing scream shattered the sky, much closer than it should have been, and he turned his head sharply, his hand tightening on the handle of the knife. *How does anyone think in this world?* he thought. *It is so busy*!

A black-eyed raven glared at him from the warm stones of the tower. The sharp beak pointed north, but one jet-black marble eye bore into him. Unblinking.

The black-clad man of shadows and the silken Corvus stared at one another for a long moment. He knew better than to shoo it away. Ravens were not like cats. Not at all. Cats were indifferent. Ravens were just different.

The black bird screamed again and rose into the sky with a

great flap of its wings. It climbed higher and higher and joined a throng of its brothers above the Minster. They swirled and tumbled together, a mass of black bodies against the blue sky, a jumble of dark shapes, but within the chaos there appeared a glimmer of order—a swirling, indefinable pattern.

Arthur sat on the warm grass of Museum Gardens and closed his eyes against the brightness of the sun as he leaned against the ruins of the abbey. He had the taste for beer on his tongue and the leftover nervous residue of conflict that made him want more. The cold bottles he bought in the off-licence rested against his leg. Unopened...so far.

He knew this wasn't healthy. He knew he should probably stop. But he also knew it would make him feel better and smooth out the edges. The only problem was, he'd been smoothing out the edges for a few years now, and there weren't that many left.

Like a poorly poured pint, Arthur was flat.

He was ashamed of sleeping in the street, angry at the duke, angry at himself for the way he handled things, angry at the world for giving him such a gift and making it so bloody hard to do anything with.

Strangely, he felt he finally understood that annoying kid in those Christmas movies whose dad becomes Santa. You have the greatest gift of all, but you can't tell anyone. Although Arthur wasn't entirely sure it was the greatest thing of all—one man's blessing being another man's curse and all that. Knowing Santa was real was a damn sight better than knowing ghosts are.

Jolly Old Saint Nick or the lecherous old pervert in the Cock and Bottle?

No contest.

Arthur tapped his fingernails on the side of a bottle and listened to the enticing *ting-ting-ting* of the glass. He wanted another drink, but drinking by yourself in a park in the middle of a summer afternoon was yet one more thing to feel bloody wonderful about. He lit a cigarette instead and ignored Steve's excited barks. He was angry at Steve. Angry that he ran off. Angry he had to chase him through the city, across busy, dangerous roads, and down to the bustling riverbank. By the time he caught up and took hold of the young puppy, he was breathless and annoyed, and they walked to Museum Gardens in stony silence. Most of all, though, Arthur was angry with himself.

The afternoon shifted lazily toward evening. The park was full. Families played with balls and frisbees, gangs of teenagers and students sat in circles, couples lay together on blankets as rogue children ran through them all. Indistinct music drifted from portable speakers all across the park as groups smoked and drank and laughed and even danced in a few places. The sharp, citrus smell of weed filtered through the scent of flowers and freshly cut grass. It was the perfect summer day. You could almost *taste* the sun.

Arthur was surrounded by people and life—twice as many people as most when you think about it—and yet he felt utterly alone. And that level of self-pity made him even more alone and even angrier. You could escape anything except the inside of your own mind.

That took something special.

Or someone special.

Someone, for instance, like a cute redhead with dimples and a knowing smile, standing in front of the sun holding your dog.

The dead man had made it halfway up the tower at the west end of the Minster and pulled himself onto the terrace above the great west window. The intricate tracery detail of the Heart of Yorkshire had never been so ignored by so many cameras pointed in its direction. Zoom lenses and the occasional pair of binoculars were all focused on the strange man as he continued his climb without so much as a pause for breath. The crowd was silent, reverent even. Police were everywhere. Bright, high-visibility vests glistened in the sun as they raced back and forth beneath the stone edifice, keeping the crowd under control and trying to find someone, anyone, who could lead them into the many hidden stairwells of the tower. Whispers of missing keys filtered through the crowd from those big-eared people near enough to a police radio.

They say it's all locked up, they can't get in.

They'll never let them knock down the doors in there.

They couldn't if they wanted to. Big oak things like that.

Aye, but what if he jumps?

He doesn't look like he's going to jump, does he?

Can you see him?

Yeah, he's—no, wait, that's a gargoyle.

A grotesque.

What?

A grotesque. Gargoyles have water coming out of them...

There wasn't so much an air of panic as there was a distinct sense of awe. The climb was impressive. Undeniably so. The man was now too high for camera phones to clearly make him out, and so far, the police had done a good job of keeping the news vans away. A live broadcast of this nature often led to copycats, and the last thing they needed was a group of students trying to re-enact *Assassin's Creed* across the rooftops of the ancient city.

The roads were closed. The crowds controlled. All eyes raised to the lofty heights of the Minster Tower...which goes some way to explaining why no one noticed the cats gathering on the rooftop of Saint Michael-le-Belfrey next door.

Hundreds of the sleek felines sat on the angled roof of the small church at the foot of the Minster. They came from all over the city, and much like the dead man, they paid little heed to normal laws of physics. They were perched on tiles and on the stepped roof that rose like a pyramid above the main door, filling every space. And above them, two sleek black ravens watched everything.

Like the humans below, the eyes of the gathered creatures were raised to the sky, but unlike them, they weren't watching the shrinking figure of the climbing man—they were watching the sun.

And in the shadows of the tower, in the gaps and the dark places where the warm light feared to go, hundreds of *other* eyes watched and waited.

It was time.

The ghosts of York stirred, restless and confused. They moved openly through the city, unseen in the bustling streets as they left their places of haunting and wandered in the daylight, no longer tied by the bonds that normally held them. For most, this had never happened before, and it took time to realise something had changed.

Habits, even in death, were hard to break.

Duke George Villiers stood by the river with the Cock and Bottle at his back. He had never ventured this far from the pub.

He had chased the girl in the flowery dress out of the inn like he often did with the pretty ones, but something this time had been different. The normal tug he felt as he strode away from the building was missing, and so he kept walking, across the street and between the offices. Now he stood beside the river and didn't quite know what to do.

The duke looked at the sun glistening on the water and marvelled at the colour and majesty of the world on a beautiful summer day.

Then he saw the pub on the far bank and all the people sunbathing and drinking, all that flesh on display, and he grinned.

Ann Barber stood in the middle of Low Petergate and let the crowds drift through and around her. She went entirely unnoticed except for the occasional shiver from a sensitive soul. Ann stared at the sky, oblivious to all.

No one paid any attention to her.

No one except Kay.

In the shop window beside Mad Alice Lane, hundreds of beautifully framed photographs and paintings looked out into the crowded street as tourists looked in. An unseen figure drifted from frame to frame—a bedraggled, angry spirit trapped in the reflections of glass and mirrors, unable to move anywhere except for within the confines of reflective, water-like surfaces.

Kay danced from a mirror to a shining frame and to the glass door of the shop where she peered through to the world outside. The real people, the living ones, seemed to her as insubstantial as grey smoke, but Ann, that bitch, was right there! Standing in the street. In front of the shop. Clear as day.

Kay lifted her eyes to the sky and smiled a toothless smile as water dripped from her sodden hair and down her face. Condensation grew at the base of the door and the wood began to rot.

In various churches throughout the city, grey ladies and headless earls, bakers and guards, sinners and saints, all clamoured in the graveyards or in the places the graveyards used to be. A great gathering of the dead was taking place.

The ghosts of York moved together in a swarm, and the cats fled from the streets to gather on the rooftops. Other creatures moved in the dark places. Creatures not seen or spoken of for hundreds of years. Forgotten sprites and those called demons.

The fae and the Folk.

There had long been a misapprehension that the word folk referred solely to people, and while that was true, it was not entirely accurate.

The common people, such as it were, included anyone below the elite—anyone not part of the establishment.

Anyone.

The Folk were the inhabitants of the land.

Yorkshire was full of Folk.

And full of lore.

And the veil was wearing thin.

On the border of Museum Gardens, just a few hundred feet away from where Arthur found himself looking nervously into the eyes of a good-looking woman with dimples, the courtiers of Queen Katheryn Howard drifted into the courtyard of King's Manor. They paced slowly among the ghosts of convalescing soldiers who filled the area in front of the university and the City Art Gallery. They, like many others, had not left their places of haunting for a long time—some never at all. Others had made their way to the manor knowing therein resided a queen, one who could give a semblance of order to this strange and unexpected existence. But the queen was gone, and the bonds were breaking, the barriers falling.

The city lay open before them.

In the museums and ancient stately homes, in the pubs, inns, hotels and ruined castles, in the antique shops and the rebuilt halls, in all the places where the anchors of the dead were transported and stored, the ghosts moved.

Romans walked the streets.

Vikings stalked through Starbucks.

The fae and the Folk roamed unchecked.

All those souls trapped and unable to move on gathered…and watched…and waited.

And a saint left her home, gripping the hands of a small boy, to offer aid to all who might need it.

CHAPTER 5

"I'm Nae."

"Neigh?"

"Yes."

"Like the horse a noise makes?"

"Pardon?"

"Erm, the noise a horse makes. You know, *neigh*!" Arthur gave his best horse impression and blew his lips out in a snort. He instantly regretted it and looked to his feet. In the arms of the woman, Steve whispered the truth.

"Dickhead."

"You know, I've never heard that joke before," the young woman said, and there might have been an uncomfortable silence if not for the fact that she filled it while Arthur blushed. "It's short for Renae," she added with a smile and a perfectly raised eyebrow.

"Oh!"

"You're not very good at this, are you?" She laughed, her eyes flashing.

"Good at what?"

"Never mind," she said, laughing again. It was musical, and Arthur blinked at those dimples as they did something strange to his cognitive ability.

The woman was very pretty—arrestingly so—in the sense that

you would happily commit a crime if she were the one with the handcuffs. She grinned with amusement and a hint of mischief as the man squirmed in front of her.

She stared at Arthur as though really seeing him, he thought, her eyes wide and bright and interested. It was a look impossible to miss but entirely possible for him to fuck up. Arthur clambered to his feet and awkwardly brushed down his jeans before holding out his hand in a valiant effort to do so.

"I'm Arthur," he said. It wasn't a bad start.

"Pleased to meet you, Arthur," she replied, gripping his hand briefly while holding Steve with the other arm. "And this gorgeous little guy?" she asked, bringing the happy little dog close to her face and peering at Arthur from between his inside-out ears. "What's his name?"

"This is Steve."

"Steve!" she laughed, and her smile stirred something deep inside Arthur.

Despite his romantic inclinations, he generally believed the idea of love at first sight was complete and utter bollocks, but he very much believed in pretty redheads at first sight. Unfortunately, a decade plus change of awkward interactions and a general sense of being crap with women threatened to override everything he wanted to be and say. Arthur had been in a relationship with the same girl for most of his late teens and early twenties. He wasn't what you'd call skilled, and suddenly his tongue was apparently five sizes too big for his mouth.

"He was already called that when I got him," Arthur stammered, then coughed. "It's a cool name though, I think," he added when Steve barked.

"Steve," the woman repeated with a grin. "Well, hello, Steve. Or are you a Steven? No, Steven is too formal. You shouldn't run away from your dad like that," she added with a mock tut.

Arthur and Steve looked at each other at that last comment, and Arthur couldn't help but grin. It was hard not to when your dog raised an eyebrow and cocked his head in confused amusement.

Nae patted Steve on the head and ruffled his ears, and the little puppy yapped with excitement and licked her face. She laughed and placed him gently on the ground where he ran around in a tight little circle and then stopped suddenly between Arthur and the woman. He sat down and looked up at his best friend. Steve tilted his head.

"You're welcome," he said, in a voice only Arthur could hear. "Don't fuck it up."

Arthur knelt and grinned as he patted the side of Steve's face.

"That'll do, pig," he said. Then, acting as if he couldn't hear the stream of profanity, added, "Do you want to go chase squirrels?"

Steve barked and spun in another little circle, his tail wagging so hard his fluffy black bottom vibrated from side to side.

"Go on, then," Arthur said, and Steve darted away between the ruins and vanished under a sign warning people to keep their dogs on a lead at all times.

"Well, that was a bit cute," Nae said, and Arthur's Spidey-senses tingled. They looked at each other, and there was that flash of amusement again an unmistakable attraction. They both looked away quickly, each growing red at the awkward moment. Silence sat between the two strangers with all the subtlety of a drunk aunt playing matchmaker at a wedding, and they cast their embarrassed gaze over the park, each desperately trying to think of something to say now that their distraction, Steve, was busy hunting squirrels.

In the deep shade of the trees and bushes, a squirrel ventured down the wide trunk of an oak, descending cautiously toward the littered undergrowth, nose twitching and searching for unfamiliar scents and, more importantly, familiar ones. The dog had gone, sniffling somewhere on the other side of the park, and so the little creature was free to roam and forage once more. A searching paw touched the mass of fallen leaves and twigs at the dark, cool base of the tree, and the nose twitched. There was something there, something different. But it was too late. A small dark green figure burst from a hole beneath two roots and dragged the terrified animal under the tree. A dead leaf lifted into the air and floated gently back to earth. There was a sharp crack and a wet thud, but these were tiny sounds, and so no one heard.

High above, the ravens circled.

A bead of sweat trickled slowly down the pallid face of the Shadowman; that in itself was new. He lifted a questing finger and felt the moisture falling from beneath the flat cap.

And so it begins, he thought.

He didn't turn when he heard the noise behind him but rose slowly to his feet, the knife gripped tight in his fist, the knuckles white and straining against the skin. His hands trembled, and he swapped the knife from right to left, flexing the fingers of his open hand. His heartbeat sounded like thunder. He marvelled at the feel of it, the roar of blood through his body. It hadn't even begun yet, and already everything was so different.

A cool breeze lifted over the parapet and brought with it the smell of soil and chemicals. He turned slowly and watched as a grey arm appeared over the stone. A resting raven leaped into the sky with a startled shout. The Shadowman watched as the revenant clambered up and over, crushing the masonry in its cold, dead grip.

He remembered this man. He remembered the night he died. How could he not? This had been the first life the Shadowman had taken with his own hands, and now here he was, right on time.

He looked at the sky. The sun was still bright and clear, shimmering and painful to look at. The dead man stood before him, expressionless and dispassionate, neither truly living nor entirely dead; not one thing or the other.

The stones shivered at his step as he moved steadily toward the man in black. The Shadowman took a step back, then another, over the top of the book so that it sat on the roof between the two men. He lifted the knife in his left hand, held the other out. Then, in a moment he had not planned, he raised the blade to his lips and kissed it before slicing down in one swift, savage movement.

The Shadowman blinked in surprise. He had planned this for a very long time, and it had been far easier and yet infinitely more painful than he expected.

He heard the wet thud, but didn't dare look down as he raised the stump of his right arm. Hot blood fired in bursts from the severed limb and covered the shining stones in a crimson mess, each pulse accompanied by an electric shock of agony that ravaged his body. He almost stumbled as a wave of nausea flooded through him. He had no idea! Pain coursed up his arm and rippled across his chest. Why did his whole body hurt? The knife suddenly burned in his hand, and he dropped it to the floor where it burst into flames. There would be time to process that later, but for now, there was only the revenant...and the pain.

The Shadowman blinked in the bright light and noticed the splash of blood on the jeans of the dead man. He was close now. Too close. And the time wasn't right. Not yet. But the pain was too much!

The Shadowman bent down as quickly as he could manage and picked up his own severed hand, trying not to grimace at the thick warmth and stickiness of the blood. The contrast it made on the pale white skin seemed to him like paint on a clean canvas. Abstract but all too real. The revenant reached for him, and the Shadowman lifted the severed hand toward the reanimated creature and whispered three words.

Two things happened.

The revenant thrust a grasping hand at the Shadowman and punched a hole into his chest, the dirty fingers piercing skin and flesh, finding the gaps between his ribs to grasp at the heart...and the Shadowman's severed hand burst into flames.

The Shadowman screamed in mortal agony, but it was a sound heard only by the ravens and the grotesques before it froze in time, snuffed out and trapped in the world between worlds. His burning hand, now a Hand of Glory, stopped the revenant at the exact moment the dead man's fingers clasped around the Shadowman's heart.

They stood there, frozen in a macabre dance, the spell almost complete. With a desperate last gasp of shock, the Shadowman realised he couldn't hold on, but neither could he drop the burning hand for fear the flames might go out.

There was so much he hadn't considered.

Pain being the most immediate.

He blinked in agony as his strength abandoned him, and he did the only thing his shattered mind could think of.

With the last of his strength, the Shadowman forced his burning severed hand onto the head of the revenant, pushing the ulna and radius bones into the corpse's skull until it stood fast.

Finally, it was done.

A spasm rippled through his body, and blood trickled from his lips as his head bowed, and his shoulders sagged with pain, his chest rising and shuddering as he sucked in small sips of air.

The revenant and the Shadowman stood together like two fucked-up decorations atop the world's largest wedding cake. The flames of the severed hand flickered and wavered in the gentle breeze, casting thin plumes of smoke like calligraphy into the sky. Then they too froze in a pocket of trapped time.

High above them, high above everything, the heavens moved.

CHAPTER 6

Arthur and Nae sat side by side in the strange seclusion of the abbey ruins in Museum Gardens. It took them both by surprise when two black-suited wardens warned them the park would be closing in thirty minutes, and could they please make their way to the exit. The bottles of beer were empty, having been shared long ago. They now rested against their legs, acting as ashtrays while the man and the woman smoked and talked and laughed.

They had walked around the park a few times with Steve yapping at their heels and chasing anything that ran, but they eventually settled back in the ruins and barely noticed the passage of time.

A summer day in England could be endless, the light often lasting until nearly 11:00 p.m., and the park still glistened gold as it had since early that morning. The grass was a deep green, and the flowers stood out in bright clumps of purple and pink. Large patches of gilded daffodils were everywhere, and even the stones of the old ruins appeared to glow in the evening sun, just as much a part of the world as the nature around it.

Arthur was smiling. In fact, his face ached from it. He was relaxed and happy, stroking Steve's soft head as the tired dog slept between him and Nae.

Nae.

He was amazed by her. So confident but with an underlying nervousness that came out masked by laughter and overflowing observations about anything and everything around them. She had travelled and seen the world while Arthur and almost everyone he knew had graduated from the playground to the student's union to the office staff room, a straight run from start to finish. It was only the events of the past year that had given Arthur himself any personal deviation from such a linear and formulaic existence, but of course, that was one subject he couldn't talk about.

First impressions counted, and telling someone you can talk to the dead is, to put it mildly, a bit of risk.

Arthur's thoughts flashed back to the castle in Richmond and the fight with the witch. Images of swords and chains flashed before him, and with an effort, he closed his mind to it all. There were some things you just couldn't talk about. And, he realised, you didn't need to when you're sitting beside a pretty girl on a long summer day.

So, while Nae talked, he listened, and it suited them both perfectly.

She filled the silences, and Arthur encouraged her to talk by listening intently. Every time there was a small pause, they'd catch each other's eye and look away, nervous perhaps at what they saw there. Nae looked wonderful when she blushed, and Arthur could feel the heat on his own cheeks.

The day had fallen away as the world turned around them. Arthur was completely oblivious to the shadows and the shades wandering through the park, no longer checking the dark places. In fact, he barely looked anywhere except for Nae's face and his own feet, though he forced himself to look away when she yawned and stretched, arching her back and sighing. She laughed at his strained gentlemanliness, the reason for his aversion fully clear in the flush that crept up his neck. She wanted him to check her out. She grinned to herself, and the dimples flashed again. For Arthur, that was even worse than the pull of her shirt.

To sit in the sun, to talk and drink and smoke and laugh while the world turned around you, lost in time with nowhere to be and nothing to do, was perfect. Neither of them had checked their phones other than to show the occasional photograph—Nae of her time in Australia and Arthur of the cottage below the castle in Richmond where he grew up. There was no need to. No need to scroll mindlessly, to find something—anything—to occupy your attention when the person you were with was doing a perfect job of it on their own. But the excuse to show photographs allowed them to move closer, and once the phones were away, they remained where they were, a dog's width apart.

The only moment that offered a potential concern was when Arthur asked Nae what she did for a living, and she told him she was a psychologist. He made a joke about how he was surprised they hadn't met before as he'd seen just about every shrink in North Yorkshire, and then instantly regretted it. His biggest hang-up with the whole counselling thing, apart from the fact they all thought he was mental, was the impression it gave other people. He realised the irony of this as he tried to stammer an explanation to someone whose entire career was predicated on people asking for help and receiving it, but he needn't have worried.

"It takes strength," Nae said.

"What do you mean?" Arthur asked.

"To ask for help. To open up to someone," she explained. "It takes a lot of strength. You'd be surprised how many people sit in my office and don't say anything at all. It can take a while to get going."

"What? Like *Good Will Hunting*?"

"Exactly!" she laughed, and Arthur inwardly congratulated himself on a joke well-received.

"I bet people talk to you," he said. He hoped it was a compliment.

"Not all the time, but we tend to get there in the end."

"Have you..." Arthur paused and picked at the grass, not entirely sure he wanted to ask the question but then throwing the grass away because he didn't want to seem like a teenager. "Have you ever had anyone utterly convinced of something that isn't real?"

"What do you mean?"

He thought fast. "Have you seen that movie, *Candyman*?"

"Is that the one where you say his name in the mirror, and he comes to get you or something?"

"Yeah, that's it. He's got a hook for a hand."

"I saw it years ago. Probably when I was much too young. Why?"

"Well, there's this scene in it where the woman wakes up and her dogs are dead, and the baby's cot is covered in blood."

Steve lifted his head off Arthur's leg and mumbled, "What the hell are you doing?" Arthur ignored him and went on.

"Obviously, no one would believe her if she told them about the Candyman, but she wasn't lying. It actually happened. Well, in the movie, anyway. I mean...to her. The Candyman did it. She wasn't mad or delusional. It was all real. I guess I just wondered if you ever had a patient that was so convinced something was real that you, I don't know, believed them."

"Oh, I always believe them," she said, surprising him.

"Really?"

"Yes. The thing is, it is always real to that person. To deny that would be dangerous."

"But you don't think it's *really* real, do you?" Arthur asked.

"What? The Candyman?" she laughed. "Are you asking if I believe the Candyman is real?"

"No, of course not. But, well, maybe?"

"Look, it doesn't really matter what I think. My reality doesn't negate the reality of my patient. And, anyway, I was always more scared of Bloody Mary myself," she said and reached for a cigarette. Arthur stared at her bottom lip as she took a drag, the way it stuck to the filter for a moment when she pulled it away. He really wanted to kiss her, right in the middle of that conversation, although perhaps not in the middle of a cigarette.

"The brain is fascinating," she said, the smoke curling up and away into the evening air. "What's real to one person is impossible to another."

"Like atheists and Jehovah's Witnesses."

She laughed. Another point.

"I guess so. But it's not just belief. There are all kinds of things that can alter or affect the way a person experiences the world." She paused for a moment and blew smoke into the clear blue sky. Arthur thought he'd be content just to sit and watch her smoke, but something like a shadow crossed her face, and the dimples vanished. "My nanna had Alzheimer's," she said quietly, looking briefly at Arthur and then staring across to the other side of the park, where the water of the River Ouse was just visible behind the iron-railed fence.

The silence stretched on, but then she spoke again, softly.

"It took her early and for about ten years or so she had absolutely no idea who she was. It started out funny, you know. Like she'd forget our names and go through the whole family before she got to us. Sometimes she'd give me pocket money...twice." She laughed a little at that and Arthur sat up straight, turning his shoulder toward her, giving her his undivided attention. He wanted to put his arm around her as she spoke but stopped himself and just sat still and listened.

"But then it got really bad," she said, stubbing the cigarette out angrily on the grass. "Really quick, and instead of forgetting names, she'd forget where she lived...or the fact she had to wash and feed the dogs. And I always remember this doctor explaining to my dad that it wasn't so much that she was forgetting these things but that her brain was living in another time. So, she didn't *forget* to feed her dogs because in her mind, wherever she was, she already had, because that's what she always did. It's hard to explain. After Grandad died, the dogs were her world and so we knew something was really wrong when they started getting all scruffy and thin." She stopped then and patted Steve who was looking at her with big brown eyes. Arthur placed his hand on top of hers and gave her fingers a small squeeze.

"You don't have to talk about this if you don't want to," he said.

"No, it's okay. I want to. It kind of shaped my life, you know. The big important event. We all have one. Well, Nanna got worse and worse, and she spent the last few years of her life in a hospital bed getting flipped four times a day, so she didn't get bed sores. It was no way to live, and Dad and his brothers used to talk about maybe ending it for her, easing her pain, you know. Can you imagine having that conversation?" She shook her head. "I never knew, of course, they never talked about it in front of me or my brother, but we found out later. And you know what, Nanna would've wanted it. She was a country girl and always used to say if she ever lost her marbles, we should take her out back and shoot her like one of the dogs. Put her out of her misery."

Steve looked up and whined.

"Not you," Nae said, patting him on the head. "But here's the thing, we didn't really know if she was miserable. Not really. Maybe she was living in a world where Grandad was still alive. Dad used to say that Nanna died when Grandad did, it just took years for her body to catch up. But maybe, what if..." she stammered, a small catch in her voice, and Arthur squeezed her hand.

"The big question," she went on, "the one that no one could answer, was where was she in her mind in those last few years? What was true to her? Did her mind exist in a place where Grandad still existed? If so, isn't that actually kind of beautiful? She was living in a different time, in a different world. I wish I'd spent more time with her, asked her questions about what she was seeing, you know."

They fell quiet for a while, and Arthur knew that the silence was more important than any words he might utter, so he just sat and held her hand, this wonderful redheaded woman he hadn't known existed this morning who suddenly filled his world. He ran his thumb gently over the knuckle of her fingers and couldn't help but think of how many times he'd stared at his own hands in a therapist's office, terrified to say the words that needed saying, knowing what they would think of him when he eventually did. And here was this girl, this woman, who just... who just got it! "My reality doesn't negate the reality of my patient," she'd said, and

Arthur had felt some of the tension in the back of his neck let go and fall away. He thought of the little boy in *The Sixth Sense* and the words of that famous quote almost found their way to his lips but then Nae laughed loudly and snorted, which made her laugh more.

"Fucking hell!" she said. "That got totally morbid, didn't it. What a way to ruin the mood, hey?"

Her eyes were shining and her face flushed as she looked at Arthur. "And here's you being so sweet and lovely and listening to me dribble on about my Nan when you asked about a movie."

She ran her hand through her hair and tucked it behind her ear and then her voice changed. Softer.

"I guess you've gotta love a chick who talks about her dead gran rather than stealing a quick snog on a lovely summer day," she said, and before Arthur had time to react, she leaned in and kissed him on the lips. Just for a moment. A quick meeting of warm flesh that lingered ever so slightly before she pulled away.

It would have been a wonderful, perfect moment, if it wasn't for Steve laughing his head off at the look on Arthur's face.

Officer Boardman whistled a jaunty tune as he stood at the gates of Museum Gardens. His shift was nearly over, and he was in a great mood. A full day without a single incident of anyone being horrible to each other. He'd chatted to tourists and shopkeepers, walked his beat with a colleague, and generally enjoyed being in the sun. His regulation stab-vest was a heavy reminder of the darker potential of his job, but on days like this, he remembered why he loved it so much. It was the people. Good people.

A long sweltering summer Saturday usually meant an extraordinary number of drunk and disorderlies, but so far everyone had behaved themselves. The police had kept an eye on a few rowdy stag-dos, but the worst they did was sing loud and off-key in the middle of Coney Street.

I'll never forget the smell of the sweat from under your armpit!

Old rugby songs. He couldn't fault that. And the hen parties were always fun...if they kept their hands to themselves.

He'd spent a large part of the day on duty outside the Minster after some incident with a cat that he still wasn't sure he entirely understood, and then there was the idiot who decided to climb the west tower. That was odd, but it was something interesting to tell the wife, not just for the speed at which the man ascended, but the way he vanished when he got to the top. Officer Boardman wasn't in the team that finally clambered up the internal stairs (thank the Lord, there were hundreds of them!) but he heard on the radio their shock that the roof was empty. And then suddenly they were all ordered to pack up and disperse the crowd, and that was that, back on the beat.

He could say one thing for the job. It was never dull.

But a day of hot weather and too much booze had a way of descending quickly into dehydrated, emotional chaos, so he was glad to be heading home before it got much later. He'd enjoy the last of the day's warmth in the back garden with his girls, far away from the drunken crying, fights, and vomit that would no doubt be in store for the night watch. He knew his daughter would still be up even though it was nearly 8:00 p.m. The long hours of daylight were confusing the poor girl, and most evenings were spent trying to convince her that it was indeed bedtime despite the blatant lies of the blazing sun outside her bedroom window.

Boardman did a double take as a young couple with a dog walked through the gates, and the man nodded thanks to him. They were all smiles, and he was glad to see them placing their rubbish in the appropriate bins. He was tempted to say something about the lack of a lead on the dog, but the little terrier trotted obediently alongside them, and so he decided not to.

There was something about the young man, though—something familiar he couldn't quite put his finger on. That was the thing about being a bobby in the same city for so long; you got to know a lot of people, and you got to recognise a lot of faces. He was sure he'd seen the young woman as well. A girl as pretty as her with hair that vibrant really stood out. He smiled as they jogged across the road to beat the traffic and vanished into the throng of people still packing Lendal. The man leaned in and said something, and the young woman responded with unbridled laughter. Oh, to be young and in love. He tutted at himself for the cliché but grinned anyway. This was the city in which he met his lady wife after all; it was nice to think others might be starting out on the same journey.

Officer Boardman turned on his heel and put his hand on his truncheon as he took up the whistle once again, smiling at a group of American tourists who surreptitiously tried to take photographs of his distinctive helmet. Time to go home. A beer and a bag of cheese and onion crisps to relax with. Champion. The longest day of the year was nearly over.

For others, it was just beginning.

The book and the blade of the Shadowmen were much like the notebook and the truncheon of the police force. They were symbols as much as tools. They bound the owner to duty and to service. The book—that strange leatherbound beast that seemed to be almost sentient, acting much like a copper's notebook. The words changed and fled as if they didn't want to be read, scribed in a language so old no scholar could ever translate it. It kept a record of the truth. It also recorded the lies, the deceits, the mistakes, and all those things that needed to be done, fixed, crossed out...

Dealt with.

Each book, each blade, belonged to one being, and misplacing them was unthinkable.

The Shadowman on the roof of the Minster knew exactly where his book and his blade were. He stared at the blood-spattered leather cover of the tome as he tried desperately to control his breathing. The blade was gone—nothing more than a pile of ash at the top of the world.

It should have blown away in the breeze by now, but the flames from his severed hand had put a stop to that. He trapped them in moment of stillness, outside of time and movement and motion. There was nothing but pain. So much more pain than he thought possible. Perhaps more than he could bear.

The Shadowman was dying. But the time wasn't right. It couldn't happen yet.

He fixed his gaze on the book, tracing with his eyes the strange contours as familiar to him as his own hands. Sacrifices must be made.

"No death shall come from mortal birth," he gasped, his voice nothing more than a whisper. "No death shall come from mortal birth."

He said it again and again—a pained, desperate, breathless mantra. The words of a dying man.

CHAPTER 7

"So, this is me," Arthur said a little awkwardly as they stood at the entrance to Stonegate—that long, ancient artery leading to the Minster. A gang of singing drunks in plastic Viking helmets crashed into them as they charged from one pub to the next, and Arthur stumbled into Nae with an apology. It was hard to have a private moment in a crowd. Steve pressed against their legs, trying not to get trampled but trying equally hard to catch Arthur's attention. They were in the city now, and the city had a lot more dark places and hidden shadows than the park.

"Something isn't right!" the little dog barked, but Arthur could barely hear him for the press of people and the surge of his own pulse elicited by his proximity to Nae. If he did hear, he might have noted the tone in Steve's voice, but then, he hadn't even noticed the way the poor dog was shivering and had his tail tucked between his legs since they entered St. Helen's Square. Steve butted his head against Arthur, but his friend wasn't paying any attention. He tried his luck with Nae. She reached down and picked him up.

"So, where are you two going?" she asked, unknowingly cutting the little dog off before he could speak. "Who are you ditching me for?"

"Erm, well it's a bit embarrassing, to be honest," Arthur said. "But I've had it booked for months."

"What is it?" she asked, curiosity and amusement lighting her eyes. She tucked her bright red hair behind her ear with one hand and juggled Steve with the other. He was squirming and wriggling in her arms. He barked and she laughed. Arthur shushed him.

"Well, it's…"

"Oh, come on," she teased. "I told you damn near everything about me today, and all you told me is that you grew up in Richmond, you went to uni here, and you work at the council. Give me something. Unless," she added with a raised finger, "unless you're visiting a dominatrix. I don't really want to know if you have a fetish for getting whipped by women in leather."

"*Women*? No," Arthur laughed, and Nae punched him on the arm. They retreated to the relative safety of a shop doorway on the corner. The crowds drifted past, and they stood huddled together as though on a rock protected from a surging river. Steve couldn't believe Arthur wasn't seeing what he was seeing.

Arthur sighed. "I'd kind of prefer if it was something like that," he said. "It's a bit embarrassing, really."

"Oh, now you have to tell me!" Nae said with a grin.

"I'm going to a séance."

He said it quickly, perhaps hoping she wouldn't hear, but the look in her eye told him she had. "I guess I'm just really interested in what some people think is real," he added by way of explanation.

"You know, I never would have picked that," she said. "Of all the things you could've said, I would never have guessed *that*. You, you don't actually believe it, though, do you?" she asked with one perfectly raised eyebrow. "That people can speak to the dead? I mean, there's being whipped by the lady in leather and then there's, well, there's…that. At least with the dominatrix, you get something for your money!"

"It's complicated," he said, looking at his feet.

"Oh, my God! Do you?!" Her eyes widened in surprise. There was amusement there, for sure, but something else, the first hint of concern. This was a big moment for Arthur. This was the type of thing that plagued his mind and had done for the better part of a year, the balance between what was real and what was not, but more than that, what *he* knew was real and what others didn't. What they couldn't.

Nae was an educated woman. Worse, a psychologist with experience of the world. She didn't just go from school to university to the office and pretend to know everything. She had lived. And every day she dealt with people existing in their own worlds.

Arthur knew just how quickly this day would change if he told her the truth, but he also didn't want to deny it.

He would be denying himself. There were convictions, there were certainties, but in the face of a cute smile, he forgot all of that.

"Of course not!" he laughed. "It's total and utter bollocks! But you've got to admit it's interesting. I mean, these people earn money by convincing others they can speak to the dead!"

"Like you?"

"Well, yeah. But I'm doing it in an ironic way," he said.

Nae laughed, which was proof enough for Arthur that she was into him. It was a terrible line.

"Like a hipster?" she asked.

"I guess so."

"So, you were talking to dead people before it was cool?"

"Something like that." He grinned. "Look, in all seriousness, I know it's weird. I know it's something lonely old widows do to nag their dead husbands, but I'm really interested in it." He almost added that loneliness, above all things, was what motivated him the most to seek out others who might be able to do what he could do, but he figured that might be one revelation too far. "You must be too," he said. "Interested in it, I mean. What with being a psychologist. Why don't you come with me?" he said suddenly, his eyes growing wide with the idea. "Call it a research trip? You'll be able to diagnose everyone there and figure out what it is that makes them think it's all real!"

"Terrible idea," Steve said. Arthur ignored him.

"I don't know…"

"Oh, go on! I'll buy you dinner after?" he added with what he hoped was a cheeky smile.

"I might not feel like eating after talking to the dead."

"Well, I'll buy you a beer then. Everyone knows beer makes talking to the dead easier to handle." He should know.

"I do like beer," she said with a smile that hid a lingering question, like she still wasn't sure.

"Look, I know it's odd, but…" And here Arthur told his second lie of the evening, hoping it would make him seem enigmatic and cool. "I made a vow that I was going to try something new every month this year and, well, this was on the list."

"What did you do last month?"

"Dominatrix."

She laughed again and sighed. "Okay, when you put it like that, I guess I have no choice. Nothing like a little adventure."

"Awesome!"

"This is really not a good idea," Steve grumbled, but once again Arthur wasn't listening and was completely unaware of the concern in the little dog's voice.

There were a lot of things that Arthur wasn't aware of—which is a statement that could fit most men when distracted by cute redheads—but in this particular moment, it was very specific to Arthur's unique abilities. As they walked down the crowded Stonegate, a street he hadn't visited for well over a year, he was completely ignorant to everything but the girl.

The last time he'd been here, he wasn't walking, he was running. Fleeing, even.

Back then, Arthur saw everything…every demon, sprite, spirit, ghost, and physics-defying cat. This was a street he now avoided for that very reason, but the séance was being held in a reputed 'haunted house,' and you know what they say about curiosity and cats.

Arthur wanted to see just how haunted the place really was.

The great irony here was that on his way to see something he felt sure would be little more than a gimmick, Arthur was entirely blind to the reality. Ghosts filled the street and alleys around them, but he didn't notice.

Neither did he notice the cats fleeing over the rooftops and along the walls, the creatures dancing through the shadows, or the small figures darting in and out of shop doorways.

There was a hell of a lot *not* to notice, really. But finally, after a painfully long few years, Arthur no longer felt lonely.

He was one of the normal people again, and so the shadows didn't seem to matter. His habit of checking the dark places was momentarily forgotten.

Arthur walked slowly and happily down Stonegate, heading toward the towering, sunlit Minster. He thought only of the beautiful woman by his side and the way she smiled at him. They were relaxed and carefree.

Only Steve seemed agitated, but as he was being cuddled tight and called a good boy, his focus began to shift as well. His tail wagged under Nae's arm as she played with his ears, and he closed his eyes in delight.

This was probably for the best.

It meant he didn't see the shadow creep across the towering Minster, or the small creatures run through the forest of legs like rats abandoning ship. Nor did he see the ravens circling high above. Steve did, however, feel a cold shiver run through his body and sensed that the world had grown darker. When his eyes snapped open, he saw that he was right. They were inside, huddled in a dark doorway with a set of steep stairs leading straight up. The narrow hallway made a mockery of the summer behind them and stretched away with a line of thin, guttering candles that faded into dim nothingness. Steve looked up the stairs, and his tail stopped wagging.

The day was still bright and warm, but it was changing rapidly. The heavens moved, and a great, dark line encroached on the blazing sphere of the sun. It touched the bright light just as Arthur, Nae, and Steve crossed the threshold of the haunted house, and so they never saw the change, but the people in the streets did. The crowds looked up and fell silent. People always do in the face of an eclipse. There is something primeval about the dance of the sun and moon that cuts through even the most stubborn drunk. The bars and restaurants still pulsed with the noise of summer revellers ignorant to the world outside, but the narrow streets and the parks of the city grew quiet as eyes lifted heavenwards and arms hugged bodies to chase away sudden shivers. Sleek cats and other creatures raced across the rooftops, and the small ones dodged through the tangled forest of legs in a blur. The small ones followed the cats to the Minster under the watchful eye of the circling ravens. They were so fast—a flicker in the peripheral vision, easily dismissed.

The world turned, and the moon moved slowly in front of the sun, a clear black curve now prominent in the sky. A dark shadow spilled through the streets, shrouding the statue of Emperor Constantine in unnatural darkness as it caressed the warm cobbles and slowly climbed the sandy-gold towers of the Minster.

At the top, the Shadowman and the revenant waited, frozen in time. The flames from the finger of the severed hand rose straight to a point without so much as a flicker. A thin, inklike plume of smoke rose from each fingertip like a pen line drawn onto the sky itself, and the Shadowman turned his eyes slightly as he sensed the shadows approach. He knew them well. He was born of them. The corner of his mouth turned up in what might have been a smile.

"Not by daylight nor by night," he said in a barely audible whisper. He looked down at the fingers protruding from his chest, and slowly, painfully, lifted his own hand to grasp the cold flesh of the dead man's wrist.

"Not by weapons of steel or flight."

He stood up straighter, grimacing in agony as the fingers pulled at him and raked against his bones. He shuffled his left foot and planted it as firmly as he could.

"Not in the sky nor on the earth."

The Shadowman was panting now, gasping and barely conscious, his head swimming as the darkness drew nearer. With a tremendous effort, he lifted his head and looked in wonder at his own severed hand, sitting aflame atop the dead man's head.

"No death shall come from mortal birth," he gasped.

Tears streamed down his cheeks as he uttered one more line, one final verse in a language unknown, and the flames went out.

Time returned as the sun vanished, and the revenant crushed the heart of the Shadowman beneath dirt-encrusted fingers.

He couldn't even scream.

The life was ripped from his body in a blazing white-hot wave of agony. His mouth opened in silent, desperate anguish as the organ he paid no attention to was destroyed in an explosion of blood and gore.

Finally, the Shadowman fell into the embrace of the dead.

They held each other upright for a moment, two bodies entwined at the top of the city, and then they collapsed to the still-warm surface of the roof. The Shadowman's severed hand skittered away into the corner of the tower as the moon drew a blanket of darkness over the world.

CHAPTER 8

Arthur and Nae giggled as they followed the sombre old lady who had suddenly appeared in the hallway. They filed up the stairs and through a heavy velvet curtain, but they stopped when they entered the small room beyond. It wasn't that there was nothing to laugh at; it was that there was too much, and their brains simply couldn't process it all in one go.

"Oh, this is awesome," Nae gasped, and the old lady preened, completely unaware of the real meaning in the young woman's voice. Her heavily made-up face cracked into a mass of wrinkles and crow's feet, and the thick black eyeliner seemed to make her eyes vanish into her head. The old lady's hair was silver but so bright it couldn't possibly be natural, though maybe it just stood out in sharp contrast against all the black. A voluminous velvet dress, probably designed to billow dramatically, clung with defeated purpose to her heavy form, spreading like a bridal train at her feet. The effect was probably not what she was going for.

She looked like a tea-cosy, albeit a tea-cosy for goths.

"I'll leave you here for a moment," the lady said theatrically as she grasped another curtain with a flourish. It would have been a more impressive exit if she didn't have to pause to squeeze past a table overflowing with ornamental snow globes. She swore as the table wobbled and then vanished through the curtain.

On the other side, Arthur caught a glimpse of people enjoying tea and biscuits. He did not like what he saw and was about to suggest to Nae that they go somewhere else, but she leaned in close and whispered, "This is so cool. It's like a cliché had sex with a stereotype!"

He laughed out loud, grinning as Nae shushed him with a giggle.

Arthur looked around the room, trying to take it all in.

It was full to the brim with what he could only guess was every single item from the occult lovers home catalogue. Tall shelves reached to the ceiling on all four walls. Skulls and various bones nestled between leather bound books, and dusty scrolls lay in piles on small tables. Arthur counted at least three different Hindu deities, a number of fat Buddhas next to what looked like a bobblehead Jesus, and, he was pretty certain, a large brass figurine of Satan. Paintings hung from the shelves themselves, some large, some small, all from different religious traditions and massively contradicting ideologies. Thick, dark drapes fell in suspended waves across the ceiling, and incense burned in three or four different braziers filling the confined space with thick, sweet smoke. The only light came from a smattering of strategically placed electric candles and a single red bulb hanging over the table beneath a black lightshade.

The room was square, but somehow—with the sheer volume of bric-a-brac, knick-knacks, and trinkets, plus the tables in each corner—the confined space felt like a circle centred on the round table in the middle. Arthur knew instantly what nonsense he was getting himself in for. As always, the more popular the séance—and the more stereotypical the set-up—the further away from being able to achieve its purpose it was. This was a tourist attraction for a place he doubted any of them could visit. It was the Disneyland of the occult. Music filtered in from somewhere, and Arthur almost cracked when he spotted the bright pink portable Bluetooth speaker and mobile phone with its diamanté case sitting between two stuffed ravens and a ferret. He leaned over to

Nae as the sound of heavy bass notes and howling winds filled the room.

"I'm sorry," he hissed.

"Are you kidding?" she said. "This is awesome! They've really gone all out with their colour pallet, haven't they?"

Arthur's cheeks ached from trying not to smile. "I see a red door and I want to paint it black," he sang quietly, and Nae hung her head, letting her hair fall over her face to hide her grin.

"What's the betting the playlist is called something like Ominous Tones for the Discerning Goth?"

"Supernatural Smash Hits."

"Top Ten Vampiric Beats."

"Smells Like Teen Spirits."

"Nice one."

"Welcome!" a voice boomed, causing them both to jump. They turned as the curtain parted dramatically to reveal a smiling man with a long white beard and the world's most ineffectual combover.

"Oh, this is ace," Nae gasped almost to herself. She gripped Arthur's arm in both her hands, and he suddenly couldn't care less that the bald man was wearing a bright purple robe, with—*for fucksake*—golden stars and moons!

Arthur had made his peace with occult jewellery and atmospheric rooms. He'd been in many of them over the last year and there was a lot to be said for the creation of a ritual atmosphere, but he drew the line at fancy-dress. Wizard robes and witch's hats normally caused him to turn around and walk straight back out, but the excited woman gripping onto his arm made him stay exactly where he was. The man beamed in delight at Arthur and Nae, and no wonder, the group filing into the room after him drove the average age higher than his receding hairline.

The black-clad woman who greeted them squeezed around the table and directed Arthur and Nae to sit in two of the high-backed wooden chairs. They settled in and waited for the others. It seemed to take an age for the jewellery and clothes to be positioned comfortably, but eventually, an expectant hush fell across the room and the bald man grinned at them all.

"Wonderful to see you all on this auspicious eve," he declared in a deep, sonorous voice. It was too deep though, too theatrical, and Arthur had to drop his gaze from the balding man rather than risk the impoliteness of letting slip an accidental smirk. He shuffled in his seat and tried to affect a nervous interest to mask his amusement. A small cough beside him let him know that Nae was also struggling to compose herself. He couldn't help but grin as they gave each other a quick sideways glance.

"We have newcomers today and we welcome you both," the man said. "Know that you are safe," he added in a serious tone. That caused Arthur to look up, but the purple wizard was staring at Nae. "I will protect you, you have my word," he said with a smile. "It is no trifling matter to commune with the spirits."

Around the table, the other guests nodded in sage agreement.

There were four others, two men and two women, bringing the total to eight. Nine, if you included Steve. Wordlessly and seemingly without prompting, they all grasped each other's hands and held them up together. Nae's left hand was taken by a smiling Indian man, and Arthur's hand was taken by the Gothic tea-cosy lady. The rattle of her jewellery was almost as loud as the ominous music. Arthur and Nae looked at each other for a moment, then grasped hands and raised them together, completing the circle. On Arthur's lap, Steve crossed his paws and rested his head on them, closing his eyes with a grumble.

"We are all now connected," the man said in a low voice. "The bond has been made betwixt brother and sister, and now we wait to see if that bond can reach to the other side."

He lifted his head and closed his eyes, as did all the others in the circle, double chins waving in unison. Arthur glanced around the room. The purple wizard had women on either side of him—either by accident or design—and he held their hands tight and high, elbows off the table.

The woman on his right was stick-thin and heavily made-up with bright aqua eyeshadow that glimmered in the dim light, as did the dress that appeared to be made of silk. She gripped hands with the small Indian man, but she leaned close to the wizard, her head tilted toward him, nodding and smiling each time he spoke.

On the other side of the purple-robed man, the woman sitting in quiet anticipation seemed perfectly normal in comparison to the rest of the company. She had short, cropped hair and thick round glasses, and she wore a simple blouse that stood out in a stark contrast, sitting as she was between the robes of the leading man and another man in a tweed waistcoat and bowtie.

The sleeves of this final man's white shirt were rolled up past the elbows, and his arms were covered in indistinct tattoos. Not a single patch of skin was visible apart from his fingers, and even they were laced with intricate lines and patterns. The man had a full beard, cut to a point, and wore a flat cap to match the waistcoat. It was a look that had been making a resurgence of late, although it seemed odd on a man who must have been pushing seventy. Thick black spacers the size of two-pound coins sat in his ears and pulled the lobes so low he looked like the statue of the Buddha on the shelf behind him.

He in turn held hands with the Gothic tea-cosy and the circle was complete. Arthur shifted in his seat and looked back to the bald wizard who was staring at him with narrow eyes.

"We say there are two kinds of spirits in this house," the man said to the room. "Those that you drink...and those who are our guests." He paused and waited for the dutiful laugh to come from the woman next to him and smiled in delight when she obliged. He went on, lowering his voice.

"You are here to witness a phenomenon not many people experience and only those with the gift can truly appreciate."

He turned to Nae, speaking directly to her.

"This will change your life forever. You are sitting on the site of a spiritual vortex. We are all of us here different, though all welcome. Some are Christian, Hindu, Buddhist. We have those who welcome the New Age, and we have the Wiccans of old. Welcome"—he nodded—"to our table."

"Welcome," they all intoned together and lowered their hands.

Steve's head shot up at the chorus of voices and he mumbled, "The greater good," mimicking the cult-like villagers of his favourite movie, *Hot Fuzz*. Arthur ignored him with difficulty and nodded politely to the leader, not trusting himself to speak, his cheeks burning with the need to grin.

"This evening," the bald man said, "we are going to place our hands lightly on the table to see what the spirit world has for us. Hopefully, the table will move. But"—and here he raised a crooked finger as if to warn them all—"that is not all."

He turned in his seat and rummaged in the pile of items behind him, pulling out a long dark tube. It looked like one of the drinking horns carried by the stag parties roaming the city outside (minus the long straw and alcohol), but it elicited an excited response from the table. The thin lady beside him made a noise of wonder. She reached her hand out before snatching it back and holding it to her red-painted lips as though she didn't dare touch.

"Tonight, we use the spirit trumpet!" the man declared, placing the strange horn on the centre of the table to a chorus of gasps and an excited smatter of clapping from the goth lady.

"Fuckin' hell," Steve grumbled.

From the corner of his eye, Arthur saw the way Nae bit her lip as she looked down, and he knew he couldn't look at her. It would set them both off. He fixed his own gaze on the 'spirit trumpet' and tried not to think too hard about it.

"We might hear a tapping," the wizard said, rapping his finger-nails on the horn, "as the spirits try to break through. But nobody really knows for sure what is going to happen." He paused for a long time, way too long, looking at each person in turn. Finally, he sat back with a heavy sigh.

"We are not in charge here," he said simply.

The man took a deep breath, rolled his shoulders, then slowly and deliberately placed his hands on the table, his fingers splayed like a pianist about to rock the Royal Albert Hall. Those around him followed suit, and both Nae and Arthur sat up straight and copied their actions, still unable to look at each other for fear of laughter.

"Are we ready to begin?" the wizard asked.

"Oh, yes!" the thin woman breathed in something bordering on ecstasy, and Arthur was very grateful when the lights suddenly flickered and went out.

Fierce winds blew across the darkening roof of the Minster and whistled through the ancient stonework with an eerie cadence that was far more appropriate than the lovely weather they'd been having so far.

The ghost of the Shadowman looked at the scene before him with the critical eye of a professional. It was a mess. There was a lot to do. And truth be told, he wasn't entirely sure he was the man for the job anymore.

Doubt.

That was new.

A thought occurred to him as he stared at the prone figures on the stones near his feet, and he lifted his hands until they were in front of his eyes. He turned them over and back, staring at each in turn. Back and front. Knuckles and palm. Both complete. He flexed his fingers as he looked at the figure on the ground. At the injuries. The blood. The ruined stump. A wave of emotion flooded through him, and he gasped at the rawness of it. Another new experience. The day had been full of them.

The dark spectre knelt and peered intently at the bodies entwined over the black book. Above them, the ravens circled, drifting in and out, lines and lines of birds following each other in intricate patterns beneath the eclipse.

A final bright flash of sunlight pierced the vortex of the twirling birds, and something else caught the eye of the Shadowman. He looked to his left, and there, on the roof of the Minster, covered in a mixture of blood and ash, was the ghost of the blade. He reached forward with a trembling hand, trying to ignore the grisly seeping stump a few feet away, and grasped hold of the handle he had known his entire existence.

Was it real?

Was *he* real?

And *which* him?

The Shadowman kneeling or the Shadowman lying face down on the floor?

Confusion and doubt rattled through the man as he realised he felt absolutely no different from before. He touched his face with his free hand and pulled the hat from his head, scrunching it in a tight grip.

It was all so *normal*.

Was this how the humans felt when they crossed over?

And what had happened when he...died? He had no memory of it. The Shadowman prided himself on memory.

There must have been something, a moment between this state and—he looked down—*that*.

He closed his eyes as he remembered the crushing agony of the revenant's hand on his heart and then...nothing. It just ended. Then he was here.

Was it instant? Was there a delay? Did he suffer?

For the first time in his existence, the Shadowman realised he wasn't sure. And that was a great and wondrous thing.

He smiled and reached out with the blade. There was work to do.

The shadows cast by the moon blanketed the city in a false night. Many of York's streets lived in near permanent shadow anyway, with their narrow roads and high-walled buildings blocking the natural reach of the sun, but now the darkness had spread, and with it came the cold.

People shivered and laughed nervously, hugging themselves tight and pulling jumpers or jackets over their shoulders. Those outside were in awe of the unexpected solar activity and stared at the sky, pointing and trying in vain to capture the majesty on camera phones ill-equipped for the job.

It was fortunate their eyes were cast heavenwards as it meant they didn't see the small creatures dashing through the shadows at their feet.

The Short Ones.

The Folk.

They moved swiftly beneath cars and danced between slow-moving people. They clambered out of drains and ran along stone gutters or anywhere the light couldn't touch. If the Short Ones didn't want to be seen, they wouldn't be. They lived in a place of shadows between worlds, and they knew where the gaps were.

Usually, those gaps were tiny and difficult to traverse. The summer solstice always did a fair job of thinning the veil on its own, but the addition of the eclipse had ripped bloody great holes in it.

The Short Ones spilled out of the dark places and descended on the city like English football fans in a Spanish beach resort.

Because everyone likes foreign food.

Outside the city, by the banks of the winding River Ouse, Emily Lovell knelt beside a small, smoky fire. Her face was smudged where she rubbed tears with ashen hands, but she didn't care. Her long black hair hung over her shoulders, hiding her face, and for a moment she wondered what would happen if it caught fire.

Would anyone care?

Oh, that's not right. They'd care, all right. Especially her mamma.

The black hair of the Lovell girls was a trademark in the caravans. A symbol of their status among the people and—she gripped it tightly and twisted until it hurt—the cause of all her anguish.

She was beautiful. They all said so. Beautiful just like her mamma. Perhaps even more so.

And tomorrow was her wedding day.

The lucky lass.

Emily poked angrily at the fire, and the meagre flames flickered and died, fading into ember as thick white smoke curled over her face and away across the river. She hadn't needed to light the fire, but she liked the smoke. She liked the way it smelled, the way it moved. She loved the artistry of it, and so she perched on her heels and watched as the smoke danced over the water, catching the eerie glow of the eclipse, and twisting the remaining light into grey lines and shadows.

The birds were quiet, and the water lapped gently against the bank. It was a moment of perfect peace and tranquillity, though the eclipse made her shiver more than she cared to admit.

Perhaps this wasn't a good time?

Or perhaps it was the perfect time?

Emily reached into the pocket of her dress and pulled out five white stones. She was pretty certain this wasn't going to work; it was just another of the many myths and fireside stories that did the rounds among the caravans, but stories would soon be all she had left.

As far as Emily was concerned, the next time the sun rose, her life would no longer be her own.

If it ever had been.

When you're a Lovell girl, when the world has expectations, when you're told for so long what is best for you, your own desires become lost in the mire of others.

Emily crawled around the fire to the riverbank and looked over the edge. The water was flat and still—a mirror for the sad lonely girl to see herself reflected in nature. She looked at her pale, perfect skin, her black hair, the dark hollows of her eyes, the sharp, pretty nose, and she dropped the first stone, smiling as it destroyed her reflection.

Five white stones in the River Ouse and the water would show you anything you desired—that's what the old ones said, anyway.

The second stone followed the first, and Emily wondered if she was supposed to put them all in at once. The ripples settled, and her face swam back into focus, so she quickly dropped the last three, gripping hold of the grassy bank to peer into the depths as they landed with a musical *plink, plink, plink.*

"Show me what I desire," she said, her words barely a whisper, her cheeks flushed red. This was a kids' game—girls asking to see their future husband or their dead relatives—but Emily had no idea what her own desires even were. Her mamma barely gave her time or space to have them.

The water settled, and for a moment, Emily's heart raced as the image shifted and changed, but it was nothing more than a trick of the light.

It was still her own reflection.

There would be no more kids' games. No more make-believe. No more magic.

Emily closed her eyes and tears fell from her cheeks, rolling down her face and gathering until they hung and fell, splashing silently onto the surface. She dug her hands into the dirt until it hurt and stifled the cry that threatened to rise from the depths and escape her lips.

No. She would not give in to self-pity. She was a Lovell after all.

Emily's head hung low against her chest, and her arched back rose and fell as she tried to control her breathing. Calming herself, she let out a small laugh at the silly childishness of the game and her own wild emotions. Then, she opened her eyes.

The reflection was gone.

The water no longer showed a picture of her own sad self but the smiling face of another girl.

It was a girl she instantly recognised. A girl she had met in year eleven, that wonderful winter she spent in school.

Emily screwed her eyes shut and shook her head, but when she opened them, the girl was still there, dancing in the water.

Rosie.

A name more suited to a traveller than her own, but where Emily was dark and tall, Rosie was blonde and short...and beautiful. She came from a loving family who had lived in the same house in the same street in the same town their whole lives. Rosie had been new to the school as well, moving from her last due to bullying and arriving on the same day as Emily.

The girls didn't really speak in class. Emily didn't bother making friends as she was never sure how long she would stay, but when the prospect of a school trip came along, the two found themselves thrust together, the infamous 'last pick.'

To Emily's surprise, her mamma had signed the permission form, and she was free to go on the excursion to the Lakes District. A two-day outward bound course with a one-night stay in the dorms. Rosie and Emily had been put together in their own room because neither of them had any friends and all the other girls had already partnered up.

It was one of the shining memories of Emily's brief experiences of school.

She looked at the reflection and cried out as Rosie smiled at her. She remembered that smile. Sitting close on the bed as they spoke all night. The downward cast of her eyes and that slight lean forward.

Her heart raced faster, and she moved closer to the water, remembering. Rosie's eyes closed and Emily was transported back to that wonderful, breathless moment, but suddenly the water churned as slimy grey-green hands burst from the depths to take hold of her hair.

She would have screamed if she had time.

The creature snarled in the sudden broiling mass of the river —it had the face of a woman, but it wasn't her Rosie. The mouth split in a wicked grin. It laughed as it dragged the stricken girl in... and under...and away.

The ripples on the surface of the Ouse settled quickly, and the small fire smouldered on the riverbank as wafts of thinning smoke danced over the still water.

~

The summer solstice was a night of spirits when people like the wizard man—who was currently crooning a song to a distinct lack of them—would say that the boundaries are thin, and the veil has been pulled aside. And, annoyingly, in this respect, he was absolutely spot on.

For centuries, the events of midsummer had been tied to the land. Bonfires were lit and smoke was driven over crops and livestock as a means to ward off evil spirits and to bless the harvest. Unfortunately for Emily, those bonfires needed to be far bigger than a few meagre twigs smouldering on a riverbank. The smoke had to be thick and heavy to roll slowly over the farms and villages. The fire represented the sun itself, and sometimes the young men would create burning wheels and run them across the hills while the villagers traversed the fields with lit torches.

Boys would burn bones, offal, and filth to create a thick noxious smoke that would confuse the demons and even—according to some stories—the dragons.

These creatures, supposedly driven mad by the summer heat, would fly into the air to have sex and poison the rivers and wells with their falling seed, which, when you think about it, leaves an awful lot of unanswered questions.

It was perhaps best, then, to say that Midsummer's Eve celebrations started out with agrarian intentions but devolved over the years into a party.

Any excuse for a piss-up.

The fact remained that fire and smoke were essential ingredients and absolutely key to the whole business.

The Shadowman knew this.

The fire he'd created on the roof of the Minster burned white-hot, the smoke billowing into the sky, rising through the centre of the ravens like a chimney, reaching for the sun and moon. It was huge...a great pyre atop the cathedral, and deep in the white glow of the pulsing flame, the leatherbound book sat in scorched defiance. The pages trembled, the edges curling, and a black stain spread across the dirty white edges while the cover tried in vain to hold back the heat.

Suddenly, the book shuddered and burst open. Flames roared and tumbled across the exposed paper. Pages flickered and rolled as the fire ate at them, and the smoke grew thicker and thicker.

Satisfied, the Shadowman turned to the bodies.

They lay in a tangled heap where he had dragged them, the revenant's fingers still clasping the ruin that used to be the Shadowman's heart. The man in black leaned down and took hold of the dead man's thumb, bending it back until it snapped and came away in his hand. He broke three more fingers before he could extricate the ruined organ, and not once did he utter anything about a little piggy, which just went to show how different he was from the rest of us.

The Shadowman lifted his heart to the strange half-light of the sky.

His own heart.

Nothing more than a chunk of meat, he thought, though he did marvel at the tubes, turning it this way and that, exploring with questing fingers.

With a shake of his head, he placed it on the stones. So many distractions when there was work to be done. How did the humans manage? He turned to the revenant. The heart of the dead man was still in the chest. Intact. He needed both.

Taking a tight grip of the ethereal blade, the Shadowman made four deep cuts, much bigger than needed, but he couldn't risk harm to the organ within. The knife slid through flesh and bone with a satisfying hiss, and the man in black placed the blade on the stones beside his heart.

He reached between the ribs with his gloved fingers and lifted the grisly rectangle from the corpse. A few stubborn muscles and veins fought back, but with a swift tug and a noise like a shucked mussel, the dead man's chest lay exposed to the world.

And there, right where it should be, but perhaps a little draftier than normal, was the heart of the revenant.

To make this grim spectacle even more surreal, the Shadowman had gone about his task with a soft smile and the occasional whistle. It felt good to enjoy his work again. He reached into the chest and carefully pulled the heart from within, holding it up in wonder. Then he picked up his own and stared at them both, turning them back and forth.

One intact. One broken.

One human. One not.

Both flesh.

"Mine's bigger," he mumbled, proving he might be a man after all, before placing them gently back on the roof.

The two hearts touched, and just for a moment, it seemed that they both beat slightly, but that was probably just a trick of the light...or the dark.

The Shadowman rose to his feet and grabbed each body by an ankle, dragging them to the roaring fire where he dumped them unceremoniously into the flames. They had served their purpose. The fire flared, devouring the two bodies so quickly it was as though they fell through a hole in the roof and vanished. The spirit of the Shadowman shielded his eyes until the blaze finally began to dwindle, reduced somehow to a small flame no bigger than a camping stove, but still white hot. The fire had scorched the stones black, and piles of ash drifted gently in the heat.

There was one more thing.

The Shadowman placed the hearts in the centre of the small flame and watched as they cooked, the last residues of moisture bubbling on the rapidly blackening surface. They sizzled as flames burst over the flesh, the smell of roasting meat filling his nostrils. The fire reached from the broken heart to the full, knitting them together, fusing the flesh with flame.

Finally, they crumpled together and turned to ash.

One last white flame flickered for a moment and died.

And suddenly it was done.

The smoke drifted away, and the birds fell silent, hanging in the air in a wide spiral beneath the shadowed sun.

In the shade of the eclipse, on the cold, dark roof of the Minster and under the watchful eye of the ravens, the Shadowman scooped the ashes into a black mug filled with a dark liquid. He stirred it once with a gloved finger, raised it to the heavens, and drank.

Behind him, shrivelled and forgotten in the shadows where it fell, the severed hand curled one slow finger into the air. An errant spark drifted out the dark sky and settled on the grey flesh.

Slowly, it began to smoulder.

CHAPTER 9

The single red light hung above the table and lit the gathered circle in an eerie glow. Arthur could feel the tension in the room as the odd assortment waited in anticipation. What they were waiting for, he had absolutely no idea. There were no ghosts here. He cast his eyes around, trying to take it all in without moving his head too much, but he was certain they were alone. Despite this, the wizard began to talk in a deep, sonorous voice.

"Spirits, you are welcome to come in. Use the table. Use the trumpets. Use our energy."

"Yes! Use us!" one of the women said in a low gasp.

Once more Arthur was glad the lights were so low. He was painfully aware of Nae sitting beside him and couldn't begin to wonder what she might be thinking. He thought he heard her gasp or laugh, and his cheeks burned with his own barely suppressed amusement, but the group was just gearing up. Soon enough, the room filled with increasingly excited voices as they communed with absolutely nothing.

"Tip the table, please."

"Welcome."

"Use our energy."

"Tip the table, please."

"You are welcome here."

"The table is starting to vibrate!"

"Thank you. Oh, thank you!"

"Welcome."

"It's good."

"What the flying fuck is going on?"

This last voice couldn't be heard by anyone else, but Steve was fully awake now and sitting on Arthur's lap looking around in utter bemusement. "These guys are mental," he gasped, and Arthur had to resist the urge to shush the little dog, knowing if he did it would be completely misconstrued by the assembled people.

"How much money did you pay to be part of this shit?" Steve asked, and then he jumped suddenly as the table tipped and rocked. The little dog scrambled to stay on Arthur's lap, and the volume of the people increased.

"You're here!"

"It's good!"

"Welcome!"

"Fuck off! That woman is rocking it. Look at her fingers! She's pushing and pulling!"

"The table moves!"

"The table moves!"

"Of course it bloody moves! You're—"

"The spirits are here."

"Sing to them! Bring them closer!"

And then the group began to sing, and Arthur couldn't help but stare, open-mouthed at them all.

"Row, row, row your boat, gently down the stream!"

"What..."

"Row, row, row your boat gently down the steam!"

"...the fuck..."

"Row, row, row your boat gently down the stream!"

"...is happening?"

Arthur was almost certain he could see Nae's shoulders shaking as she tried to contain herself, but the group were in full stride now, and the table rocked violently beneath their hands.

The trumpet rattled loudly as it rolled and bounced around, bumping into people and crashing back. Steve whined as the noises grew louder and louder—the singing, the trumpet, the table. It built and built until the wizard man shouted, "They are here! Open your eyes. Commune with the spirit world!"

"Are you here for someone in this room?" the hippie lady asked loudly, and Arthur thought he saw a quick flash of irritation cross the wizard's face, but the table rocked violently toward Arthur and Nae, and the collected people gasped and laughed.

"Yes!"

"Yes, you are!"

"It is good."

"He fucking pushed it!"

The table rocked back with a crash and then lifted again, and the trumpet bounced and landed in Nae's lap. She looked up at Arthur with wide, unfathomable eyes as the movement slowed and the trumpet settled between her breasts.

"You are chosen," the wizard man said to Nae, and all eyes turned to her.

Arthur mouthed, "I'm sorry."

Nae grinned, her eyes bright in the dim red light.

"Don't think," the man said, "*feel! W*ho do you think it might be?"

"He just bloody said don't think," Steve complained.

Nae looked at the wizard and spoke without hesitation, causing Arthur to blink in surprise.

"My father," she said.

"Oh, shit," Steve said.

"Say his name."

"Alan."

"Are you Alan?" he asked loudly, lifting his head to the ceiling. The table rocked again, nearly pushing Nae back in her seat. The trumpet bounced and hit her in the face, but everyone laughed and cooed.

"It *is* Alan!"

"Welcome Alan!"

"Alan, you are so welcome!"

"It is good."

"What do you wish to ask your father?" the wizard asked, raising his voice over the others.

"Are you happy where you are?" Nae said instantly, and the table bounced back with a clatter, moving in a circular motion, pushing and pulling everyone's arms around in an arc.

"He is happy!"

"He has found the spirit world!"

"Oh, bless you, Alan!"

"The spirit world is love!"

"Thank you, spirits!"

"Thank you, Alan!"

Nae reached out and took hold of Arthur's hand before leaning close and whispering in his ear.

"My Dad's called Bob. He's not dead."

That was too much for Arthur. He burst out laughing and then tried to cover it with a cough, but the table crashed to a halt, and everyone stopped. The trumpet did one last slow bounce on Nae's lap and then rattled against the table and became still.

"Sorry, sorry," Arthur said, but no one spoke.

The room was utterly silent, eerily so after all the noise, and Arthur looked up slowly, expecting judgemental stares and shaking heads. Instead, he found himself staring into the cold, black eyes of the Shadowman as he crouched on the table.

Nae leaped from her seat with a scream, tumbling backward over her chair and crashing into the shelves behind them. She stood up in a fluster and backed away.

"What the fuck!" she gasped and then laughed nervously, casting her eyes around the dark room. "Where did they go?"

Arthur blinked. She was right. All the other members of the séance were gone.

"Who the fuck is that?" she said. "Is this some sort of show?"

Arthur reached out and took her hand, his mind whirring.

"You can see him too!"

"See him? What? Of course I can fucking see him. Where did he come from?"

She turned to the Shadowman, who stepped down from the table, standing where the wizard had been.

"Who are you?" she demanded. "What the hell is going on? Wait..."

Nae looked closely, trying to take it all in, trying to process what her eyes saw but her brain couldn't translate. The people were still there. They were just...washed out. The wizard had his hand in the air and his mouth open, but it looked as though someone had set the translucency on a photograph too high and the background was now the foreground.

Nae tried desperately to hold on to something that would make sense, but then Arthur's words filtered back through her frazzled mind. She pulled her hand away from his. There was a hiss of static and purple sparks, but she barely registered them.

"What do you mean, *can I see him*?"

"Well," Arthur began, "the man in black. You *can* see him, can't you?"

"Of course I can see him! What is going on? Is this some sort of magic show?"

"No, I don't think so..."

"Why are you so fucking calm!" she shouted. "Those hippies have just vanished! Nearly. Almost. Look!" She waved her arm at the man who was in the seat next to her, and it passed right through his face. Nae tried to scream, but no sounds came from her mouth as she gripped her own hand in horror and stared at it.

Steve barked at the top of his voice and jumped onto Arthur's now vacant seat.

"Mate, this is fucked!" he said. "What do we do?"

Nae turned sharply at the sound of the dog's voice and stared wide-eyed at the little terrier.

"Did you just fucking talk?" she gasped.

If it were possible, Steve would have blushed. But he couldn't, so he didn't. Instead, he wagged his tail, grinned, and said, "Yeah. Sorry about that. Hi."

Arthur tried to catch Nae, but he wasn't fast enough. Her suddenly unconscious body crashed into the table. The unbalanced central leg gave way and broke in two as the tabletop and the girl fell to the floor.

Arthur knelt beside her and gently stroked her hair as she breathed deeply in a stupor. His eyes flashed at the Shadowman. "What—" he started, but the man in black raised his hands and interrupted.

"To use your parlance, I think I fucked up."

CHAPTER 10

The biggest problem with magic is that it exists. Thousands of years of evolution and technological advancement does nothing to change that one salient fact. It is no wonder that in its infancy, science as we know it was regarded simply as another form of magic. And wouldn't a person from as little as a hundred years ago marvel at the revelation of a smartphone? All that computing power, all that knowledge, all that potential for learning. That is magic in its own right. It would, however, maybe surprise them less to discover the smartphone had not been a turning point in humanity's stately march forward but rather an excuse to be really shitty to each other while watching unlimited pornography and cat videos. Humans hadn't changed, but the world had.

For some people, magic was just science we didn't yet understand. For others, it was entertainment—rabbits and hats and all that. But believing something isn't real didn't stop it from being so, and banishing it into the realm of storytelling didn't necessarily make it fiction. The magic was still there, still here. It was just that we'd forgotten how to use it.

Take Arthur, for example.

Arthur could *do* magic. He could create flames and balls of fire and speak to the dead and release them from the bondage of their afterlife, but he didn't have a Scooby-Doo how it all worked or what else he might be capable of. And deep in his soul, he had doubts. It all seemed a little too easy, a little too obvious. Electric magic was an awful cliché after all.

But if you were watching closely when it all went tits up at the séance, you might have noticed that Arthur was holding Nae's hand.

They were connected.

When the Shadowman completed his spell under the shade of the eclipse, the effects were felt far and wide, his own goals and aims a mere drop in the ocean.

There were always consequences for breaking the rules, and more often than not, others got dragged along for the ride.

Magic is a power, and power flows both ways.

In short, he did, indeed, fuck up.

"Run that by me again," Arthur said in a level voice. "Just one more time."

He was angry. Furious even. Nae was awake and groggy, and she sat against a pile of books with her knees held tightly to her chest. Arthur sat beside her with his arm protectively over the young woman's shoulder. She hadn't spoken yet, and she didn't look likely to, but neither had she pushed him away. The scared woman watched and listened, taking it all in and trying her best to process what her mind wouldn't let her believe.

The Shadowman pinched the bridge of his nose and smiled, opening his arms wide.

"I'm alive," he said.

"Haven't you always been?"

"Well, yes. And no."

"Helpful."

"This is new to me. All this..." He made an indistinct motion that could have meant anything—his head, the room, the events, the life cycle of an African swallow. Arthur didn't care.

"Just tell me what you did."

"A spell. An ancient magic. It was hidden across many pages of the book."

"Your book?"

"Yes."

"And what does it do, this spell?"

"It makes me live."

"Something you were not doing before."

"Quite."

"Do I want to know the details of this spell?"

"Probably not."

Arthur rubbed Nae's shoulder, and she moved away from him slightly. It was the first indication that she was really there with them, and he didn't like it. It had seemed like a flinch. This was all wrong. He turned on the Shadowman again.

"Tell me what happened here?"

"Well, the spell worked."

"Get to the point!"

"I broke the bonds of the Shadowmen, I burned the book, I died, and I came back. As a man."

He seemed terribly proud.

"And?"

"And other events occurred I had not anticipated."

"Like this?" Arthur nodded to the barely visible shapes of the gathered séance who sat, frozen, in their seats. You had to concentrate hard to notice them, but once you did they were difficult to miss.

"That appears to be part of it, yes."

"And the rest?" Arthur asked slowly, not liking the tone in the Shadowman's voice.

"These are not the only ones who—"

"How many?" Arthur interrupted.

"Well..."

"How many?"

"All."

"What do you mean, *all*?"

"The entire city."

Arthur stared, his mouth open. Beside him Nae barely reacted, but then Steve spoke for them both, and she twitched at the sound of the little dog's voice.

"What the bloody hell do you mean, the *entire* city? The entire city what...has vanished? Has become translucent? Has turned into ghosts?"

"Your dog can say the word translucent," Nae said in a small voice. They all looked at her, and she giggled slightly, then shook her head. She gave Arthur a look, and all of a sudden it seemed she was back with them, but her eyes were hard. Abruptly, she pushed Arthur away and got to her feet, glancing with purpose around the room.

"Tell me what is going on," she demanded. "No bullshit, no lies, just the truth." She smoothed down her clothes and ran her fingers through her hair, then rubbed her palms against her face to wake herself up. Arthur was impressed at the self-control, but he couldn't find the words. Nae took his hesitation for reluctance and turned on him.

"I don't know what you're playing at or how you pulled this off, but I want answers now or I'm calling the police!"

"That won't help," Steve said.

"What the fuck does that mean? Is that a threat?" She paused, then laughed at the realisation she was berating a small black and tan terrier. She stepped away. "Ventriloquism? Of course it is! I'll admit, it's pretty bloody good, but it's not funny! Did you drug me?" she demanded suddenly without giving him time to answer.

"Look," Arthur began, raising hands in what he hoped was a calming gesture.

"Don't fucking *look* me!" she shouted, her face twisting with anger. "Tell me what is going on or get the hell away from that door!"

"Calm down," he said, and he knew instantly it was a mistake. Nae's eyes narrowed, and a red flush ran up her neck.

"Don't tell me to calm down! Never in the history of *calm down* has anyone ever calmed down by being told to fucking calm down! Door! Now!"

"I..." Arthur began and turned, noticing that he was indeed standing between Nae and the only way out of the room. This was not a fact Nae had missed. Women never do. "No, you can't," Arthur stammered. "I don't think it's safe out there."

"What?" Her voice was low, a hint of snarl. "So, I can't leave this room. Is that what you're saying?"

"No, I..."

Again, Arthur couldn't find the words, and he stepped around the table to try to prove to her that he wasn't purposefully blocking the door, but as soon as he moved and before he could explain, Nae exploded into action. She threw a chair at Arthur and yanked at the door in one motion.

"Wait!" Arthur shouted, diving over the chair and trying to grab at her arm, but she yelled and rolled her shoulder away, punching him in the side of the head with her left fist. It was a short, sharp jab—hard enough to shock Arthur into pausing, and that was all she needed.

With a crash, Nae was through the door and halfway down the stairs before he had time to react.

"I like her," the Shadowman said.

"Fuck off!" Arthur shouted.

He raced after the fleeing woman but tripped over the chair and fell.

By the time he got to his feet and pushed through the door, Nae was already gone.

Arthur ran down the stairs and bolted along the narrow corridor toward the open door, not quite registering the darkness of the world outside.

A shame really, for it was through the darkness the Shadowman travelled.

He appeared in front of Arthur, and the young man crashed into him, stumbling backward with a grunt as the breath left his body. It was like running into a wall! He gasped but his chest was empty, and he couldn't breathe. Panic welled inside Arthur, and a hot flush crept across his cheeks as he fought for air, reaching a hand toward the door. Purple sparks crackled along his fingers, but the emptiness in his chest caused him to gasp again and clutch at his sides. The sparks spluttered and died.

"In through the nose, out through the mouth," a voice said beside him. It was Steve. With an effort, Arthur nodded, gesticulating and pointing sharply toward the door. The little dog instantly understood. "I'm on it," he said, and dodged through the Shadowman's feet, into the street after the fleeing girl.

Arthur tried to stand, using the wall to steady himself, bent double as he forced air back into his lungs. It hurt.

"Sorry about that," the Shadowman said. "I'm not quite myself. Ha!" he laughed suddenly at a joke only he knew. "I guess I don't know my own strength."

"How?" Arthur gasped and leaned against the wall. He nodded up to the room and back to the man in black.

"How did I move through the shadows if I am alive? I was going to ask myself that very same question. I guess old habits die hard," he said, lifting his nose to the air as if in deep thought. "It is how I found you, after all. A curious thing."

"But?"

"But I'm a man now, yes? A living breathing man. Just like you!" the Shadowman grinned, and it was a deeply unnerving sight. It was the grin of a man who had *seen* smiles but never bothered to master the necessary musculature arrangements. It put Arthur in mind of a hyena. No one doubted the buggers could laugh, but you wouldn't get close enough to tell one a joke.

With an effort, Arthur straightened and made toward the door, but the Shadowman raised his hands, blocking the way.

"Stop. I need your help."

Arthur ignored him. He was determined to follow Steve...to find Nae. He pushed the man in black to the side and made for the door.

The Shadowman saw the way Arthur clasped his stomach as though trying to keep in what little air he'd managed to steal back and reached a logical conclusion. Effortlessly, he slammed the man against the wall.

There was a bang and a crack as Arthur hit the brickwork and what little breath was in him exploded from his body once again. He fell to the floor without making a sound, and tears sprang to his eyes as pain rocked through his body. He rolled to his knees, his face red, and his forehead resting on the dark carpet.

The Shadowman knelt next to him and then patted him on the back.

"Good. Now we can talk. I think I need your help, Arthur. I'm not sure I completed the spell properly. I'm definitely a man now, isn't that wonderful? But I'm not sure I did it right. I have all these conflicting thoughts. Emotions, I think. And this body suddenly does not want to do what it is told. I am...I don't know the word...I want something. This body needs something, but I do not know what. I feel as though I am being pulled in different directions."

Arthur tried to speak but couldn't manage it. He felt as though he was suffocating, and his lungs burned with the absence of air. He held his sides and grimaced at what he thought might be a cracked rib.

The Shadowman was different, that was certain. They never talked this much before, and the patting of his back was a lot like the smile...there was nothing particularly wrong with it...but neither was it right.

Arthur turned his head and tried to speak, his lips forming a question, but the man in black beat him to it.

"Why you? Dear Arthur, you set me free. Not in the same way you set my brother free, of course. He passed over. Truly broke the bonds. None of us even knew that was a possibility until you came along and suddenly one of our number was...no more. Free. But then you had the chance to do the same for me...to end my existence...and you didn't. Do you remember, Arthur? Do you remember the castle? The witch? I know her name, you know. As do you. It was written in the book for centuries. She was little more than a story, forgotten and locked away, and none of us knew why her name was still there. Then you set her loose upon the world."

He patted Arthur on the back in what he probably thought was a companionable gesture, but the bent man winced in pain and slumped to the ground.

"Witches and barghests, warriors and wizards, demons, sprites and hobgoblins," the Shadowman mused, not noticing Arthur's pain. "There hasn't been that much trouble since Merlin. She should not have had the power to bind me like she did, but then you came along, Arthur. You, again. And this time, *you* freed *me*. You could have killed me, sent me off in the same direction as my brethren, but you freed me, and you let me live. Then you freed all those trapped souls. You gave them a choice, Arthur. A choice!"

Arthur thought of the bonfire in the middle of Richmond. The magic fire that drew the ghosts in and set them free if that's what they chose.

The Shadowman sat back and leaned on the opposite wall, pulling his knees up to rest his elbows on them.

The man's boots were in front of Arthur's face—jet black and functional, like a goth farmer, he thought. What he wasn't expecting were the socks. Somehow the idea that the men of shadows wore socks was almost impossible to wrap his head around. The thought that this creature might get up in the morning and sit on the edge of the bed like anyone else just didn't compute. But the more he looked, the more he realised there was something off about the clothes.

Before, the Shadowmen looked like they had been cut from the world itself. The black they wore wasn't a colour; it was a hole. But now...now he seemed real. He was even wearing a waistcoat beneath the black jacket, Arthur noticed. Admittedly, it was a black waistcoat over a black shirt, but they were *real* clothes.

There had always been a quality to the Shadowmen that made them seem to Arthur as though they did not belong to this world. And yet here one was, sitting on the floor with his neatly tied boots and impeccably ironed trousers.

Arthur reached out and touched the cloth. It felt like cotton.

"A choice," the man said again, and Arthur groaned as he shifted his body to look at him. "It is not something I have ever had but you showed me it was possible. So, I made a choice, Arthur. I made a choice, and I chose to live. I chose to become human, like you."

Arthur shuffled into a sitting position. He glanced at the open door and noticed the darkness there. A cold breeze drifted in from the empty street, and he shivered, his brain trying to catch up, to piece it all together.

"Where is everyone?" he managed to say with a pained effort.

"Still there," the Shadowman said. "It is *we* who are on the other side."

"What?"

"The other side," the Shadowman repeated. "We're in the place where the ghosts live. It took an age to find you."

"I thought...I thought you did the spell just now," Arthur croaked.

"Yes, well, time is relative."

Arthur glared at him, and the Shadowman shrugged. His face was still deep in the shadows beneath the brim of a flat cap, but the mouth was moving, animated, as though he was chewing a sweet and rolling it around his tongue. The skin even seemed to have more colour than before.

The flesh of the Shadowmen had always seemed to Arthur to be one shade short of dead. Pallid.

"Look closely," the Shadowman said, and a smile curled the corner of his lips.

Arthur looked out of the door at the empty street and suddenly realised what he meant. The street wasn't empty at all. It was like the room upstairs. The people were still there but they could barely be seen. It was as if they were frozen in time and space. If he moved his gaze quickly, they vanished, only reappearing when he really concentrated. A shopper here, a couple there, a group of drinkers with arms over shoulders in a line on the far side of the street. The usual throng on Stonegate on a long summer day but somehow barely visible. A sharp throbbing started above Arthur's right brow, and he closed his eyes tight, screwing them up until the pain subsided.

"Slide the brightness until the symbol becomes barely visible," he said to himself.

"What?"

"Nothing," he said. "So, we're on the other side?"

"Indeed."

"Where the ghosts live?"

"Quite."

"Why aren't they moving?"

"They are. In their own time."

"Wibbly-wobbly," Arthur mumbled but then stopped as a black cat appeared in the doorway and licked itself. He raised an eyebrow.

"Cats don't count," the Shadowman said.

The animal's ears twitched, and it hissed at them, the sleek black back arching high, the hairs prickling with angry static. Suddenly, the eyes grew wide and frightened. The ears flattened, and the creature turned to run, claws scratching furiously to get some purchase on the cobbled street. It ran in place for a few moments then raced out of sight. A cluster of tiny, green creatures clambered over each other in their haste to catch the fleeing feline.

Arthur gasped. "What were they?"

"The Folk," the Shadowman sighed. "Short Ones. Savage little buggers. For some strange reason, your kind used to call them fai—"

A loud, terrified cry cut him off as it echoed from the street and then died as quickly as it had come. The cat came back the other way, but this time it was in two halves and being carried above the heads of the tiny creatures. They moved in complete silence, and Arthur shivered as the dismembered corpse bounced out of sight.

"I need a drink."

"*I* need you to help me."

"How? What can I do? I can't fix this!"

"Oh, this doesn't need fixing. This will end when the eclipse is over."

"And how long will that take?"

"In your world, just a few minutes."

"And here?"

The Shadowman shrugged.

"Great."

"I miscalculated. I did not, as it were, account for...everybody."

"You've lost me."

"I need you to set someone free."

"What? Who?"

"A man I used."

"What happened to him?"

"He's dead."

"And now he's a ghost?"

"In a manner of speaking."

"And why do you want me to set him free?"

"It is the right thing to do."

That made Arthur pause. He stared hard at the man before him—if he could even call him that—and the man stared back.

They looked at one another, and the Shadowman reached up and took off his hat, scrunching it in his hands and looking to the floor. It was a curiously shy gesture. Like a child. Everything about him was different. Arthur could see a fleck of purple deep in those black eyes. The colour of magic. Not for the first time, he wondered just how much Sir Terry Pratchett really knew.

The Shadowman even looked younger, perhaps in his late thirties or early forties, but truthfully, he was far older than Arthur could possibly comprehend. He had a pointed chin and angular nose. Everything about him seemed sharp like a blade. Nose, chin, cheeks, eyebrows.

His hair—and Arthur wasn't sure he'd ever seen the hair of a Shadowman before as they all wore hats—was neatly trimmed. Black, of course, but well groomed. Yet again the strange oddity of this entered Arthur's mind. Was there such a thing as a barber for the Shadowmen? He stared at the bony chin. Did they shave? Or were they just made that way?

The man said he was alive, and if it were not for their history and the fact he moved through shadows, Arthur might have believed him, but he certainly wasn't of this world.

Arthur glanced to the door and the street beyond. His world. The other world. Wherever it was.

"Nae," Arthur said. The Shadowman looked puzzled.

"Like a horse?"

"No, it's her name. Renae. The woman I was with. What about her?"

"What about her?"

"She's *in this world* too!" Arthur said, using his fingers to mime inverted commas. The Shadowman tilted his head in confusion at the gesture. He lifted his own hands and did the same.

"I *do not know* why this is important."

"She doesn't have any power! She's trapped in what...a bloody ghost world? With absolutely no idea what is going on!'

"That is not important."

"It is to me!" Arthur shouted.

"It is not to me," the Shadowman replied in a level voice. There was no malice there. He was simply stating the facts as he saw them.

"Well, I'm not doing shit to help you until I know she's safe," Arthur said, rising to his feet with an effort and bracing his back against the wall.

He closed his eyes for a moment, and when he opened them again, the man in black was standing right there. He hadn't seen or heard him rise.

Arthur gulped and took a step back. A cold chill rippled down his spine, and the Shadowman's eyes narrowed, looking over his shoulder. Arthur turned quickly and realised his body was halfway through the wall, his elbows and back vanishing into the brickwork. This was another of his *talents*, though it wasn't one he had ever grown comfortable with.

Arthur shivered and stepped away, moving to the side of the

Shadowman and out of the brick. The man in black stood between him and the door. Arthur grimaced again. Being able to walk through walls sounds great until you think about the weight of all those bricks. He hated it.

"I do not see what this woman's safety has to do with your ability to do what I want," the Shadowman said, placing the flat cap on his head.

"It is the only way I'll help," Arthur replied, standing his ground, and hoping his voice didn't betray his nerves. He could still feel the claustrophobic sensation of the brickwork surrounding him, wrapping him in the world's most concrete embrace. The sudden thought flashed across his mind that he might make a run for it through the walls, but the Shadowman could move through shadows. How far would he get? And anyway, he was rubbish at the wall trick. It made him panic and feel sick, and more often than not, it didn't work—just left him with a concussion and a viral YouTube video.

"This is most irregular," the dark man said, almost to himself. "I need you to do a thing and yet you will not do it until I do a different thing."

"That's right," Arthur said.

"But I asked first," the Shadowman replied, and despite himself, Arthur laughed.

"Are you fucking kidding me? Are you a child? That's life. A grand don't come for free, mate!"

"I do not understand."

"No, you wouldn't." Arthur sighed. "Look, help me make sure Nae is okay and I'll see if I can help you with your...problem. Deal?"

"Deal?"

"It means we have an agreement," Arthur said and held out his hand. The Shadowman looked at it and then held out his own in the exact same fashion, but Arthur was ready for this and unwilling to take part in such a hackneyed cliché. He moved and gripped the man's hand, shaking it firmly, just once, while looking him dead in the eye, just like his dad had taught him.

"A deal," he said. "You help me, I help you."

"A deal," the Shadowman repeated. "I will find the girl and make her safe."

Without another word, he let go of Arthur's hand and turned away. It seemed as though he would walk out of the door and into the street, but instead, he walked behind the door and into the shadows. Arthur strode forward and snatched at the handle knowing full well what he would see when he did...nothing.

Arthur swore and ran into the false night of the frozen city.

CHAPTER 11

Arthur turned left where Nae had turned right because sometimes that's just the way these things go. The frightened woman had raced out of the doorway and headed toward the Minster, knowing instinctively that's where she'd find the biggest crowd, and she was halfway there by the time Arthur extricated himself from the tangle of chair legs and got beaten up by the Shadowman.

As she burst into the open space beneath the watchful eye of Emperor Constantine, Nae was more concerned with what lay behind than what lay in front, and so when she finally looked up, she skidded to a halt in shock.

There were hundreds—no, thousands—of people filling Minster Yard. They gathered around the base of the giant Gothic cathedral, filling the paths, the steps, the grass, everywhere, and not one of them moved. Every single person had their face turned to the sky, where above them, the black disc of the moon covered the sun.

Nae strangled her terrified gasp, backing away toward the upside-down Roman column. The set of keys gripped between her clenched knuckles rattled as she trembled in fear.

"What the..." She sobbed as she looked closely at the crowd and clamped a hand over her mouth. Some of them weren't people. Some of them weren't *all* people. There were missing limbs, missing heads, missing eyes. There were claws, scales, and teeth. Cats clambered through legs that didn't always go all the way down, and the ravens—the ravens flew in a spiral!

Nae's legs gave way, and she fell to the ground in a heap, biting her hand in fear. What the fuck had he done to her? How could she have been so stupid? She let out a strangled sob, and a tall lady at the back of the crowd turned and smiled. Half her face was missing. The woman was beautiful, and the smile was kind, but with only one remaining eye and half a mouth, beauty and kindness do very little to alleviate fear. Nae tried to make herself small against the terror, but there was just too much.

"There you are," a voice said, and she jumped in fright, clenching the keys tighter.

It was Steve.

Arthur's little terrier stood beside her with his tongue lolling and his ear turned inside out. He panted, paused, cocked a leg against the column and then spoke again. "This is all a bit odd, isn't it?" he said.

Nae scrambled to her feet, and—going against everything in her nature—kicked the dog in the side and legged it.

She ran, fleeing back the way she came, away from the swearing dog and the mad gathering. She turned left onto Low Petergate, heading away from the haunted house, and moved deeper into the city.

The street was empty. There were people in the windows, shadows on the other side of the glass, but nothing moved. They were frozen and almost translucent like the people at the séance. Nae caught a glimpse of some strange horror in the shadows as she ran. A dark mass writhed on the moonlit cobbles, and ten or more tiny creatures clambered over it like ants over rotting meat. She heard a strangled meow and kept going, racing down Low Petergate. She had to get away, to find safety, to find help.

Lights glimmered in the distance. The road ahead was narrow but clear, leading all the way to King's Square. There were always people in King's Square! Or the taxi rank at the end of Colliergate.

If she could just get to a taxi, she could get home, maybe the police? Or the hospital?

It had to be drugs, she thought. But what? And when did he do it? How? The mangled head of the woman at the Minster flashed in front of her eyes, and she forced down a strangled sob and ran on, tears streaming as the panic threatened to overwhelm her. It had to be drugs. Nothing else could explain it!

A woman stepped from one of the shops and walked into the road, and finally, Nae felt a surge of hope.

"Help me! Please!" she cried out, stumbling to a halt.

The lady smiled at her. She was real. Perfectly normal. A plump old lady with curly white hair in dusty overalls over a nondescript dress. There was nothing wrong with her face, no bits missing, no scales, or glowing eyes. Just rosy cheeks and flour-covered hands. *She must work in one of the cafes or bakeries*, Nae thought. She'd wait there while calling the police.

"Whatever is the matter, dear?" the woman asked, her eyes wide with concern. "Is someone chasing you?" She looked behind Nae at the empty street.

The nearly empty street.

A lone figure jogged up behind them, and the woman smiled.

"Oh, hello Steve. Friend of yours?"

"Hi, Alice," Steve said, trotting up and wagging his tail happily. Nae froze at the sound of the voice.

"Now, young man, I've told you before, my name is Ann."

"You'll always be Mad Alice to me," Steve panted, then looked sharply toward Nae who had made a strange, strangled sound in her throat. "Catch her," he said with a nod.

"Pardon?" said Ann, who turned a fraction too late. "Oh." She looked down at the unconscious form of the strange red-haired woman. "I bet that hurt."

Arthur came to a stop in St. Helen's Square and looked around. The grand buildings formed tall walls on four sides with narrow roads leading off on each corner. Nae could have gone down either one. The glass facade of Betty's was on his left and the bank on his right. Harker's was ahead, along with the red and white Mansion House, but there was no one there.

The square was empty.

Arthur had never known the square to be empty. Well, hardly ever. There was that time last year when Sarah Brocklebank ran toward him waving her father's lost keys. It seemed pretty empty back then.

Sarah.

She was beautiful. Whether he'd known she was a ghost at that point, he couldn't quite remember, although, it was typical of his mind to drag up memories of Sarah when he was looking for Nae.

All he needed now was to remember Wendy.

Christ. There it was.

Arthur tried to focus, banishing the memories of yet another drunken night in the city and walked across the cobbles. The Mansion House was covered in scaffolding and shrouded in green cloth. Maybe Nae had gone through there. Everywhere else seemed empty.

He slowed as he got close to the imposing building, a nervousness creeping into his limbs and holding him still. He felt eyes on him and shivered as he checked the dark places. He was alone, but he couldn't shake the feeling of being watched.

Then he saw them—the people reflected in the glass of the shops. They were everywhere.

Arthur did a double take. The streets were empty, but the reflections were definitely there. He turned back and forth, dizzy and confused, then narrowed his eyes. Suddenly, there they were, the shades and shadows of people filling the world as normal, going about their business—shopping and walking and taking in the sights. They weren't frozen, he realised, but rather moving so slow as to be barely noticeable.

Suddenly, a great animal roar shattered the night. Arthur had been breathing so hard he hadn't noticed just how quiet the world had become. He jumped at the noise, spinning back toward the open entrance of Stonegate.

And finally, he noticed the eclipse.

The sun and the moon appeared to hover just above the city, large and portentous in the false dark. A thin piercing white light bordered the jet-black moon, flickering and wavering over the edge of the abyss. There were other colours there too, deep in the blinding white, dancing like motes in the corner of the eye. Lines of purple and blue that flashed and vanished.

Arthur couldn't tear his gaze away. He had never seen anything like it.

The sky was full of birds, a great murmuration frozen in mid-flight, tracing a spiral that connected the celestial bodies to the earth—all focused on the Minster.

A fierce wind burst violently into the square then, carrying with it a cacophony of furious barks, discarded chocolate wrappers, and cardboard coffee cups. The litter danced in the sudden gust and Arthur backed away as the sounds increased. Thoughts of giant, slathering black beasts and devil dogs assaulted him, and he stepped back, suddenly tense and ready to run, but then another sound swelled over everything, building and rising until it was louder than all the rest.

Sssssssssshhhhhhhhhhh

A man in a well-tailored suit thundered out of Stonegate and grabbed desperately at a lamppost to swing himself round. His feet left the ground as he made the turn, then hit the stones before he was away again, screaming as he headed toward the centre of the city. The noise trailed behind him as though it had a life of its own.

iiiiiiiiiiiiiiiiiiiiiittttttttttttt!

A snarling and ferocious pack of dogs tumbled into the square, skidding and skittering on the stones. They crashed into each other and rolled, kicking out to get purchase. Arthur stared in horror as he realised some of the animals had bones poking through rotten flesh and a smorgasbord of open wounds. Tiny creatures darted beneath their legs and clambered over steaming backs, not caring where they trod or what they yanked on to get purchase. The barks weren't just vicious, they were frightened.

The hunters were being hunted.

The whole mob vanished down Davygate after the fleeing man, the echoes of their howls and barks drifting back through the street, and Arthur once more found himself alone in the suddenly silent square. He stared at the sky, at the birds, at the streets, at the reflections in the shop windows, at the way everything appeared normal on the surface and yet completely fucked underneath.

What the bloody hell was going on?

Arthur had never experienced anything like this, and for him, that was quite a statement. Arthur had dealt with ghosts and demons and giants and witches and vague Arthurian mythology for over a year now, but this was different. It's all well and good having a sneaky peek into whatever comes next, but when the whatever comes next becomes now, it was kind of taking the piss.

"And I'm sober," he grumbled to himself. "Well, mostly."

Arthur wondered if either of the others had found Nae yet. Three men looking for the same woman. Well, two men, and a dog. Well, one man, a dog, and...whatever the hell the Shadowman was. There were the makings of a joke in there somewhere, he thought, but now probably wasn't the time.

There was no logical place for Arthur to go, no rational decision to make, no phone call to be made to a friendly neighbour or helpful policeman, and he was buggered if he'd sit and wait at the séance in the company of the slow-moving wizard and his friends. So, he chose the illogical decision and followed the dogs.

Nae was conscious long before she opened her eyes. There were people talking. She recognised one voice. It was the voice that supposedly belonged to Steve, Arthur's dog. So, did that mean that Arthur was there as well? Was he throwing his voice to make it seem like the dog was talking? What a psycho! She had seen a ventriloquist act at the Barbican last summer and loved the way the woman had been able to throw her voice between different puppets. Of course, you could see her neck strain or small movements in her cheeks if you looked for them, but part of the magic was in not looking. But this? This was just creepy. She listened as the two people spoke and realised the second voice must belong to the little old lady, who somehow, impossibly, was wrapped up in all of this.

"She's a pretty one."

"Arthur seems to think so."

"I guess it's all gone a bit skewwhiff, hasn't it?"

"You could say that. Things haven't exactly gone to plan."

To plan. So, it was some sort of weird set-up!

Nae screwed her eyes tight and bit her lip to stop herself from crying out. Before she went travelling, her dad had made her watch a marathon of movies about backpackers getting kidnapped and sex-traffickers stealing away young women—which was either the very best parenting or the very worst—so she knew of the theoretical existence of groups who did those sorts of things. Was this that? She loved her dad, but he was no Liam Neeson. He didn't have money, but neither did he have a particular set of skills that could make him a nightmare for anyone. She was on her own. She had to use her brain.

All those hallucinations, all the images and visions, and yet she didn't feel any different. There was no blurred vision, no grogginess, no sense of being out of control at all. It had to be drugs, but what drugs could do this?

She needed to know what was going on.

Nae faked a groan and shifted her body to try to get a sense of where she was. The voices fell quiet, and she felt cold stone beneath her and rough brick behind. Her feet touched something that bent and shifted. A wheelie bin perhaps? Maybe they were in an alley? Mad Alice Lane. Someone had said that, hadn't they? Someone had said Mad Alice?

"We know you're awake, dear." A voice broke the silence. It was kind and gentle. The old lady. Nae opened her eyes.

It was an alley, but whether it was Mad Alice Lane or not she had no idea. One alley looked much like the rest from the ground. Dark. Narrow. Lined with dirty red bricks and an ever-present odour of stale piss and old cigarettes.

In fact, Nae was sitting in the exact same spot Arthur had woken up just that morning, right before they clapped eyes on each other for the first time. If she had been willing to chat with Steve, she might have discovered that he thought there was some sort of wonderful, cyclical poetry in that, but she probably wasn't in the mood.

"How's your head?" the dog asked, trotting to the side of the kneeling old lady and sitting down. His ear twitched as though it had a mind of its own, and his back leg sprang up to scratch away at it. "Sorry," he added when he was finished, but Nae never said a word. She just looked at him, then looked at the woman. There was no one else in the alley.

"Are you doing that?" she asked.

"Doing what, dear?"

"Doing that! Making the dog talk."

"Oh, no. That's got nothing to do with me."

"But he's talking."

"It's getting him to shut up that's the problem."

"Charming," said Steve.

"Dogs can't talk," Nae snapped, hoping the words would make sense of the world. Steve just grinned.

"I don't know what to tell you," he said and wagged his tail.

"Fucking nothing," yelled Nae, "because dogs can't fucking talk!"

"That's no way for a young lady to speak," Ann Barber gasped.

"And who the fuck are you?" Nae demanded, glaring at the old lady.

The two women looked at each for a long moment in stony silence, and Steve whined. Neither of them gave until suddenly Ann grinned.

"Oh, I like you. You've got spunk."

But Nae wasn't listening. She clambered to her feet and cried out in pain as her head spun. She lifted her hand to her hair and felt the tenderness there. Ann stood with her.

"You took a bit of a tumble, dear," she explained. "So, I brought you in here to get you out of the street."

"Where's here?" Nae demanded. She looked left and right and wondered which way would be the best to run. She was pretty certain she could push the old lady over easily enough, but then, if she'd dragged Nae down here, she was stronger than she looked.

"This is where I...live." Ann explained. Nae noticed the hesitation and reached a logical but entirely incorrect conclusion.

"You're homeless?" she asked, her voice softening a fraction.

"Oh no, dear. This is my home."

"This is Mad Alice," Steve said and barked. He seemed incredibly pleased with himself.

"Mad Alice Lane?" Nae said in a flat voice. She wasn't exactly comfortable talking to the dog, but at least she was getting answers. She glanced to the left. *That must lead to Low Petergate.* She shifted her weight, ready to run, but the dog spoke again.

"No. Well, yes. But what I meant was *this* is Mad Alice. *The* Mad Alice. Pretty cool, right?"

Nae stared at the dog, then at the old lady, who blushed (best not to think about that too much).

"I prefer Ann," she said, stretching out a hand. "Pleased to meet you."

"Fuck off!" Nae laughed.

"Dear, do you know any other words?" Ann scolded, folding her arms across her bosom. "You know..." But whatever she was going to say didn't leave her because Nae threw a wheelie bin at her and ran.

As soon as she left the wall, Nae saw the dim lights of the street and raced through the narrow passage. She pulled over milk crates and bins and whatever else she could lay her hands on, anything to help make her escape.

The noise was tremendous as smashing glass and crashing

plastic clamoured in her wake, but then she burst into the open street and was away.

She made it less than two steps before running into a horse's arse.

This was not a metaphor.

The giant animal barely flinched but stamped irritably, and Nae, though winded, still had the presence of mind to move away from its back legs in case it kicked. She'd been on the receiving end of that while working as a jillaroo in Australia. It was not an experience she ever wanted to repeat. But there was a horse! A horse ridden by a man in uniform. At last, the police.

"Sorry! God. Shit. Sorry. I'm sorry, officer, but I'm so glad you're here, I need…"

She stopped. She stared. She giggled a little and tried not to cry. She backed away.

The rider on the horse was indeed in uniform, but if it was a police uniform, then they had rolled back the dress code a few thousand years.

The Roman soldier gave the frightened woman a dismissive glance, then forgot about her. He raised a horn to his lips and blew hard. The noise shattered the night and bounced around the tall buildings, filling the world with the echo of a hundred horns all blowing in unison. It was the same note. The note to charge.

Nae pressed herself against the wall as a regiment of mounted Roman soldiers thundered down Low Petergate toward King's Square, where—she stared—where a line of screaming Vikings waited behind a shield wall.

Nae laughed.

Then she nodded.

Then she turned and walked quietly back into the alley, picking her way over the rubbish and scattered crates.

"So," she said, when she reached the wheelie bins. "You're Mad Alice, and you're a talking dog."

CHAPTER 12

Arthur heard the horns as he ran across St. Sampson's Square. He glanced down Church Street in the direction of the noise just as the charging Roman cavalry hit the Viking shield wall in an explosion of bodies and steel. From this distance, he couldn't quite work out what he was looking at, but he had his own problems to worry about. The dogs had gone. Vanished. There was absolutely no one to be seen in the wide paved area of Parliament Street.

Sometimes the absence of action could be far stranger than a surplus of it.

The dogs had been right in front of Arthur and now they were gone. He stopped and caught his breath, turning to look around the city centre. The buildings looked...wrong. There was a church tower sticking out of a coffee shop he was certain hadn't been there before. And the fountain was missing. The fountain was a staple of York. A permanent fixture. If it was gone, then something had gone seriously tits up.

His vision blurred, and a sharp, needle-like pain worked its way deeper behind Arthur's eyes as the world refused to play by the rules. He was in a crowd. He was alone. There were thousands of people. There were none. It was day and night at the same time.

Arthur groaned as a wave of nausea washed over him, and he

clamped his eyes shut against the mixed signals. When he was a child, his dad had an old black and white television in the back room. When you turned it off, the picture wouldn't just blink out, it would fade slowly as though the people on the screen were reluctant to leave. Arthur could never quite pick the point the image vanished.

The world felt like that.

None of it made sense.

If this truly was the ghost realm or whatever supernatural bloody name he was supposed to give it, then where the hell were all the ghosts? Why was it so quiet? Sure, he'd seen the dogs, and whatever the hell was happening down Church Street, and some of the buildings couldn't quite decide where they were or what they wanted to be, but other than that it was oddly calm.

This was, of course, the narrative equivalent of buying a boat called the Live Forever on the day you get run over by a truck carrying coffins from the coffin factory. So, it was with little surprise that the man in the well-cut suit suddenly sprinted out of Market Street with a pack of ghost dogs and other creatures hot on his heels.

They raced across the open expanse of Parliament Street with the man's terrified refrain struggling to keep up.

Shitshitshitshitshitshitshitshitshitshitshit!

Arthur watched in horror as the dogs gained on him in the open space. They were close, teeth and slathering jaws reaching and snapping, but the man was fast. He ran straight toward the shops and burst through the door of Marks and Spencer's. The glass door slammed shut behind him, and to Arthur's amazement, the pack of dogs crashed into the glass and let out a furious clamour of angry howls and barks. They scratched and clawed, but they were stuck, unable to go any further.

Arthur breathed a sigh of relief for the man, then nearly choked on it when he realised he was alone in a street with a pack of wild animals. Dead wild animals, admittedly, but that distinction did little to ease the tension.

Arthur was about fifty feet away and trying to move quietly toward the narrow market lane of Jubbergate when they saw him.

The Shadowman was lost, and though he would never admit it, he had been since the moment he left Arthur. Moving through shadows, stepping in and out of the dark places, arriving and leaving in secret as he had done for millennia was nothing new, but something was different now.

He *felt* it.

At first, it had been interesting, a sensation he was not familiar with and one not entirely unwelcome, but the more he moved, the more it became a strain. The Shadowman had to *try*. He had to focus his mind on making his body do what it had always done naturally, and it was causing him some discomfort. This was entirely new, and the more it went on, the less pleasant it became. The mind and the body suddenly seemed like two very separate entities, and he wondered if this was how all humans felt. One thing fighting against the other. Fighting for control.

Fighting yourself.

The man leaned against a table in a dark room and marvelled at the shaking in his legs. How did they do this? How did they manage with such weak vessels? With an effort, he stood up straight, determined that his body wouldn't fail, but there was a strange emptiness inside him, a heaviness even, as though something was missing.

Then there were the other feelings, the other emotions. The longings and the cravings. The desires. He did not realise how base humans really were. Little more than animals.

And yet he did not regret his decision. It had been his choice after all, and to make a choice is to truly live.

The Shadowman crouched and clambered into the shadows beneath the table. When he stepped out of the other side, he was in a park, deep in the shadows beside a wooden bench. The eclipse sat heavy in the sky, and a cool breeze blew through the trees. It was almost pleasant, but a sudden pain in his chest made the man gasp and stagger. A strange prickling sensation rippled through his arms and up into his head. The man groaned, pulled off his hat, and sat down heavily.

This was all wrong. This was not how it was supposed to go. What were these aches and pains? What was that horrible smell? And why couldn't he find that stupid girl?

Normally, he'd walk through the shadows and arrive exactly where he needed to be, but then, he always had the book.

The book.

The book was the key.

The man sat back and waited for the pain to subside. How was he going to find the girl if he no longer had the book to direct him? What was the point in moving through the shadow paths if he did not know the destination? He slumped forward and put his head in his hands. He felt weak, though he did not know what that meant. His hands were hard and rough on his face, and his skin felt brittle and heavy. He looked at his hands and saw the wrinkles that never used to be there, the spots and the withered skin. His eyes widened at his own sudden frailty, and he sat back again, touching his face gently with the fingers of an old man. There were bags under his eyes, wrinkles and hanging flesh.

"Oy! Gerroff!" a voice grumbled, startling him. What he had taken for rags or discarded and abandoned clothes turned out to be a man who had been sleeping on the bench. Suddenly the smell made sense. The Shadowman wrinkled his nose in disgust.

"I said gerroff! Go on! Off, ya fuck! Get yer ain bench!" The man kicked at him from beneath the rags, a filthy sock with no ends and protruding black toenails jabbed him in the side, and the Shadowman grunted.

"Do not do that again," he said. His voice was calm, but a new emotion simmered inside him, hotter than all the others. It made his skin prickle, and he noticed for the first time how the hairs on his body reacted to stimulus.

"Intriguing," he said to himself, turning his arm over and rolling up the sleeve to look at the bare flesh and rising hair.

The stranger on the bench kicked out again and swore, sitting up to shove the intruder away. The Shadowman grimaced, taking the hit, and then thrust his hand out to stop another one.

There was a wet thud, and the kicking legs went limp.

The man in black turned his head and blinked. Slowly, he pulled his hand away and there was another thud on the bench beside him, but he didn't pay any attention to it.

He stared at his fingers in the dim light of the eclipse. The blood shone like oil, but the smell was something else entirely.

"Very intriguing," he said.

As her eyes adjusted, the shadowy world came into slow focus for Nae. There was Steve, the little old lady, and the mess she'd made as she fled. There were bins and crates everywhere, rubbish littered the floor, and a dark slick of old beer pooled in the cobbles. Nae looked at Mad Alice, about to offer an apology, but the woman ignored her and Steve began to growl. It was low and dangerous. His hackles were high, and his teeth bared. For a small dog, he suddenly seemed very savage. Maybe this wasn't going to be as easy as she thought?

"Look," Nae said, "I didn't mean to call you Mad Alice. You said your name was Ann, right? Well, I'm Nae, and I don't know what is happening, but I'm scared, and I just want to go home."

Ann didn't respond. She just stared at the rubbish on the floor, and a look of deep concern creased her brow.

"I'm sorry about all this," Nae said, "I didn't mean to cause a mess. I just wanted to get away. I don't know what is going on, and I don't feel well. I can pick all this up and leave. It won't take long..." She drifted off, realising that no one was paying her the slightest bit of attention. Both the lady and the dog were looking at the pool of beer.

Nae glanced down just as the surface of the puddle broke and a hand thrust upward, reaching into the air and grasping for the cobbles. It was grey and rank with grease or slime, and as the fingers searched for a grip on the slick surface, a second hand followed. Fingers dug into the gaps between the stones and heaved. A head broke through, then shoulders, and a torso. Long, lank hair dragged up from the puddle as the creature appeared.

It was a woman, or at least, it was shaped like a woman.

Nae stifled a cry and backed into the wall as wet feet slapped on the stones, and the puddle vanished. The creature stood up straight and staggered forward. *She* was the puddle. Nae grimaced at the strange damp shucking noises the woman made as she moved, stepping closer to Mad Alice and Steve. Had she really thought she was in control? How the hell could she rationalise any of this? She took a deep breath and closed her eyes. None of this was real. She just had to realise that none of this was real!

And then the creature spoke.

"Hello, Alice!" it hissed. "Long time." The voice was thick with malice and heavy with grease. The woman chewed the words and spat them out. The rasping noise filled Nae's world. She opened her eyes again and shuddered at the sight of the dripping creature.

"Kay," Ann said with a nod. "You look like a drowned rat."

"No talk, Alice," the creature hissed. "I've watched you for too long. I know your games. No talk." She lunged at the old woman with a cry and clawed at her face with long, raking fingers. Nae watched in horror as four jagged lines of flesh were ripped from the old woman's cheek and fell in tattered rags to hang from her chin.

There was a pause as the creature known as Kay stared with glee...and Alice laughed.

Slowly, she lifted the flesh back into place. The wounds blurred and melted into her face as though nothing had happened, and the sweet old lady turned her head and smiled.

There was nothing sweet or old ladylike about that smile.

She grinned like a shark chasing a cellist.

"My turn," Ann said.

The meagre light leached away, and the shadows grew in its place, rising from the cobbles and the stones themselves. Nae gripped the bricks of the wall behind her as the world descended into complete and total darkness. The fingernails broke as she dug into the hard surface, knowing that it might be the only thing she could count on as real. The world vanished, and the alley filled with the sound of screams and barks and the occasional wet thud as Nae remained frozen in place, unable to make her legs move. She was caught up in a world she had no control over and could do nothing about. The urge to run was overwhelming, but the fear was stronger, and she hated herself for being unable to act while chaos raged around her.

A long, strangled scream echoed through the shadows and was suddenly cut short by a loud splash, and then someone laughed.

Slowly, the dim grey light of the eclipse filtered back into the alley as the shadows melted into stone. Nae winced as she pulled her hand away from the bricks, leaving one or two nails behind. Mad Alice stood in the centre of the alley, dusting herself down while Steve lapped at a rapidly decreasing puddle on the ground, his little tail wagging so fast it was a blur.

"I, I just want to go home," Nae sobbed. "Please!"

"Of course, dear," Mad Alice said sweetly. She smiled. It would have been a much nicer smile if her ear hadn't been hanging somewhere near her shoulder. Nae stared, giggled, then vomited onto the stones. Alice reached up and tucked the hanging flesh back in place with a tut, then stepped over to pat the shaking woman on the back. "It's okay, dearie. You've had a big day. I think a good night's sleep will do you good."

"But I can feel you touching me," Nae sobbed. "How?"

"These are strange times," Mad Alice said. "The shaded sun changes things."

"But you're not real. You can't be."

"Why not, dear?"

Nae stood up, her eyes wild and red. "Because I just saw your face get ripped off, and then you put it back together, and that's not normal."

"There are lots of normals, sweetheart. That was nothing, just a trick. The silly girl should have known better than to attack me like that. You should see my other tricks."

"Don't!" Steve said, pausing for a moment, then going back to his drink.

"Dogs can't talk," Nae said in a small voice.

"That one can," Alice said. "And you can hear him. Why deny the evidence of your own experience?"

"I've been drugged! Arthur spiked my drink!"

"Arthur?" Mad Alice exclaimed. "Our Arthur?" she said to Steve, who looked up briefly and nodded. "Oh, he's a lovely boy. Wouldn't hurt a fly."

"He did this to me!" Nae cried.

"He didn't," Steve said.

"Shut up! You can't fucking talk!"

"Woof," said the dog. "Bark, bark, growl."

"My dear," Alice interrupted, taking hold of Nae's shoulders and shaking her gently. "It's time you started paying attention to what is happening around you."

"I'm hallucinating."

"I don't know what that means."

"I'm seeing things."

"We all see things, but you need to know that the things you are seeing are very much real...in a way."

"In a way?"

"Well, they're not *not* real. I am dead and Steve is a reincarnated young man from the city council, but we're still, in our own way, real."

"You're a ghost?"

"Yes, dear."

"I don't believe in ghosts."

"Tough."

"And there's no such thing as reincarnation."

"Tell that to the Buddhists," Steve said without looking up from his puddle. He licked the last few drops from the cracks in the pavement and then turned to the two women. "Look," he said, "I know it's a lot to take in, but you have to admit it makes sense."

"Stop talking! You can't talk!" Nae screamed. She was crying now, tears streaming down her face as her heart raced in fear and her mind raced in confusion.

"There's no talking to some people," Steve said. "You might as well show her your party trick."

Alice laughed and lifted her hand in front of her face, holding it between her eyes and Nae's. Then, she stuck her fist through the centre of her head, turned, and gave a little wave and a thumbs up. When she turned back, Nae was on the floor. Her eyes were open, but she wasn't seeing anything.

"Ah, well." Alice shrugged. "You pop off and get Arthur while I look after her."

"I've never seen someone faint so many times," Steve said to himself, then sat and looked curiously down the alley. His head tilted to one side. "First things first though," he said to Ann as he headed toward a row of bins Nae hadn't tipped over. "I've got to get rid of swampy."

"Not in my alley, you won't!" Alice snapped. "Piss that silly girl out somewhere else."

Arthur ran into the marketplace and ducked between the stalls and tents. On a normal day this would be teeming with people, but right now, it was empty, and he raced as fast as he could between the tables. It made no difference. Wherever he moved, no matter how fast he ran and dodged, the barking seemed to be right behind him. It filled the world, bouncing off the ramshackle buildings and coming back at him from all sides. The dogs were ferocious, and they were close.

Arthur gripped a pole and spun himself round a stall, aiming to double back and make a break for Marks and Spencer's like the man in the nice suit. The doors there had been enough to hold the creatures back. He figured there was something important about the place, something he needed to look into...urgently.

Perhaps the man was like him?

Perhaps he was alive?

Alive and trapped here with the dead and the decayed.

Arthur bolted down a narrow passage at full tilt, fruit and veg flashing by on one side, handbags and novelty T-shirts on the other. The horde was behind him somewhere, lost in the maze of the market, and the city was ahead.

He almost made it.

Arthur stumbled in terror and panic, grabbing hold of a table to slow himself down. He tried running backward before he'd even really stopped going forward.

Wolves have a habit of eliciting such a response from their prey.

The great grey beast leaped over a stall and landed, snarling, on the cobbles in front of him, blocking the way.

It was definitely a wolf. The large paws, powerful body, and savage teeth were testament to that. They screamed wolf. The fact that the top of the head was missing didn't seem entirely important when all the sharp bits were still very much in place. Somehow, despite the lack of eyes, Arthur knew it was looking right at him. He stepped slowly to the side and the wolf's head followed. He stepped back and it followed again, saliva dripping from the open muzzle onto the cold stones. It made no sense. But Arthur had been paralysed by these logical conundrums before and found it better to just ignore them and act as though the thing in front of him wanted to kill him, which often, it did.

The beast snarled and snapped and stalked forward, its claws clicking on the stones. The space between them vanished swiftly, and Arthur stumbled back, finally reacting on instinct as the great wolf bunched its muscles and leaped.

Arthur had been here before.

Swords and hounds.

He didn't have the sword, but he did have magic.

He hit the animal with a purple fireball and didn't even bother shouting anything from *Street Fighter* or *Star Wars*. There was no time. The wolf exploded in a blinding flash and turned to ash right before Arthur's eyes.

That was new.

He grimaced and gasped. The teeth had been inches from his face when he hit it, and the residue flew into his open mouth. Arthur choked and spat, waving his hands over his face before he realised it wasn't ash at all; it wasn't anything. It was just...gone.

There was no time to stop and wonder. Something growled behind Arthur, and he turned just in time to shoot down a snarling Shih Tzu with its ribs showing through open, rotten flesh.

An earless Doberman appeared over the top of the bananas, and Arthur stumbled through a rack of hanging shirts as he blasted fireball after fireball at the attacking creatures. A wolf, a Labrador, a cat, a strange green thing that looked like a tiny man— they flooded over the stalls and lunged toward Arthur who tripped and fell, firing and screaming.

He hit the ground and rolled under a table, narrowly avoiding what appeared to be a badger swiping at him with dirty claws. Arthur cast fire into the shadows, kicking out at anything that growled or snapped beneath the bench. They were all around him, and he was growing desperate. The darkness under the market stall flashed purple as Arthur fought and rolled into another aisle. The dull, colourless sky was above him. He pulled himself to his feet and raced away.

Arthur threw fireballs in all directions without giving a second thought to where they might land. A terrier leaped at him, and he kicked it in the head without breaking stride sending it spinning away over a stall of handmade soaps. Part of his brain registered the horror of what he had just done, but the fact that the terrier had bright, glowing red eyes and was being ridden by another of the strange green creatures made him feel a little less shit about himself. Survival made a mockery of morals.

"This way!" a voice shouted in the lamplit dimness of the world, and he veered toward the sound, leaping over a grasping creature and heading toward a tall, grey stone building.

There, in the shadows, a dark figure beckoned Arthur on.

They wore a long dark robe, and the head was covered by a shawl or hood. For a moment, Arthur thought it was a Shadowman but realised quickly the voice belonged to a woman. With no other option available, he raced toward her, pulling at the last trestle table and spilling its contents over the ground behind him.

The woman vanished around the corner of Shambles, one of York's oldest streets, and Arthur followed. Ancient timber-framed houses leaned in from both sides, and the light of the eclipse struggled to break through the narrow gap between the rooftops. Even without the current situation, it was like running into a different world. The dull orange streetlights did little to penetrate the gloom, and Arthur spun in the darkness to cast a line of purple flickering fire across the small gap between the buildings. The creatures surging toward him skidded to a halt and snapped and barked at the flaming barrier. Arthur grinned wickedly and turned on his heel, running after the woman who stood now, holding open a door halfway down the street.

Arthur felt amazing. He felt powerful. He felt like he could do anything.

And then he tripped on the cobbles and fell over in the street, crying out in fear as the barrier behind him collapsed.

In a panic, Arthur Crazy scrambled to his feet and dove through the door. The woman slammed it shut behind him.

CHAPTER 13

They were in a room of total darkness and nearly complete silence. The only sound was Arthur's heavy breathing, the roaring of his own pulse in his ears, and the rasping of cloth and metal as the unseen woman pushed bolts into place.

Arthur had never used the magic like that before, and he was buzzing. He felt like he'd just drunk three double-vodka Red Bulls and made a facedown snow angel in a pile of cocaine. His heart punched against his chest and sparks crackled down his fingers, flashing in the darkness. The hairs on his arms and neck were on end, and his thighs ached from the exertion of the run. Arthur wheezed as he tried to calm the roaring in his ears.

He could feel his teeth. But my God, he felt alive!

"This way," the woman said, taking hold of his arm in the dark. Arthur let himself be led but put his other hand out to trace the wall as they went. His fingers ran across open brickwork and wooden beams, and he heard another door open. "In here," the woman hissed. "You'll have to stay hidden until I let you out. Don't make a sound."

"Who are you?" Arthur asked.

"A friend. Now, be quiet and pray to the Lord the demons of hell don't find this place, nor the servants of the false church."

"Erm. Come again?"

"Quiet now. The Lord be with you."

Arthur was pushed through an opening and banged his head on a wooden door that closed quickly behind him. He heard heavy metal bolts slide into place. The sound filled the world with its finality, and his own hot breath rolled back to him in the confined space.

He knew instantly that he was trapped before he even tried to move. He could feel the walls around him. A cupboard perhaps or even a wardrobe? He reached out and felt brickwork behind and wood to the sides, and suddenly his senses came flooding back. He rapped his knuckles on the door and strangled a gasp.

He had just let himself get locked up without even so much as a protest.

"Hey! Wait!"

"Quiet, child!" the voice came back, muffled and dull from the other side, and Arthur groaned. He was such an idiot! He didn't even see the woman's face, just her long hair flowing out from beneath the hood of a full-length dark robe. Why the hell did he just decide to follow her? His mother always said he was a sucker for following women into trouble, but he figured she meant the more obvious paths.

Arthur was trapped.

He was safe, perhaps, but he was trapped.

The Shadowman felt wonderful. He had eaten, which was an entirely new experience, and he marvelled at the way it instantly rejuvenated his body. It even seemed to have an effect on his mind. His thoughts came quick and fast. Sharper than ever. He could barely comprehend the impact of a good meal, and the tastes were a revelation. He had, of course, spent years watching humans eat, but it had never really dawned on him just how important it was. A lot of them died while eating, and so it had always seemed a mystery to him that they would want to do so over and over again. He was beginning to understand. And the problem of finding Nae was a simple one. It was embarrassing how he had been ducking in and out of shadows, following the dark ways without a clue. The key was focus. It was always focus. Back when he had the book, it took much of that from him, but now he understood. It was how he'd tracked down Arthur in that strange room, after all. It took time, but when he really concentrated and pictured the strange, frustrating man, he had arrived at the table, and there he was.

Sustenance and focus. Fuel and mental fortitude. Being human was easy once you understood the processes.

The Shadowman wondered if he would ever need to sleep. He had never slept before. It was something to look forward to. But first, he had to find the girl. He had to find the girl so Arthur would help him with his final task. The task that niggled at him and tormented him, that tugged at his mind and assaulted his very ability to persevere. This was not something he could do himself.

The spell had given the Shadowman everything, but it had also taken some things away. Finding the balance was key, and he needed Arthur to tip the scales in the right direction. The thought occurred to him that he could just *make* Arthur do what he wanted, but a deal had been struck, and hands had been clasped together in promise. This was important. This was the same as the writing in the book, and he would be held to the duty of that promise.

So would Arthur.

His thoughts turned to the woman, to Nae—Renae—and he pictured her in his mind's eye, focussing his will on her, seeking her out, feeling for her through the shadow paths, for her heartbeat, her life. And there she was—a slow, relaxed beat, resting. He smiled.

And then the world exploded into chaos.

The Shadowman lost the thread of the missing woman as magic flashed and shattered the still night. Explosion after explosion rocked the city in a way that no normal person would have been fully able to comprehend, but those accustomed to the dark paths spun in the direction of the chaos, toward the centre of the city.

Purple flashes danced in the sky above the tiled rooftops, reaching the spires of the city's churches. An errant fireball rose into the night like a stately firework before sputtering and vanishing into nothingness.

"Arthur," the Shadowman said and stepped into the darkness between two ferns.

CHAPTER 14

As the door locked behind Arthur, the pack of dead dogs and other beasts slunk carefully into Shambles proper. They prowled the narrow, cobbled street, sniffing and clawing at the doors and walls of the tall buildings. Thick wooden beams held the old houses and shops steadfastly together against the unnatural night, but they all appeared squat and sagging with age, their upper levels bigger and heavier than the bottom.

Deep shadows filled both sides of the winding lane, and they teemed with the creatures of the dark places. Hobgoblins kicked dead dogs out of the way, sprites dragged boggarts into the gloom, and the Short Ones danced through it all in a whirlwind of chaos.

The ancient streets of York were awash with the dead and the different.

And from out of the dark mess strode a man in black.

His skin was pale but free from blemishes and wrinkles. He looked young and strong. He walked with purpose, and the shadows melted away from him, easing back and letting him pass. He was a newcomer who had been around forever, and now he stood before the black-framed door of a shop with windows full of interesting items designed to separate dazzled travellers and tourists from their hard-earned money.

But the image shifted, turned, and twisted before him.

It faded in and out as though not quite wanting to be seen. Layers of time and places of residence sat on top of one another and fought for dominance as the moon danced in front of the sun and made a mockery of the normal order of things.

A shop, a grocer, a butcher, a house. It was all these and none.

The black-framed door, however, did not change, and the Shadowman stood before it, raised his fist, and knocked.

Once.

The effect was instant.

The creatures in the shadows whined and turned, slinking away from him, vanishing into the dark places or skittering up the walls. The man in black stared at the dark glass, and for the first time, really paid attention to his own reflection. He was not displeased with what he saw. He pulled the hat from his head and ran his hand through his hair, which was another first. He enjoyed the way it felt and the way it fell. He turned his face from side to side but kept his eyes focused on the reflection. They were sharp features but strong and youthful.

Power.

The power of a man, he thought.

He smiled and looked into his own dark eyes until suddenly they became the eyes of a black-haired woman with a high forehead and a small chin. She stared at him from the other side of the glass and smiled politely, though there was no warmth in it.

"You have a man with you," the Shadowman said.

"You are mistaken, sir. My husband is not at home. He works."

"Your husband does not concern me. You have another man in this residence."

"I assure you, you are mistaken, my lord. There is only myself and the serving boy." The man in black looked through his own reflection at the woman on the other side of the glass. He liked being called 'my lord.' It felt...fitting. He looked beyond her into the dim gloom of the house and reached for the handle. The woman grew wide-eyed as he rattled the door violently. It was a large door, heavy and thick, and the man did not appear to be putting in a lot of effort, yet the whole house shook with his actions. She bit her bottom lip in anger and offered a silent prayer before setting her shoulders and lifting her small chin.

"Dear sir. I must ask you to refrain. What on Earth will people think? It is not seemly for a man to force his way into the home of an unaccompanied woman."

"I assure you, I mean you no harm," he said, but he wasn't looking at her; he was glancing down the street. The wind had picked up, and the sky above seemed to be more blue than black. The moon was shifting. The shadows moving. Even here where time ran different, he was running out of it. Arthur was close. He knew he was close, and though he would have to find the girl to complete their deal, he couldn't risk harm coming to Arthur.

Arthur was the key to everything.

But where was he? The paths had brought him here, but Arthur was nowhere to be seen. He was close, either hiding or being hidden, but he was certainly nearby. There was no one else who used the magic with such reckless abandon. He closed his eyes and sought the heartbeat of the man, sought his magic, his presence, but there was nothing there in the dark paths. No trace of Arthur at all, and that in itself was entirely unusual. He wasn't dead; he would know, so where was he? There were other forces at work here. Forces he did not understand, and this made him angry. It was the same sensation that had washed over his body at the bench...hot and sharp, but also wonderfully enticing.

Anger.

Fascinating.

He turned back to the woman and almost gave in to the sudden urge to shatter the glass and drag her into the street. He could feel himself doing it—feel the impulse, picture the way her expression would change and the damage that would be done as he pulled her weak frame through a gap too small, but he hesitated and took a breath, musing on the impulse as he looked into her eyes.

The woman did not look away.

There was no fear in her gaze. He knew he didn't frighten her at all even as he pictured how easy it would be to reach through and crush her pretty face. He wondered what base instinct allowed the thought of such violence against her to enter his mind. It was a strange compulsion and one he actively quelled as he felt his fingers twitch. It would be so easy. Why wouldn't she just do what he said? The creatures had all been gathering at this door, and even now they were slinking through the shadows on the periphery of his vision, surrounding the building as best they could, climbing the walls of the neighbouring houses and stalking across the uneven rooftops. They could sense Arthur, these beasts, or they had seen him, so he must be close. The Shadowman reasoned the pack had attacked Arthur, and he'd reacted with a flurry of magic in his rush to escape.

The woman knew something.

He lifted his hands and rested them against the glass on either side of her face and breathed deeply for a moment, ignoring the baser instincts that threatened to overwhelm him. He was not used to such a lack of control. He wondered if all humans felt this way. And if so, how on earth did they decide what course of action to take when parts of their brain and even their bodies appeared to make decisions independent of anything else? It must drive them crazy.

The woman was speaking, but the words were an indistinct murmur behind the glass, and the Shadowman realised she was not talking to him.

Prayer.

What odd creatures these humans were. Even in death, they clung to their beliefs as strongly as their bodies clung to the memory of old forms. He decided to approach the matter differently.

"He is my friend," he tried. "I am worried he is in trouble."

The lady stopped her mumbling and crossed herself. The man flinched at the unusual action, and they continued to stare at each other through the glass. Her dark eyes were curious, and he felt as though her gaze missed nothing. Her face was pleasing to him in yet another way he did not quite understand.

Having come to some sort of decision, the lady moved. She

reached to the top of the door and grasped hold of the lock. The sleeves of her long dark cloak fell back, and the Shadowman's eyes widened at the stump where her left hand used to be. His own fingers itched with memory as he watched her manipulate the bolts with her right hand, bracing the door with her stump and then stepping back. She opened it wide, and the two faced each other on the threshold.

"It would be un-Christian of me to deny you help in your search for your friend," she said with a small bow. "And you are welcome to look for him, but as I say, there is only myself and the boy." She beckoned behind her, and a young lad of about nine years old appeared in the hallway. He stared at the man filling the frame and looked to his own feet, shuffling as he clasped his pale hands together. The woman turned back to the door. "Are you hungry?"

"I am not."

"Are you thirsty?"

"No."

"Who is it that you seek? Perhaps I know of them or can help point you in the right direction."

"His name is Arthur."

"I am not sure I know an Arthur," she said. "William? Do you know of anyone local by that name?" She turned to look over her shoulder at the young boy, who shook his head without looking up. "There you have it."

"I believe he is in this house, lady," the Shadowman said with a strained voice. "He...may be hiding." There was something going on here beyond his control and understanding. Something important that eluded him. He felt suddenly adrift and lost. Alone even. The feeling washed over him and made him pause on the threshold. He hadn't yet crossed over into the house, but the woman was talking, and so he forced his attention back to her.

"There are few places to hide, my lord," she said, laughing. "This is a humble home. I am sure I would have noticed a strange man in my house." She stepped back from the door but made no motion to the tall stranger. The boy squeaked in fright and disappeared into another room. The man in black looked at the open door and didn't move. A deep line creased his brow, and a puzzled expression crossed his face as he peered inside the candlelit hallway. He cast his eyes over the door and the frame and then stepped back, looking up and around the dark entrance.

"Something troubles you, my lord?" the lady said with impeccable manners.

"Not at all," he grumbled.

"Your friend?"

He ignored her, shook his head, and stepped forward as if to come in, but then he stopped short and stayed where he was on the step, his tall, lean body framed in the doorway. He shook his head again and moved forward slightly, but no more than a shuffle. The man swore under his breath and stepped back. The lady hid a small smile.

"It will have to wait for another time," he said. He was confused. He was certain Arthur was in this house or perhaps one next to it, but he couldn't bring himself to step inside. What was that emotion? Fear? Nervousness? That couldn't be right. And how could such an emotion hold sway over the body? The muscles simply would not obey him. None of this made sense, and he knew it must have something to do with the last piece of the puzzle.

He needed Arthur, but he couldn't get to Arthur.

It was infuriating. He felt incomplete. This had to be remedied and fast.

He thought then of the girl. If she was the key to Arthur's cooperation then he would fetch her and if need be, bring her here. Then Arthur would do as he had promised. And if he broke that promise there would be consequences. The man in black did not know what game was being played here, but he did not like it. There was a magic at work he was not familiar with, and it unnerved him. He suddenly realised how much he missed the book, missed being able to find what he needed—anything he needed. He was adrift. Unmoored.

Without a word, he turned on his heel and walked away down

the centre of Shambles, leaving the lady in the house to let out the breath she did not realise she had been holding.

After a brief moment, she stepped forward and leaned out the door, but there was no sign of the man. The street was full of shadows, and as she looked, they began to move, twisting and turning and flowing like ink. They ran down the sides of the buildings and across the cobbles, and she knew the creatures were returning. She slammed the door shut and bolted it once more, leaned back, closed her eyes, and offered a prayer of thanks. William ran out of the kitchen and thrust his arms around her. She gathered him in and held him tight.

"I don't like that man, Mamma."

"I know, darling." She kissed the top of his head.

"Why did you call me a serving boy?" he asked.

"Hush now, dear. I did what I thought best."

"Was he a bad man?"

"I do not know."

"Was he from the...authorities?" he stumbled over the big word.

"I don't believe so."

"But you didn't like him, did you, Mam?"

"It is not Christian to dislike anyone, my boy. We are all God's creatures."

"Even him?" the boy asked, leaning his head back to look at his mother. She was the most beautiful woman in the world, and he adored her, but she often left him confused. He didn't understand a lot of what she said or the things she did, and he was scared of the authorities who sometimes came to take her away. She looked down at her son's questioning eyes and stroked his hair before kissing his forehead.

She did not answer his question.

CHAPTER 15

Nothing much had changed on the banks of the River Ouse other than the temperature and the colour of the sky, but this was the real world, this was Yorkshire. God's own country they call it, where there's nowt so predictable as unpredictable weather.

The drinkers at the King's Arms pulled jackets and coats over chilly shoulders, but if anything, the sudden eclipse had caused even more of a carnival atmosphere, albeit a quieter one. People gathered on the bridge to take photographs, lining the banks of the river with their legs dangling over the water to chat in hushed whispers and to drink. Of course, to drink. The bar staff inside the tiny, dimly lit pub rushed back and forth, trying to keep up with the orders as pint after pint and wine glass after wine glass were filled and taken outside to be enjoyed beneath the strange sky. Couples pointed at the eclipse and tried to take selfies with the odd moon and sun filling the world behind them. They laughed and joked as normal, but the voices were perhaps a little quieter than before, hushed in the presence of the astrological phenomenon. They were like wedding guests who had started early but now had to sit through the service. Despite the heavy and steady flow of alcohol the crowd was respectful, even humbled, in the face of something so much greater than themselves.

That would soon change.

Through the tightly packed throng of drinkers covering the riverbank, Duke George Villiers stalked the real world with real intent, real purpose, and his trousers down. He laughed as he wandered slowly, free and unrestrained, removing his clothes and taking his sweet time. He stroked the bare shoulder of a woman in a simple black vest and marvelled at the goosebumps that rose across her arms and chest as she giggled and shook in what she thought was a breeze. They wore nothing these days. Not a thing. Denim shorts and a singlet seemed like the most private of underwear to the duke, who was used to the bodices and corsets of his time, clothes that left a little mystery and required a whole lot of digging. In the centuries since his death, the duke realised he no longer cared for the dig. It was the treasure beneath he craved. The people here were drunk, hot, stripped down and nearly naked, wearing garments so thin it was almost like the netting cast over a roast ham. And just like the ham, it all looked tasty, but he couldn't quite get at it.

That did not mean he couldn't have some fun. He yawned and stretched. Completely naked now. This was his kind of party, and he meant to enjoy it.

When in Eboracum...

Just then the duke noticed the two women from the Cock and Bottle sitting at a table, leaning close and whispering together, their skin flushed red from wine and sun. They laughed loudly, and to his great delight, they kissed, their lips locking for a moment before they both giggled and continued with their conversation. He had never known the like. Not in the open like this. His father would be amazed!

He moved among the drinkers, touching and caressing and fondling where he could. Physical contact was exhausting though, and he swayed on his feet as he weaved in and out of the people, having never—so to speak—kept it up for this long in years. Performance anxiety was not something that overly worried the dead, and the duke was having far too much fun to stop now.

A familiar summer dress caught his eye, and he grinned lasciviously. So, this was where they all went when they left his pub. What a wonder it was to be free from his bonds, he thought.

He drifted through a table and crouched behind the seated young woman, his bulbous face over the back of her naked shoulder, his pursed lips close to her neck. She swayed gently in her seat and hiccupped. The duke tried to kiss her flushed skin, and she sighed, closing her eyes and murmuring a name under her breath. There was a giggle as she turned to her boyfriend...who was not there. He was sitting on the other side of her, staring into his mobile phone, completely oblivious to the events around him. Unable to see the perverted ghost, the drunk girl screamed at the man sharing the long bench seat and staggered to her feet, knocking the tracksuit-clad boyfriend's phone out of his hands as she did. It hit the stones and bounced perfectly between the shoulders of two students sitting on the riverbank. As the phone fell toward the water, the boyfriend made a valiant lunge to save it but only succeeded in crashing into the two students.

It was at this point it all went tits up.

As the girl slapped the unsuspecting man across the face—her second misplaced slap of the day—three bodies hit the water with a triad of loud cries and even louder splashes, and suddenly the spell of the eclipse was broken.

Individuals were generally intelligent, rational, and not overly given to unprovoked erratic behaviour, but place a sizeable number in a group together, turn up the temperature, fill them with booze, and give them a nudge...well, see what happens.

The slap led to a stumble, which led to a tray full of freshly bought drinks smashing to the ground, which led to an angry shove, which led to another splash in the water, which led to a punch, and then another and another. All along the riverbank, the crowd turned on each other as small pockets of chaos spread, recruiting fresh volunteers for mass stupidity. More and more people fell into the river as fights broke out and the crowd swayed back and forth with the bedlam of hundreds of people sharing three beer-soaked brain cells. And there were those who, for want of nothing better to do, willingly threw themselves into the turgid waters because, as they would sheepishly tell the police much later, "It seemed like a laugh."

Small green figures darted unseen between legs and contributed to the chaos where they could, stealing drinks, smashing glasses, punching, pulling, scratching, and generally being right little twats.

And through it all danced the fat, naked duke with a big smile, a big stomach, and a complete dearth of morality. He danced with his arms in the air, thrusting and gyrating and knocking over any remaining drinks he could lay his...let's say, *hands*...on.

Why?

Because he could.

All over the city—the real city—common sense vanished, and disarray spread like wildfire. The eclipse had lasted for far too long. Mobile phones were frantically searched, and bar fly self-appointed experts informed anyone who would listen, and many who wouldn't, that the longest recorded eclipse had been a little over seven and a half minutes in full totality. They were reaching close to an hour, and the strain was beginning to show as phone calls were made and panic set in. The switchboard operators watched in amazement as their computers lit up with call after call. People were reporting fights, theft, drunken behaviour, packs of wild animals, a "fucking cat walking up the side of the Minster," ghosts, strange sightings, a "horse that doesnee look like a real horse, ye ken?" And even regarding the eclipse itself, the operator carefully explained there wasn't much the police could do about the moon, and no, sir, she did not think the fire brigade would be much help either, and yes, sir, perhaps in this circumstance we are useless, and he was more than entitled to write a strongly worded letter to his local MP, as was his right.

The chaos was not helped by a city that had spent the day drinking and basking in the sun, and neither was it helped by the very real emergence of these ghosts and sprites and spectres and, more significantly, the Short Ones.

The ghosts, for the most part, could largely be dismissed as a trick of the light, a moving shadow, or too many Jaeger bombs, but the little green men were a different story. They were adept at finding the gaps between the realms at the best of times, but with the combination of the solstice and the eclipse they ran rampant through the city. Difficult to spot and almost impossible to catch, the little buggers had free rein to cause as much trouble as they liked.

And they really, really liked.

The Folk, or the Short Ones, were known by many names, and there were many legends and myths attributed to them, either mistakenly or deservedly so, but hardly anyone knew who or what they really were. There were some who said they were the true leprechauns, though the idea that catching one would bring fortune clearly came from a person who had never come face to face with the little sods.

Stories twisted and turned and meandered around, and people placed their own agendas onto long-told tales in order to create something new or serve a specific purpose. The closest to an accurate identification of the truth is the oft-told tale of the faerie folk causing mischief on the nights of the solstice when the veils are thin and magic leaks into the world, but this got two things fundamentally wrong. To begin with, they were not fairies, or faeries, or fae, although the people who did meet them often used words beginning with the same letter. The second misconception was the word *mischief*. This implied they were nothing more than wee little scamps—opportunistic, harmless apple-rustlers—no more dangerous than a rambunctious youth on a long summer day with a slingshot and some time to kill.

Right now, they had time, but what they were killing were cats.

And pigeons. And squirrels. And rats. And one unfortunate fox who happened to be raiding the wrong bin at the wrong time.

But mainly cats.

They hated them.

The Short Ones might've looked like little green men from a distance, but up close, they looked like *right evil little fuckers*. And they were entirely silent. They didn't have mouths, which, perhaps, is one sign that a potential creator was at least marginally proactive in their genesis. Their skin appeared green because it was scaled like a snake, but other than two legs, two arms, and connecting bits in between, the similarity to humans ended. The creatures killed for sport and for food, but with no mouths, their feasting shared little resemblance to what anyone might recognisably associate with the word *eat*.

They were, in a way, much like plants. Though where plants fed on the sun's rays via photosynthesis, the Short Ones used their skins to feed through a process similar to osmosis. This meant, of course, that they existed on an entirely liquid diet, which did not bode well for the cats, pigeons, squirrels, and fox.

The Short Ones were green. But when eating, they didn't stay that colour for long.

S teve was scared. Terrified even. He made his way carefully past what he initially thought was a discarded and torn rag. On closer inspection, it turned out to be a fox.

Well, it used to be.

The shattered body twisted and lurched beside an old metal bin, and occasionally the head crashed into it with a sound like a steel drum. Two of the Short Ones were deep inside the fox, feeding.

Steve tucked his tail firmly beneath his little body and tried to quell the overwhelming urge to whine. Everything in his doggy-DNA wanted to whine, to let it out, to vocalise the fear, but something of his latent humanity told him to remain as quiet as he could and, if possible, to hide.

He had felt Arthur's magic as he ran through the city and knew immediately his friend was in trouble. There was no way Arthur would let loose such a volley if he didn't have to, and so Steve had been racing to help his friend when a charging horse startled him, and he ducked down the nearest alley.

Now, like Arthur, he was trapped.

The fox's head clanged against the bin, and Steve's little body shook with fear. He tried to make himself small, pressing up against the wall of the narrow tunnel, squeezing between a stack of plastic bins while a mural of Queen Elizabeth looked down at him from her place on the wall. It was always a good idea to keep one eye on the things that frighten you, but Steve was petrified and so had both eyes fixed firmly on the writhing body of the dead animal.

This, of course, meant he was not watching where he was going.

Steve's shoulder hit the tower of black plastic, and the bins teetered above him. He had just enough time to glance up as the stack fell, and then the lights went out.

The smell was appalling, and he gagged and stumbled, the plastic box dragging with an alarming scrape across the cobbles as the rest crashed around him in the alley. He froze and shivered in the darkness, barely able to breath, his nose assaulted by the rotten ghosts of a thousand dead cigarettes. The plastic bins were those found in beer gardens up and down the country, usually half-filled with sand for the smokers to discard their dog-ends.

Ironic, really.

They had been cleaned and stacked to dry but as any bartender will testify, the smell of old cigarettes was ground in like grease in a plumber's pocket. Steve coughed and clamped his mouth shut, shaking in the darkness. He had never smoked when he was human and hated the smell as a dog; it was too sharp, too chemical. The thought that cigarettes might be the death of him was almost too much to bear.

The echoes of the crashing plastic settled, and silence spread in the dark. He didn't dare move. His nose was useless, and he couldn't see a thing, but his ears twitched and turned as he cowered and strained to listen.

A small, wet thud. Barely audible.

A soft, almost delicate *pad pad pad*.

Silence.

Steve shook violently with the effort not to whine or run. His heart rippled in his chest, the pulse coursing through his body, making his fur stand on end. He shivered in abject terror in the dark, noiseless world. Something was there. Outside the box. Inches from him on the other side of a flimsy piece of a black plastic. His hackles rose as every instinct told him to run, but he forced himself to stay. Good dog.

The box moved. Slightly. But the noise was like thunder to his terrified ears. He whimpered, and tears rolled from his eyes, soaked up by the fur around his nose.

The box moved again. Differently this time.

Pad pad pad.

Above him.

They were on the box. Searching. Steve could feel rather than hear the gentle pressure as soft feet moved and turned.

And then silence returned.

He began to count. He got to five and started again. Over and over until his body stopped shaking. He kept counting. *One, two, three, four, five*. Repeat. *One, two, three, four, five*. Repeat. He opened his eyes, but there was no discernible difference beneath the black plastic. He couldn't remember ever being this afraid, not even as he raced up the stairs of the castle to fight the witch, but Arthur had needed him then.

Steve paused.

Arthur needed him now.

He stopped trembling and cocked his head.

And this, dear reader, is why we don't deserve dogs.

Fear had nothing to do with it when your best friend was in trouble. The mighty canine rose on shaking paws and growled quietly.

He waited.

There was silence.

He growled a little louder and waited some more, his body poised and ready for whatever happened next.

Nothing.

His mind made up, Steve nudged the plastic with his nose and moved forward, using the box as a shield.

Demons or not, he was going to find his friend.

Steve walked warily down the street with his bin pulled way down low.

CHAPTER 16

"What's your name again, dear?" the old lady asked quietly. "I've been known as Mad Alice for so long I almost believed it myself, but the young man, Arthur, found out my name is really Ann. Ann Barber. I like to think I remember Ann, but I don't. Still, it would be nice if you called me Ann."

"I'm Nae," the young woman groaned. She sat in the alley in the exact same spot as before. She hugged her knees to her chest and shivered. Her body was battered and bruised, and her brain felt just as sore.

The thought that she had been spiked was still very much at the forefront of her mind, but there were too many inexplicable things to wrap her head around. She did not, in any way, feel out of control. She did not feel groggy or drowsy or drunk. In short, she did not feel like someone *had* popped something in her drink.

She felt perfectly fine, in fact. Apart from all the dead people, puddle monsters, Vikings, Romans, and horses, of course.

Nae looked at the old lady. Despite recent events, she seemed nice enough. She gathered her thoughts and tried to stack them neatly together, but it was like making a house of cards in a storm...on a boat...with the hiccups.

"Have you ever," she started, treating each word carefully, stacking them one on top of the other until the sentence made sense. "Have you ever had a dream you were so convinced was real that when you woke up, there was a moment when you didn't know what was what?" she asked.

The old woman shrugged.

"You're asking the wrong person, dear," she said. "I remember what dreams are, but I can't remember the last time I had one. Daydreams, yes. *Dream* dreams, no."

"You don't dream?"

"The dead don't sleep, dear. It's hard to dream if you're always awake."

The two women looked at each other and neither blinked—Nae because she was terrified and confused, and Ann because she didn't need to.

"So, this is real? You...you're really dead?"

"I wouldn't be able to put my hand through my face if I wasn't, dear."

"Candyman," Nae whispered to herself.

"You've lost me there, pet."

"Never mind. How...how long have you...been dead?" she asked. She wasn't sure about the intricacies of polite conversation when communicating with the deceased. She had two Bachelor's degrees, a Masters, and a PhD. Somehow, it had never come up.

"Well, young Arthur reckons I've been dead for nigh on five hundred years or so."

"Arthur," Nae mumbled.

"He's a good boy, you know." Ann placed a gentle hand on Nae's shoulder. It was cold but solid, as real as her own mother's. "A bit lost maybe, but he wouldn't hurt a fly."

"But none of this makes sense," Nae said. "He must've drugged me. It's the only explanation."

"There is always more than one explanation, dear. We're all the heroes of our own story. Arthur said that to me once. He's a clever boy."

"If we're all the heroes of our own story, then doesn't that mean we're the villains of someone else's?"

Ann paused. "I never thought about it like that," she said.

"You're clever too. Just like him. You two would make a nice couple. He needs a good woman."

Nae sighed. "I was beginning to think so myself, but"—she rubbed her hands over her face and groaned—"but all this is insane! It can't be real. It just can't!"

"Well, I can't tell you what is real or not, dear—" Ann started, but a deep voice interrupted them from the shadows.

"I can," the Shadowman announced, stepping out of the dark into the small pool of light. Ann got to her feet, but before she could react the Shadowman grabbed hold of Nae's wrist and dragged her out of the light. Her scream cut off instantly with barely enough sound left for an echo in the narrow alley.

Ann Barber ran through Mad Alice Lane, but she was too slow. They were gone.

The city of York was a rough circle of narrow streets and tall buildings with, purely coincidentally in this instance, Arthur right in the centre.

The animals and the dead descended on the marketplace near Shambles, the ravens hung in a spiral high above, and the waning eclipse washed the rooftops with dim blue light.

The world to Arthur was dark and confined, but suddenly, a crack of light appeared, and the door swung open, showing the smiling, apologetic face of the woman in the dark robes. Weak candlelight lit her face, and he saw a small chin, a small mouth, and a small nose. The petiteness of her features only made her large dark eyes seem bigger. She was pretty and much younger than he expected.

Arthur blinked in the light and stepped out of the cupboard as she backed away without a word. A young boy hung around the corner of an open doorway and peered at him with fearful eyes.

"Thank you," Arthur said to the woman with a small nod. He wasn't entirely sure if he should be thanking her. He had been in there for a long time, after all, though she had given him refuge from the pack of marauding animals. "What happened?" he asked.

"The creatures have left. They could not find you in the priest hole."

"Priest hole?" Arthur asked.

"A secret place to keep the children of God safe."

"Right,"

"A man came looking for you," the woman said, pushing back the hood of her cloak and revealing the fullness of her pale and pretty face. Her hair was pinned beneath a shawl wrapped tightly to her head. It looked to Arthur like a bandage.

"A bad man," the boy said and disappeared out of sight when Arthur glanced at him. He turned back to the woman with a question on his face.

"I do not know if he was a bad man,'" she said, "though there was something about his countenance that did not sit right. So, I kept you hidden. I hope this was not in error. You have power," she said with a small curtsey. It was not a question.

"Some," Arthur admitted, "but I don't know why I have it or where it came from. Who—"

"'It is not for us to question the bounteous providence of our good Lord," she said.

"Oh." Arthur paused before continuing, "I'm not sure I'd call this a gift from God."

"If not God, then who?" the woman replied, her eyes wide and earnest. "God's gifts are not to be taken lightly, nor do they require explanation. You *are* a man of God, are you not?" she asked.

"Erm, I'm not sure I am."

"But you are God's instrument."

Arthur laughed at that. "If I am, I'm the bloody cowbell!" he said, but the woman just looked confused.

"Well, dear," she said, resting a hand on his arm. "The Lord needs more cowbell."

Arthur laughed, and then sighed, and then rubbed his face violently with his hands, digging the balls of his palm into his eyes as if to wipe away the chaos of the last hour.

"Look," he said to the strange lady, "I'm really grateful for your help, thank you. I don't know if I would have been able to keep those animals away."

"Demons," the woman said.

"Pardon?"

"They were not animals. They were demons. And I think the man who was searching for you might have been their master."

"What makes you say that?" Arthur asked, choosing his words carefully. There was something very strange about her, something he couldn't quite put his finger on, and it was more than the absolute certainty of her faith. She spread her arms wide, and Arthur saw the stump of her missing hand. He tried not to stare and failed completely, but the woman had her eyes closed and did not notice.

"When thou art come into the land which the Lord thy God giveth thee," she intoned as though reading the text from the inside of her eyelids, "thou shalt not learn to do according to the abominations of those nations. There shall be not found among you anyone who maketh his son or his daughter to pass through the fire, or who useth divination, or an observer of times, or an enchanter, or a witch, or a charmer, or a consulter with familiar spirits, or a wizard, or a necromancer. For all who do these things are an abomination unto the Lord, and because of these abominations, the Lord thy God doth drive them out from before thee."

There was silence when she finished. Arthur looked at the woman, and she looked at him. A strong gust of wind rattled around the building and whistled with a sense of occasion.

He sighed in the face of her faith.

"Well, that's going to cause a bit of a problem," he said finally. The woman raised one eyebrow and tilted her head in question. "Well," Arthur went on, "you're dead, aren't you, love? And I'm talking to you. So, I guess that puts me firmly on the list."

To his surprise, she laughed. "You would not be *here* if you were such a thing," she said. "Only those who die in God's grace and friendship may enter here." She glanced around the room with a meaningful look.

"Here?" Arthur began, but a more pressing question tumbled

over his lips first, "No, wait. What about the man in black then? Why is *he* here? Why are the demons here?"

"The Lord tempts us," she said simply.

The woman saw the expression on Arthur's face and mistook it for something else. She reached her good hand to him, then seemed to change her mind and lowered it, wrapping her arms tight around her waist instead.

"You can trust the Lord. He will not allow you to be tempted beyond that which you can bear, and our time is at hand. You need not fear. Today is an auspicious day. Different from all the rest. It will soon be time to leave for the raptures of Heaven."

"You...you do know that you're dead?" Arthur asked, looking down at her with concern written across his face, but she just smiled.

"Of course, dear child. We are all dead, awaiting the Lord to take us home."

"I'm not," Arthur said.

The lady paused, a puzzled expression clouding her face, doubt growing in her eyes.

"Dead, I mean. I'm not dead, and the man who was looking for me isn't a demon. He's just a Shadowman."

"You must be dead," she said in a small voice, her eyes brimming with tears.

Arthur felt the sudden urge to reach out and hold her but stopped himself. He didn't have the first clue about this woman or what she truly needed in that moment.

"I promise you I'm not dead," he repeated. "I can just...I can walk alongside the dead."

He didn't know why he phrased it that way. There was something about how the woman spoke that made him mimic her. It was a habit he'd had since childhood. Give him half an hour with a Scotsman, and you'd think he'd been born and raised in the Highlands. The woman's eyes grew wide, and tears fell down her cheeks. Arthur tended to fumble when women cried, but he had never quite got to grips with *dead women* crying. As far as he was aware, the proper mechanisms should not have been in place, and they were much harder to comfort. But as unprepared as he was for ghost tears, he was absolutely not ready for her next words.

"You're an angel of the Lord!" she gasped and fell to her knees, grasping hold of his hands with her fingers.

It happened before Arthur realised what she was doing, and by then it was too late. The magic sparked and flowed between them both. The pain was instant and everywhere. Arthur's whole body flashed with it, and he couldn't move. But it wasn't his pain. It was hers. Margaret. Margaret Clitherow. The young mother sentenced to death by the church and the sheriffs of the city. The flashes of her life were vivid, sharp, and blinding. They wouldn't stay still or come into focus. The pain was just too much.

Arthur couldn't breathe or move. Somehow, he found himself lying beside Margaret and in some strange way, he also *was* her.

He turned his gaze and saw those large black eyes. Then, he blinked, and they were his own, staring back.

He tried to move, tried to cry out, but he was being crushed. He felt his bones break and his skin split as the weight intensified above him. Her. Them. A sharp agony in his back made his chest heave, but of course, it couldn't go anywhere, and the ribs snapped and collapsed in on themselves.

Arthur panicked and tried to move but there was nowhere to go. No air. No space.

It was his worst nightmare.

Trapped. Inside a wall of stone.

There was absolutely no way for his body to move. He was pinned. His face crushed and twisted to the side, leaving him staring at a thin strip of daylight and booted feet moving over cobbled stones.

But he could see. So not inside a wall then.

The realisation provided no relief, and he tried to scream with the agony, but as he breathed in, the weight crushed down, and the scream died on his lips.

Margaret's dark, agony-filled eyes drifted in and out of his vision as the images blurred and twisted together. He saw her and saw her tormentors. He saw passing feet stop and kneel. He saw gawking faces peering at them with tears in their eyes. He saw the trundling wheels and shod hooves of a horse and cart as it moved slowly over the stone surface. He saw the pile of stones as one by one they were picked up by shaking men and brought forward. And each time they came close there was a thud, and the weight increased. Arthur's skull cracked, and he screamed.

CHAPTER 17

Arthur fell backward with a cry and crashed to the floor. He was back in the house with the dark-eyed woman. She knelt in front of him, her eyes wide. He flung his hands to his head and checked all over his face, neck, and body in a panic of remembered pain. He wrapped his arms around his chest and gasped and cried at the memory, at the agony and slow torment. It was unlike anything he had experienced before. The woman—Margaret Clitherow—clasped her residual limb in front of her chest as though in prayer, but Arthur knew she was holding herself just as he was, fighting the memory of pain. Tears streamed down her face as she looked at Arthur, who shifted slowly to his knees.

"You're Saint Margaret," he gasped.

The woman blinked back her tears and shook her head. "I am no saint," she said in a quiet voice.

"You are!" Arthur said. "They made you a saint for...for that. That horror. For what they did to you. For your faith. I remember learning about you on a...on a school trip. What they did was horrible."

"It was the Lord's plan," she said.

"That!" Arthur snapped. "If that was the Lord's plan, then the Lord can get fucked!"

Margaret Clitherow gasped and crossed herself. She stared at

Arthur with wide eyes, but the magic worked both ways, and she now knew something of the strange man in front of her. She knew he had power, she knew he came from a world that was far different from her own, but she also knew he had fought a witch and stood strong against the forces of darkness. He may not have been what she regarded as a man of God, but he was a good man all the same. Despite his blasphemy.

"Please," Arthur said, "let me help you."

"I know what you would say," she said with a small shake of her head. She rose gingerly to her feet and dusted herself down. Arthur noticed the tender way she moved and closed his eyes against the memory of her torment. "But this is the Lord's will, and it is not for either of us to pass judgement on God. We must hold hard to our faith and trust in him."

"What do you think all this is?" Arthur asked. "I mean, seriously. Where do you think you are?"

"This is purgatory," Margaret Clitherow said simply, "where we await the Lord's final judgement."

"This isn't purgatory," Arthur said in a pleading voice. "Don't you understand? You're dead. You're a ghost."

"There is only one ghost, dear child," she said with a soft smile, and Arthur swore. There was a degree of faith that was all but impossible to argue against. He had come across it once before when his mum got into an argument with a distant relative who decided to become a very vocal anti-vaxxer. When he was a kid, he used to call her Aunty Jean. Now his mum just referred to her as "that woman." It wasn't just the complete one-eighty from the way she used to think and act, his mum had explained, it was the fact that she had become completely evangelical about the whole thing. If you didn't believe the same as her, then you're going to hell—that sort of thing. Once a person was convinced they're correct, it was next to impossible to make them see another point of view, and the harder you tried, the more they'd dig their feet in and complain about your own blinkered view. Never, of course, seeing the irony in this.

But this was different.

Arthur knew there was something he could do to help.

Like a rational person explaining the curvature of the Earth to a nutter who believed it was flat, all he had to do was make them see it for themselves.

He instantly felt guilty for the thought. For all he knew, Margaret Clitherow lived in a time when people genuinely believed that to be true.

"Look," Arthur said gently, "I can prove to you this isn't purgatory."

"This is another temptation," Margaret said softly. "And I will not be tempted."

"It's not, it's really not. Look," he went on, "answer me this. Where are the saints?"

She blinked and took a step back. William came running in from another room and wrapped himself around her skirts again. Arthur looked at the young boy, and a flash of recognition dropped into his mind, but it was a remnant of Margaret's memories, and he couldn't quite take hold of it. It was important though. There was something there. Something behind the frightened little boy's grey eyes that might be the key to all this.

"Heaven."

The word was spoken softly, almost inaudibly, and Arthur looked into the confused but determined gaze of Saint Margaret Clitherow. He knew how to prove this to her.

"We're going to go for a little walk," he said, raising his hand to her objections. "For hundreds of years, you have lived the same experience, over and over again, am I right? You...die"—he glanced down at the scared little boy—"and then you come back here. To this house. To William. Isn't that so?"

Margaret nodded.

"You must have asked yourself, why?" He raised his hand again as Margaret opened her small mouth. "Please don't say it is the Lord's will. Please. Just trust me."

She nodded again, a steely determination crossing her face. All signs of sorrow and pain were gone now, and Arthur marvelled at the level of self-control. He was still shaking from the memory of her execution. He could still feel the weight of what he now knew was her own front door, crushing down as the executioners placed stone after stone upon it.

"You don't really venture out of this house much when you arrive back here, do you?" Arthur asked. He still wasn't entirely sure how it all happened, but he knew ghosts were tied to certain places of significance. Sometimes they had more than one, like Margaret, or just the one, like Steve, when Steve had been a ghost. As a relatively young ghost, Steve hadn't developed the strong ties that bound him to the one place, so he'd been free to wander the city. But at the beginning of every evening, no matter where he was, Steve found himself back in the basement of York council, tied to a thick metal pipe by his own red tie. He told Arthur it could be as simple as closing his eyes in one place and opening them in another, but neither man really knew the how or why of it. Arthur always suspected it was something to do with the Shadow-men, but he'd never found out.

"Today was the first time I've left these walls," Margaret admitted. "The Lord told me you needed my help."

"Okay, well, that's nice," Arthur said. "So, you haven't been anywhere else in the city since you died?"

"Just the bridge and here." She lifted her chin as she spoke, and again Arthur found himself admiring her strength. The bridge was the place of her execution. "It was not easy to leave this house," she admitted. "I felt a...a pull to come back. It is why I ran as soon as you saw me."

"Not the dogs?"

"The dogs do not worry me. What can they do to me that isn't already done each and every day?"

Arthur didn't quite know what to say to that, thinking of his own absolute terror in the face of the strange dead animals and trying not to compare it to the impressive stoicism of the woman before him.

"Well, there's an eclipse," he explained, choosing to move the conversation on, "and it's the longest day of the year. I don't know how or why, but that seems to have changed the rules a bit. You don't have to stay here. You can leave." She did not look convinced. "It's true," he insisted. "There are ghosts—people walking all over the city. Look, we won't go far. We just need to go across the street and up a little ways. There's something there I need you to see. You can trust me. You know you can and"—he paused—"I need to do something."

"What worries you?"

Arthur looked to his feet.

"There is a girl. She's like me. Not dead," he added by way of explanation. "She's lost here, wandering around the city with all these ghosts, and it's my fault and I'm...scared for her," he admitted. "But there's nothing I can do except wait. I guess, I'd rather be doing something—anything other than sitting idle with my thumb up my arse. Sorry," he said when she winced. "That's something my dad always says. He also says we are judged by the things we walk past," he finished, the words tumbling over each other as he answered her unspoken question.

"I understand," Margaret said after a pause. "Idle hands are the devil's workshop; idle lips are his mouthpiece. It is better for us both to be active in these strange end times."

"Exactly!" Arthur said. "Better than sitting with..."

"I said I understand," Margaret cut him off.

CHAPTER 18

While Arthur and Margaret carefully opened the front door of the old house, the Shadowman dragged Nae through the dark paths, and Steve ditched his bin to race toward the famous little street in the middle of the city. The dead dogs and strange creatures that attacked Arthur prowled the market square, no longer able to find the trail left by his errant magic, and so they turned back and forth in confused circles. They stalked each other and tried to make sense of the latent instincts compelling them— bizarrely, to sniff each other's backsides.

This was a tricky process when some noses, and some backsides, were not where they should be.

The ghosts that had been drawn to the raw power of the magic walked down roads and paths from their own time to join the creatures. Shambles itself remained quiet and deserted. A narrow strip of dim blue sky streaked like a ribbon above the peaceful street, though just a stone's throw away (if you're a good aim and can get a decent enough trajectory to cover three storeys) the marketplace teemed with the dead.

For the first time, in every sense of the word, the centre of the city was a shambles.

Arthur resisted the urge to take hold of Margaret's hand. He wasn't sure he knew how to stop the magic from springing up again, and he didn't want to draw attention to himself, or, if he was honest, experience any more of the pain she'd suffered at the hands of the sheriffs. He knew a little bit about the life of Margaret Clitherow, as did most people who lived in the city or grew up in the vicinity, but the experience of her death was something almost indescribably horrendous. A Roman Catholic martyr and a saint, Margaret Clitherow had been crushed to death for hiding Catholic priests in her home. He seemed to remember that Elizabeth I had sent a letter rebuking the sheriffs and the town's people, but that was the very definition of *too little too late*.

Arthur waited in the street, checking left and right as she reassured young William that they would be back soon, and he had nothing to worry about.

"If the authorities come," she said, "hide in the priest hole."

William nodded with tears in his eyes, and Margaret pulled the door closed behind her, looking back at her son as he peered through the glass.

"This way," Arthur said and walked down the street. To him, Shambles looked like it always had, a street torn out of time: medieval buildings nestled close together, a huddle of large wooden beams, ornate windows, and pointed rooftops. If you could make a fantasy street for ghosts and goblins to walk along, this would be it.

Not too far away from Margaret's house was an indistinct door. Nothing fancy. Nothing to make it stand out. Most tourists walked right on by unless they had a very specific map. The building itself was slightly different from the others in that the upper two floors were clad in white plaster, but the ground floor and entrance sat nestled beneath their heavier bulk. Beside the door, a glass window protected by a metal grill was set into the wall. Next to that was a sign. It was the sign Arthur wanted Margaret to see.

"Can you read?" he asked as they approached.

"Yes," she said. "I taught myself the second time they sent me to prison. I reasoned they could imprison my body but not my mind. Nor my soul," she added. Arthur nodded and pointed toward a prominent wooden sign on the brick wall.

Margaret stepped forward and peered at the words. They were in an unusual type and different in style to what she knew, but they were easy enough for her to understand. Very easy. She stared. She looked at Arthur, and he smiled. She looked back at the sign and shook her head. Barely able to believe her own eyes or the words that fell from her lips, she read the short sentence.

"The Shrine of Saint Margaret Clitherow."

"That's you," Arthur said.

"It can't be," she breathed, tears spilling over her eyes.

"It is. You're a martyr. They made you a saint. Queen Elizabeth herself sent a letter to the city to say your death was a travesty and should never have happened."

"The Protestant Queen! It was her laws that killed me and..." Her hands went to her belly, a movement Arthur noticed and realised was more than just a memory of the pain of her death.

"You were pregnant?" he gasped in a small, horrified voice. That was a detail they left out on the school trip.

"A girl." There were tears in her eyes. There were tears in Arthur's eyes. There were tears in the eyes of the Short One who watched from the shadows.

"How?" Arthur asked, unable to finish his question and instead settling for one word.

"I have three boys," she explained. "Three darling boys, but this"—she touched her good hand to her stomach—"She. She felt different. I just knew. I, I just know. My Mary," she cried.

"Come with me," Arthur said softly and held out his hand. Margaret took it, and the magic connected them, but Arthur was ready for it this time. He was going to use it in a way he had never tried before. Margaret Clitherow kept her pain with her. Each day she was tortured and crushed to death, and each evening she returned home to the house on Shambles. Her ethereal body was wracked with an agony that would never go away. Arthur knew from their brief contact that she believed she deserved the pain, but he was having none of it. She needed to experience this without the torment.

Arthur stepped through the open door of the small building in one world and took hold of Margaret's pain in another. They walked together into a small, candlelit room that housed a Roman Catholic chapel, and at the same time, they also lay together beneath the door of Margaret's home. Arthur could see a third plane of existence sitting just out of reach—a young couple lighting a candle and praying. They were there with them in the room but little more than a memory—a shadow of the real world —but they were there.

No longer distracted by the pain of her execution, Margaret saw the chapel dedicated to her honour. She heard the prayers offered by the South American backpackers and saw the candle they lit. She felt their devotion, and she wept. Everything Arthur had said was true. The church had made her a saint. She turned to this strange, wonderful man and saw the agony on his face, and she pulled her hand away from his. He fell to his knees, and she knelt beside him as he gasped for air. She lifted her arms to his shoulders and whispered, "No more," then waited for him to nod before hugging him close.

Arthur and the saint held each other in the candlelit chapel. In the doorway, Nae and Steve looked on. In the shadows of the street behind them, the Short One who'd witnessed the ordeal wiped his tears on the trouser leg of the Shadowman, who was utterly bemused by the whole thing.

CHAPTER 19

High above the city, two small black shapes left the frozen spiral of ravens and soared toward the roof of the Minster. It is true that cats are half in and half out, but ravens made their own rules. There is a reason Odin chose them for his messengers. These two are not the fabled Huginn and Muninn, but they are important, and they do carry a message in their own way. The time is nearly at hand.

The birds settled on the roof of the great cathedral, tucked their wings behind their backs like gentlemen, and looked with bowed heads at the scene before them.

It was not the scorched stones that interested the stately birds, nor the discarded mug that still glistened where it had fallen when the man in black vanished; it was the small flame in the corner of the roof, making a mockery of the shadows.

A black and shrivelled hand lay with fingers curled in on themselves in a withered mass. One finger still flickered with small white flames. They licked and tugged and pulled at the remaining fat and flesh, slowly unrolling the stiff digit to point at the sky. It was the middle finger, and though this meant nothing to the ravens, it had raised a smirk on the face of the watching grotesque.

One of the birds hopped down from the crenelations and

moved closer to the severed hand on the roof of the Minster, the great house of the city. The flames were still there, barely visible as they ate away the last of the fuel.

The time was close. One might almost say, at hand. And indeed, it was this Hand of Glory that held the world in the sway of the eclipse for so long, but soon the flame would die.

This had been an interesting day for the ravens. Much had happened that was previously only heard of in the songs of the corvid. The formation in the sky neared its end, and the two birds seem to reach an agreement. With a short bow they leaped into the air and plummeted over the side of the great Gothic building, thundering toward the earth like silent arrows. They stretched their wings to soar over the rooftop of Saint Michael le Belfrey, and the animals gathered there.

These strange times were nearly at an end, and though curiosity may have killed the cat, for the ravens, it was a matter of professionalism to be witnesses to what comes next.

A fluttering of wings above the narrow Shambles was ignored by the people in the street below. They made their way quickly and quietly to the house of Margaret Clitherow, away from the chapel and away from the marketplace on the other side of the tall buildings.

A susurrus filtered through the air and along the narrow alleys. It was the noise of lots of creatures moving in near silence. It was the swish of cloth sweeping across tattered cloth. It was the soft sound of padded paws on stone, the breath of the dead.

Arthur held the door open, and Nae gave him a soft, confused smile as she ducked under his arm into the building where Margaret had already gathered William into her arms.

Only the Shadowman remained outside.

"I'm sorry," Arthur said to Nae when the door closed behind them. The Shadowman turned his back and stood like a bouncer on the doorstep.

"What happened?" she said in a small voice. There were tears in her eyes, and she was shaking. "What is going on? This is all real, isn't it? But you, you—"

"I can see ghosts," Arthur said and laughed at the absurdity of saying it out loud, but there was no denying the obvious. "I don't know why," he explained quickly. "It started about a year ago. I was drunk in a bar on Micklegate and got talking to a few people, and it wasn't until much later that I realised they were dead." A small bark drew his attention, but he held her gaze as he said, "One of them was Steve."

"*Steve* Steve?"

"Steve Steve."

They both looked at the little dog, who grinned.

"Told you," he said.

"Reincarnation," Arthur answered her unspoken question. "There was a...situation. With a witch."

He sighed and pinched the end of his nose at how ridiculous all this sounded.

"Thou shalt not suffer a witch to live!" Margaret Clitherow murmured.

"I didn't," Arthur said simply. "There was a...I guess you can call it a fight. But with dead people, and I somehow have these powers that can set ghosts free, and I had to use them on Steve and—"

"Free?" Nae asked.

"Well, free to whatever comes next."

"Heaven?"

"Maybe."

"Hell?"

"Possibly."

"Don't forget reincarnation," Steve said with a wag of his tail. "Arthur had to set us all free to save us and stop the witch, but I came back."

"The door on the left." Arthur smiled, looking down at the little black terrier.

"The door on the left," he grinned and sat on his back legs.

"You're losing me," Nae said.

Arthur thought for a moment and then grinned at her. "Have you seen *Bill and Ted*?" he asked.

"*Bogus Journey* or *Excellent Adventure*?"

"*Bogus Journey*."

"My favourite."

"Mine too. Well, it's kind of like that. Only without the robots and the aliens and time travel and stuff."

"Strange things are afoot in the city of York," Nae said with a small smile, trying to force some humour into the situation. "It doesn't quite have the same ring to it, does it?"

"No, that's pretty good." Arthur grinned. "See, the truth is, I don't really know anything about any of this. For the longest time, I was convinced I was batshit crazy, and part of me still thinks I might be. I'm just trying to deal with it the best I can. I really didn't mean to drag you into it. I honestly don't even know how that happened." He glanced at the Shadowman, who was picking at his nails on the doorstep.

Arthur sighed and rubbed his hands over his face and through his hair. He was tired and on edge but happy Nae was back. "As far as I can tell, I'm the only one who can do any of this stuff. It's weird and scary and lonely, and I have to lie all the time and hide things."

"So, that's why you go to séances," she said.

Arthur nodded.

"So, were there actually dead people at that one?" she asked in amazement.

Arthur shook his head.

"No, they were all nutters. Making shit up. Or maybe they believed it, I don't know. Belief is a powerful thing."

"Tell her about the fight at the castle and the swords and the giant and the helicopter and the ogre and stuff!" Steve barked and chased his tail. They all looked at him, and he sat back to scratch his ear, his tail wagging furiously.

"I think it's best to take things a bit slower, mate," Arthur said. "There's more than enough going on."

"He got stabbed by a witch with King Arthur's sword!"

They all looked at him again. Steve, Nae, Margaret, William, and even the Shadowman who had turned to peer through the glass. Arthur laughed nervously and stammered, "Yeah, well. It's been a strange year."

"Ghosts," Nae said quietly, almost to herself. "Reincarnation, witches, magic, King Arthur. What the hell happened? I just wanted to talk to a cute guy with a nice dog."

Steve barked happily.

"So, you can do magic?" There was a challenge in her voice— not unpleasant, but certainly from the point of view of someone who was going to need a bit more evidence to believe.

Obliging, Arthur clicked his fingers, and a small purple flame appeared on the palm of his hand. He threw it casually in the air and tossed it from hand to hand, trying not to notice the fascinated looks on the faces of those gathered in the small entrance hall to Margaret Clitherow's house.

It was so easy now. So simple to manipulate the power within him. It was like a well that never ran dry, and he could turn the tap willingly whenever he needed. He remembered the thrill of the fireballs he launched into the pack of animals and the wall of purple flame he cast across the street to barre their way. It was electric.

A sharp rapping on the glass drew his attention, and the Shadowman shook his head and wagged a finger. Arthur stared at the dark-eyed man for a moment, and the flame crackled between them, reflected in the glass.

It grew brighter. More intense.

Why should I put it out? he thought. He had power enough to take care of a few dead dogs. *Why should I have to be careful?*

Arthur, of course, had no idea that a great multitude of the city's ghosts had congregated nearby. He just saw the Shadowman telling him what to do and felt the childish prickle of resentment rise from some place deep within. His thoughts were broken by the soft yet urgent voice of Margaret Clitherow.

"Those creatures are still out there," she said, "and I don't have enough space to hide you both."

Arthur held the gaze of the Shadowman for a moment longer before extinguishing the flame and turning back.

"What now?" he asked. His voice shook with suppressed anger, and he felt his chest shaking.

"What do you mean?" Margaret asked, her hand resting on William's shoulder as they both faced Arthur. Nae stood to one side and Steve sat in the middle.

Arthur closed his eyes and clenched his fists. He had no idea why he felt so strange, so on edge.

"What do you want to do now?" he asked, making an effort to keep his voice level, but he could feel the Shadowman still staring at him. He focused on Margaret and smiled, pushing the anger aside. This remarkable lady needed his help, and it was help he could give. Fuck the Shadowman. "When do you want me to release you, to set you free?" he asked.

"I don't," Margaret said, and there was a clear finality to her words.

"But..."

"You have shown me a wondrous thing, Arthur. And I thank you. The Lord truly sent you to us this day, but it changes nothing."

"It changes everything!" Arthur said.

"We still await the Lord's judgement," Margaret said softly with a shake of her head. "I am not worthy to be a saint. I did nothing to earn it other than to die so that my own children would not be tortured during trial. I could have pleaded guilty, and my death would have been swift, but in doing so, my children would have had to testify, and I could not risk harm coming their way. I did nothing special. I did what every mother would do for her children."

"But..."

"And now I must pay the price for the blessing of sainthood," she said with a warm smile. "It makes sense to me now why this purgatory has lasted for so long. Purification takes time. The purification of a saint must take longer."

Arthur stared at her open-mouthed, unable to quite comprehend what he was hearing. He had told her the truth, shown her the truth, but she still twisted it to fit her own narrative.

It made no sense. A small part of his brain that wasn't exhausted through fear and exertion urged him toward caution, his own mind seemingly split in two. He realised his hands were itching, and the temptation to simply take hold of Margaret and William and send them on to the next life was almost overbearing.

Behind them the Shadowman looked into the candlelit hall with a curious expression. Arthur and Margaret looked at each other, and it was Margaret who spoke first. She placed her hand on William's head and looked deep into Arthur's eyes. Not for the first time he got the impression that she really saw who he was. He instantly felt guilty about the direction his thoughts had taken and clasped his hands in front of him. He felt like a child again in front of the headteacher.

"Can you guarantee both William and I will go together to... whatever comes next?" Margaret asked.

Arthur paused, the truth written in his hesitation.

"I thought as much." She stepped around her son to move closer to Arthur, reaching up and placing her hand on his cheek. "You *are* an instrument of the Lord, Arthur. Cowbell or no. You have been bestowed with wondrous, miraculous gifts, but it is not for you to pass the Lord's judgement. I have been tempted and tested once more, and I passed, can't you see?" She smiled and her eyes were bright and happy. "It is not your fault that you were the instrument in this plan. And I am sorry, child, but an instrument is nothing without a musician."

Arthur hung his head and felt ashamed of the thoughts that rattled through his mind. He suddenly felt very weary. Deep down weary. In the core of his being.

"You need to take this young lady home," Margaret said. "This strange day will not last forever. The eclipse is already fading, but in the meantime, she should be kept safe."

"I can look after myself," Nae said, not quite sure where the stubbornness came from.

"Against the dead and the devil?" Margaret asked, and the younger woman couldn't maintain contact with the truth in those dark eyes. She, like Arthur, looked to her feet.

"Take her home, Arthur," Margaret said. "But be careful of that one," she warned, gripping his upper arm with a firmness that was mirrored in her voice. She nodded to the door. "I do not trust him."

Arthur looked at the beautiful saint standing before him, then at the Shadowman on the other side of the glass. Margaret squeezed his arm again.

"Ask yourself, Arthur, why does he not enter these holy places? Be wary of him. Keep him close."

"He's not too bad, you know," Arthur said. "He just hasn't exactly lived what you might call a normal life."

"Perhaps it would be best to keep it that way," Margaret said, then without elaboration, she reached past him and opened the door. The Shadowman turned on the step and looked at the gathered faces. He tried a smile.

"It is time," he said, locking eyes with Arthur. "We are close to the allotted hour. You must fulfil your promise to me now."

"Not before we get Nae home safe," Arthur said. The Shadowman stared at him and Arthur saw the strain on his face, the fight for control. He looked older than he had before. Tired. That was not something he ever thought he would see in a Shadowman.

"I have done my part of your deal," he said with a hiss. "Now it is your turn."

"Nae first," Arthur said.

There was a moment of strained silence and then the Shadowman said, "Fine! I will take her through the dark paths, and you can meet us there."

"Not a chance!" Nae said. "I'm not doing that again! I'll walk."

The Shadowman glared at her for a moment before turning suddenly on his heel and marching away, mumbling something about checking on the dogs. His exit would have had more impact if not for a slip on the cobbles, which had him stumbling and reaching out to steady himself against a shop that sold knitted llamas.

Arthur peered down the street. It was getting light. There were people there now. Much clearer. Still transparent shadows of their real selves, trapped in time, but clearer all the same.

On the doorstep of the house of Saint Margaret Clitherow, Arthur took Nae's hand without really thinking about it and smiled his goodbye to the beautiful dark-haired lady and her son.

"Can I visit?" he asked.

"I'd like that." The saint smiled. "Now go."

Arthur, Nae, and Steve walked briskly down Shambles, heading toward the street known only as Pavement. Nae said that this was the fastest way to her house, and so they walked quickly and quietly with Steve trotting ahead, their nightmares behind. Or so they thought.

The point of view of the ravens was quite different. The city looked like a map. Narrow streets and open squares. Shops, churches, roads, and rivers all criss-crossing over one another. The young couple walked in relative peace down an ancient street with high walls, but on the other side of the tall houses—a barrier of just a few metres—there was a horde of the undead.

If this was a zombie movie, this raven-eyed view was the exact sort of technique a director might use to show the potential danger our heroes were in.

So close. So unaware.

But this was not a movie. There was just a young man and a young woman walking hand in hand toward safety. Thinking, perhaps, that the dangerous part of their night was over.

And there was a dog.

A little scruffy terrier cocking a leg and peeing on one of the fake fairy doors installed by shopkeepers keen to draw a crowd to the street.

They were all, as we said, oblivious to the danger.

Oblivious, that is, until the Shadowman came sprinting from an alley, shouting at the top of his voice for them all to run.

There was an incredulous moment as Arthur stared at the running Shadowman and tried to understand what he was seeing. He had never seen a Shadowman run before. It was a bizarre sight. Like watching the Queen do push-ups. The midnight clothes flapped in the dim light as he bolted toward them with his eyes wide and his mouth a thin, narrow line. The black flat cap was gripped in a gloved fist as he pumped his limbs and pushed hard in their direction. He paid no heed to the shades of the real people in the street, more visible now as the power of the eclipse gave way. The Shadowman didn't care. He ran straight through them—men, women, and children.

If the sight of the Shadowman bearing down on them wasn't enough to goad Arthur and Nae into action, then the jumbled mass of dead dogs and demons that tumbled out of the alley behind him certainly did the trick. They spilled over the cobbles in a great clamouring mass and washed against the buildings on the other side like a wave. There was a breathless pause as the animals hit the shopfronts and crashed over each other in a great pile before individual creatures found their footing on the smooth cobbles and ran after the Shadowman in a slather of teeth and claws.

For a split second, Arthur thought, *Why am I always fucking running?* And then he ran.

He dragged Nae behind him and raced down the narrow street, but she yanked her hand free and overtook him as they aimed for the end of Shambles. Arthur, despite the situation, couldn't help but be impressed. He loved a good runner, and Nae could run! She tore ahead of him and quickly caught up with Steve, the little dog bounding around her heels as they raced toward the open end of the street.

Nae darted out into the main road of Pavement, heading left, down toward Fossgate, but Arthur shouted at her to turn and go the other way. He had an idea. The red-faced woman skidded to a halt in the middle of the road and let out a scream as an insubstantial but very real double-decker bus passed right through her. The world was catching up. She saw people packed into seats, bags on laps, a bike, even a dog. Nae shuddered, and the apparition was gone. Then Arthur was there.

He grabbed her hand again and dragged her toward the door of a large building on the corner. Nae ran with him, glancing behind and seeing the Shadowman fly out of the exit with the pack gaining. Someone was shouting, screaming at them to run faster. A man across the street leaned out of an upper storey window, hollering and urging them on, pointing to a large set of glass doors at the top of some stone steps.

Marks and Spencer's.

Arthur and Nae ran together, taking the steps two at a time and then stopped before a large set of glass doors.

They didn't move.

The sensor didn't register either of them as being there.

Arthur swore and tried to walk through the glass, banging his head sharply and swearing again.

Nae banged her fists on the doors.

"Why aren't they working?" she said. "If I can walk through a bus, I should be able to walk through these!"

"I don't know!" Arthur said.

"Move!"

It was Steve.

The little dog leaped up the steps and the mechanism clicked into gear, the glass panels sliding slowly apart. Arthur and Nae tumbled through the widening gap and ran inside. The Shadowman was right behind them, squeezing through and panting with the exertion of the chase. He accidentally kicked Steve in his haste to get inside, and the little dog tumbled over on the tiled floor with a yelp.

Arthur turned.

The doors were still opening, and the pack of dogs were close, racing toward the bottom step in a tumbling, snapping horde. There was no way the doors would close in time, and Steve was right there in the middle of the floor.

"Steve!" Arthur shouted.

The little terrier got to his feet and looked over his shoulder at his best friend, his tongue hanging out while he panted for breath. He looked at the horde and looked back. He bared his teeth. It might have been a smile; it might have been something else.

Steve the terrier barked. Just once.

And everything slowed.

The tiny black dog stood framed by the door while the mass of creatures built and tumbled up the stairs toward him. The world pressed pause for this brief moment, and Arthur saw it emblazoned on his soul. Steve's left ear popped out in its usual way, his tail flicked straight, and his hackles twitched. He stared down the pack, and then he ran.

Back the way they had come.

Back, toward the world.

Back, into the swarm of the dead.

Arthur realised what was happening too late. He started to move, but Nae had hold of his hand, and in her fright she held him tight. He stumbled backward as they pulled against each other, and by then Steve was already on the top step.

His back legs bunched and gathered, and he leaped from the rear entrance of Marks and Spencer's over and into the clamouring mass of snarling teeth and rending claws. Arthur saw his friend crash into the misshapen jaw of a half-headless dog and use the strange maw as a springboard to leap further into their midst, screaming the whole time.

"Come and have a go if you think you're hard enough!"

He bounced up once, twice, but then his little black body was ripped from the sky by a slathering wolf. Steve vanished into the violent press of teeth and claws as the horde tumbled and turned after their new prey.

Behind them, Arthur's shout of dismay was lost as the sliding

doors came together with a gentle hiss, and Nae and the Shadowman dragged him deeper into the bright lights of the department store.

CHAPTER 20

The ravens spread their wings and soared in slow, graceful arcs high above Pavement, their black eyes fixed on the careening mass of dead creatures far below. The pack turned from the grey modern building and tumbled across the road toward the medieval structures on the other side where the hollering man still hung out of the top floor window. He, like the birds, was watching the animals as they snapped and snarled and then vanished down one of the city's many snickelways. The echo of their passing bounced through the world for a moment until they were swallowed by the high, narrow walls of Lady Peckett's Yard.

Silence descended once again.

The man at the top window of the Golden Fleece Inn looked across at the department store, but all seemed peaceful. He glanced up at the eclipse and thought he saw a slight shift at the top of the glowing ring, the beginning perhaps of the famous diamond of light—that bright flash that occurs when the moon begins to move away. But something else caught his eye then. He looked down and saw the silent horde of ghosts walk out of Shambles and move slowly into Pavement. They bunched together and milled about, seemingly unsure where they should go and in which direction they should head. The man had no such doubts.

For the first time in nearly a hundred years, he closed his window and headed inside.

From the roof of the Golden Fleece, the ravens watched the dead. There was nothing particularly unnerving or scary about their movements, unless, of course, you have a thing about crowds (and missing limbs). They were simply lost spirits, still free to roam, but not entirely sure where they wanted to go. A mixture of men, women, children, and a few other things thrown in for good measure. They came from all over the vastness of the city's long memory. There were Vikings and Romans and Christians and Celts and Victorians and investment bankers. Lawyers in shoulder-padded suits walked besides soldiers from a great array of battles. Ethereal swords, guns, and axes bristled among mops, shovels, and skateboards too. There were butchers, bakers, and quite possibly a few candlestick makers, and they all came together in the middle of the road.

The ravens cast their eyes to the sky, then appeared to reach another unspoken agreement. With a loud caw, they swooped the horde over and over again, driving them back and turning them toward the city. It didn't matter if you were big and strong, short and weak, or entirely dead, the sharp cry and even sharper claws of a swooping great bird was enough to make you change direction. Just ask an Australian postman during magpie season.

The ravens shepherded the dead away from Arthur, either by coincidence or design, but I guess we'll never know. We can't speak raven.

All over the city, time was catching up with itself. Those pockets where the world turned as normal continued to fall into disarray as mischievous ghosts and spirits caused havoc with people's perceptions of reality, which was a nice way of saying the dead were scaring the shit out of the living.

George Villiers was exhausted from his exertions on the riverbank, but he sat and watched with great satisfaction as the police descended on the revellers.

From the corner of her eye, a cop caught sight of a fat naked man and turned to arrest him, but when she did, he was gone. Throughout the course of the next few minutes, she kept seeing him just on the edge of her vision, but he was never there when she looked. This was not something she wrote in her report.

In the little dark room in Stonegate the wizard said, "Welcome Alan!"

His eyes were still closed. The table shook even more violently than before, and one of the women screamed. They were really getting into it tonight, he thought. There was another scream with a slightly more masculine timbre and a collected gasp, and the wizard opened his eyes and joined in.

The women pulled their hands away as books fell from the shelves and the table cracked and broke in two.

The young couple with the dog were gone, their chairs scattered to the floor.

The wizard tried to compose himself and make sense of what was going on, but one of the more bizarre things about the human brain was that despite to the capacity to believe in spirit trumpets and necromantic tables, it quickly shut down when genuinely faced with the impossible.

"My," he stammered, "the spirits are certainly busy this evening."

You have to admit, he rallied magnificently.

A group of travellers found a body floating face down in the peaceful waters of the River Ouse. They knew who it was immediately. The angelic spread of raven hair was enough for them all to know the truth before the men found the courage to dive in and tenderly bring her body to the bank. A scream shattered the stillness of the early evening as a beautiful, black-haired woman raced across the grass and dropped to her knees beside the river. She clawed at the dirt and cursed the sky.

Heads bowed and hats were clasped against breasts as people wailed and cried, so no one noticed the figure swimming away beneath the surface of the mocking water.

Smoke drifted over the fields and hung in the air. The hint of fire, the sharp, sweet tang of wood floated over the farms and villages. It appeared to rise from the dry grass and fill the world with the memory of ritual and rite. Unseen wheels of flame rolled down hillocks, and farmers long dead lined the fields with torches. None of this was seen by the normal folk, of course, though there were, despite Arthur's fruitless search, one or two who thought they caught a glimmer of something in the corner of their eye. But much like the WPC by the King's Arms, it disappeared when they turned.

"Empty fields. Nothing there."

"Funny, I thought I saw something."

"There's definitely a smell."

"Someone must be having a bonfire."

Mike Finn walked at an easy pace while his two dogs, Jess and Rolf, raced and played over the Knavesmire on the outskirts of the city. He was surprised there were so few people out and about on such a lovely evening, but it didn't worry him. He wasn't the biggest fan of other people, more than content to spend time with his dogs and perhaps read a few chapters on the Kindle he always kept in the pocket of his shorts. But he wasn't reading this evening. The eclipse was far more interesting.

Mike wandered through the tall green trees and marvelled at

the way they moved and twisted in the dim light. It was as though the shadows themselves had come alive and walked with him along the public footpath. The main road was through the trees to his left, but the sound of the traffic was muted and hushed, just like the whole world seemed to be.

He had seen an eclipse once before, in Cornwall, but no one ever really believed his story about it. Not even his brothers. He had been walking along the cliff tops when it happened, and as he turned to marvel at the unusual sight, he noticed a black cat sitting in the middle of the dirt path behind him. There were no houses around and yet the animal was nonchalantly crouched as though it owned the place, which, admittedly, was not an unusual attitude for a cat.

As he walked in the fading light, the cat followed him, keeping distance but maintaining pace. And then, when the eclipse reached totality, the cat leaped onto his backpack and clambered onto his shoulders.

Mike laughed at the memory and then shivered, turning to the path he was walking now, here on the Knavesmire.

He stopped suddenly, then laughed again, nervous this time. Ahead of him, his two dogs sat side by side on the path. Perfectly still. Staring. He whistled but they didn't react. He moved toward them, wondering what it was that could have kept their attention, and then he heard the creaking over the top of the normal sounds of the world.

The quiet cars and the gentle wind in the trees became like background noise as the creaking came again, strained and mournful. He reached his dogs, who were sitting a few metres away from a paved square in the trees—just a small collection of concrete slabs surrounding a marker stone.

They walked past it every day. Mike knew it well.

The Tyburn.

Named after the famous place of execution in Middlesex, this was the sight of York's own gallows.

Mike *did* know it well, having walked this path every day for years, but the bodies of five dead priests hanging heavy at the end of their ropes was a new addition.

He paused and blinked and then closed his eyes tight against the horror of the decomposing bodies swaying from a large, triangular wooden frame supported on three thick legs. When he opened them again, they were still there. He would have preferred it if they had vanished, and he could chalk it up to a trick of the light, but the giant structure of the three-legged mare stood stark against the sky, the bodies dancing their slow gallows-jig.

Jess and Rolf growled as Mike knelt to them, patting their quivering flanks and whispering soothing words he didn't believe. But then, as suddenly as the mood had come on them, their demeanour changed again.

The two dogs raced away through the trees with their tails wagging, yapping happily, chasing each other through the tall grass as though nothing had happened.

Mike knew before he looked up that the gallows would no longer be there.

He just knew it.

He stood up straight, brushed off his shorts, looked around, looked up, nodded, and continued on his way.

He figured he would just chalk this one up to lunchtime Guinness.

In the marketplace of the Shambles, the only people left were the stallholders packing their produce away and the few drinkers and tourists in the pop-up bars and cafés.

In the middle of a long line of green canvas stalls, a basket of bananas crashed to the ground with no one near it, apples fell onto the cobbles and rolled away, and a lady packing away her novelty T-shirts nearly jumped a mile when a sudden gust of wind lifted them all from the hangers and crashed them back down again.

If that didn't frighten her, the power surge that rippled through the overhanging electric cables certainly did.

Purple sparks flashed in the dim evening light, and flames sprang up and down the marketplace to a chorus of screams. But as suddenly as they came, they were gone.

Men and women raced to various tents and tables, grasping fire extinguishers, but there were no fires to put out. A table was tipped over, presumably in the panic, but suddenly all was peaceful again.

There were a few nervous laughs, comments on the eclipse making them all go crazy, and offers to help each other clean up. The world turned, and life went on.

CHAPTER 21

"Steve's dead!" Arthur gasped in a small voice.

"He was already dead," the Shadowman replied, and both Arthur and Nae turned on him. He looked ill, like the short run had exhausted him. His face was peaked and grey, and he appeared to be struggling to catch his breath. He held his gloved hand close to his chest.

"That wasn't nice," Nae said, her hand on Arthur's shoulder.

"It's true," the Shadowman said, as though he couldn't understand how this fact had eluded the two people. "And we're wasting time. Arthur, you have a promise to keep."

"Fuck off, mate! My best friend just died. Can't you see I'm in a bit of shock here?"

"He was dead when you met him. Everything after that was a bonus."

"You really don't get it, do you!" Arthur shouted, tears streaming down his face. There was no point talking to the Shadowman, he knew that. The blank expression told him everything he needed to know and more, but he was in shock at the speed of what had just happened.

"It doesn't make any sense," he said, shaking his head. "Why did he do that? Why did he have to go and do that? We could've run into the shop. We could've hid."

"He was protecting us," Nae said in a small voice. She was barely keeping it together herself. Just moments earlier, she had begun to make peace with the fact that a small dog could talk, and then she watched as that very same small dog was brutally brought down by a pack of dead animals, one of which, she was sure, had actual glowing red eyes.

That in itself was enough to make a person go mad. It was the sort of thing that only happened in horror stories. Why the hell would an animal, dead or otherwise, have glowing red eyes? It made no sense. But then, she could pick any one of a number of things from this night and say the same.

Arthur slumped forward, and she gathered this strange, enigmatic man into her arms. She looked around the store, one she was very familiar with, and realised she could see the shapes of late-night shoppers moving through the aisles. They were vague and just on the edge of her vision, but they were there, and they were clearly moving.

"What the hell is going on?" she gasped, shaking her head and trying to clear her vision. It was as though two worlds were trying to come together over the top of each other.

The Shadowman sat up from where he had fallen against a shelf of handbags and groaned. He looked around, holding his sides, and saw the shift in the way the world looked.

"We're running out of time," he said. "Arthur, I need you to do this for me. I need you to do it now."

Arthur glared at him.

"Not until we get Nae home safe," he said.

"There's no time!" the Shadowman said and stepped toward Arthur. "We had a deal."

Nae held onto Arthur's shoulders and felt him shaking. She didn't know if it was in grief or anger but thought maybe the tide was turning in a very specific direction.

Arthur stood up straight and faced the Shadowman. Neither backed down, and Nae took a step back. Just then, they were interrupted by a voice.

"Who are you lot?"

A man dressed in a grey tweed suit with a waistcoat and white shirt stood in front of the fruit and veg. His shoes were black and polished to perfection except for a clear scuff mark on the left toe where he had dragged his feet while using the lamppost to turn out of Stonegate earlier that night.

Arthur recognised him instantly.

"You," he said.

The man blinked in surprise. He was short and stocky, and the suit jacket bulged against his arms as he folded them across his chest. He was clean-shaven with a square jaw and a high forehead. Piercing grey eyes stared at them from beneath dark eyebrows and slicked-back hair.

"Me," he said.

"You're the man running from the dogs earlier," Arthur said. "You came out of Stonegate and then you ran in here. Why were the dogs chasing you?"

"They always chase me," the stranger replied. He lifted a hand to his chin and scratched it, looking from Arthur to Nae to the Shadowman and then back to Arthur. "You're not dead, are you?"

It wasn't really a question, but Arthur shook his head anyway.

"No," he said. "Well, *we* aren't"—he indicated Nae and himself —"but I don't really know about him."

He faced the Shadowman, the bristling, simmering anger still just below the surface, barely held in check.

"The truth is, I don't even really know who or what you are," he said. "I've never known."

To the surprise of everyone, not least of all the Shadowman, the newcomer spoke again.

"He's a banshee," he said simply.

All heads turned toward him.

"A what?" Nae asked.

"A banshee. A shadow-walker. He is one of the Ankow."

All heads turned back to the Shadowman.

The stooped creature had a peculiar expression on his face and tilted his head to look at the newcomer with fascination. He reached up slowly and pulled the hat from his head, crushing it in his fist. The hair beneath had grown long and thin. There were patches of straggly white and silver among the black. Wrinkles and lines played at the corner of his dark eyes, and he was sweating, though still deathly pale.

"I am no more," he said, his voice taut and strained. "And I have no more time to waste." He turned to Arthur, the eyes hard and full of malice. "You must fulfil your promise," he hissed.

Arthur hesitated, but suddenly the Shadowman moved. He was metres away, then flashed forward in a rapid zigzag without appearing to move his feet. He flickered in and out of sight and was directly in front of Arthur before he knew what was happening.

The Shadowman gripped him by the arms and opened his mouth in a wide and savage scream, but to the man's dismay, there was no sound. The Shadowman's lips stretched thin, and the skin looked like it would split with the strain. The eyes bulged, and the creature trembled with the effort but still no noise left his mouth. It was like watching a horror movie with the volume down, and Arthur flinched away, but the Shadowman held him fast, his long fingers digging in like claws.

Arthur cried out.

Nae shouted and reached for him, trying to pull him away from the clawing man, but as her hands closed over the black-clad arms, there was a rush of air, and they all vanished.

The man in the well-cut suit blinked in surprise and looked around the empty aisles of the fruit and veg section.

"Well...bugger," he said to the corn because they were the only ones with ears.

Arthur, Nae, and the Shadowman appeared on the roof of the Minster and fell to the stones. The wind snatched at their clothes and ripped the air from their lungs even as they crouched beneath the crenelations of the tower.

Behind them, the deep shadows cast by the waning eclipse

writhed and twisted as though they were alive, eating at the stone roof and masonry.

A nearby grotesque raised an eyebrow in keen interest as the three people appeared from nowhere, and he slowly turned his weather-beaten body to get a better look. Not much happened up here on the roof. Other than the occasional pigeon landing in the wrong spot, it could be a lonely and dull existence, but this was proving to be a fascinating day.

The ravens circled above, faster and faster, a hypnotic blur pointing to the eclipse, joining the earth with the moon and the sun. The celestial dance was coming to an end.

Arthur scrambled to his knees and fought for breath, terrified of the dark paths. There had been...nothing. The Shadowman had stepped into shadow and stepped back out here at the highest point in the city.

The moment in between had been unlike anything Arthur had experienced.

When he walked through walls, it came with the over-whelming feeling of immense weight pressing in from all sides. It was this that caused his hesitation and fear.

But the path of the Shadowman had been the complete oppo-site. Arthur had a moment of terrifying emptiness, of being in the centre of an immense void, alone.

While there, he hadn't even been aware of the other two. He was, however, left with the unnerving feeling that somewhere on the outskirts of that vast nothingness, there were others look-ing in.

That was a thought that would take up residence in his mind and never leave.

He reached for Nae's hand and squeezed. She had travelled through the dark paths once already and seemed to be dealing with it far better than him. They both turned as a gasp rattled over the noise of the wind.

"Help me!"

The Shadowman was on his stomach, twitching and reaching toward them both with a thin, grasping hand. The skin on his face was grey and sagged, and his body shook as he tried to speak again.

Arthur and Nae got to their feet and looked down at him. He was barely recognisable, a withered husk of what he had been just moments earlier.

Arthur sneered. Anger, fear, and grief fought within him, and he just looked, unmoving and unmoved at the desperate figure.

This creature that had caused him so much trouble was nothing more than an old, bent man. He had sent one of them into the next life before, but he had shown this one mercy. Perhaps mercy was a mistake? Perhaps some people did not deserve mercy?

"Please," the Shadowman gasped.

"Arthur?" Nae said softly beside him.

He didn't look at her. He just watched the Shadowman. What was he? What did the ghost in Marks and Spencer's say? A banshee? He always thought a banshee was an old woman. He had pictured long white hair and screaming old ladies with warty noses floating over misty moorlands in flowing black robes. Not tall, thin, neatly shaven men in black suits.

There had been another word as well, a word he wasn't familiar with, it sounded like *a cow*, but that couldn't be right.

"Arthur."

How bad would it be, really, if he just let him die? What would even happen? He'd probably just come back anyway. Normal rules didn't apply to these creatures.

I could use my power, Arthur thought. *I could just get rid of him.*

The thought was there, fully formed in his mind. Use the power and send him off to whatever comes next. Like last time. No harm. No foul. Sure, another would take his place, but it would be a different creature. Not this...thing. It was pathetic really. Whatever power held it together was clearly fading quickly. It barely even looked human anymore.

He watched as the head sagged, and the hat fell to the stones. The Shadowman tried to rise on his elbows, but his whole body shook under the effort.

"Arthur!" Nae said sharply, and Arthur looked at her. Above them, the ravens circled. "Help him," she said.

Arthur looked back and knelt beside the pitiful creature. He could end it all here, now. He looked closely at the pallid skin and wrinkled his nose. He wouldn't even have to do anything. He could probably just wait. His inaction would have the same effect. But Nae was staring at him with big, hope-filled eyes. And dimples.

"How?" Arthur said, with a tilt of his head. "How can I help you?"

"Inside me," the man gasped with a voice like dry leaves.

"I beg your pardon?"

"Arsehole."

"Well, fuck you, too!"

There was a pause. The Shadowman trembled.

"No. Idiot. A...soul. Inside me."

"What does he mean?" Nae said, kneeling beside them. She was terrified of the man in black but seeing him like this made her feel only pity. He was in agony, ageing and decaying before their eyes.

"I'm not entirely sure," Arthur said, "but I have an idea."

He raised his hands, and purple flames shimmered over his fingers, throwing reflected light on Nae's shocked face. Arthur could have done it without the sparks, but part of him wanted to impress Nae, and so he let the magic ripple and shine. He looked at her and grinned.

"Wax on, wax off," he said, making circular motions in the air. Then, he laid his hands on the sides of the Shadowman's head.

Thousands and thousands of deaths. Over and over again. Turning pages of a dark book. Lines and rows and columns of names, scratched and scored across endless pages. A blade slicing through the fabric of the air. The dark paths. The dark ones. The shadows and all the things that writhe in the gaps. A spark. A flash. Something else in there with them, on the edge of vision, on the edge of reality, something that didn't belong and was…scared. Hiding.

Arthur turned in the dark, back and forth. Searching. He was in the shadow place; every twist and turn held nothing and everything all at once. A vast, endless desert like walking over oil on a pitch night, but oil reflects, and the reflections move and turn and become things…below the surface.

Doors opened and closed, and always the pages rose and fell with a sibilant hiss. Face after face pressed against the veil, and the knife flashed again and again.

And again.

This was the Shadowman.

There was nothing left in the vastness that might suggest he had been human once, other than a memory of a memory. For how long had he walked the dark paths, following the instructions in the book?

All that power and little more than a slave. Obedient, subservient, listless.

Arthur tumbled in the void as a spark flashed in the corner of his eye, or whatever passed for an eye here in the dark places.

There was something else, but it drifted away like smoke, insubstantial and nearly invisible.

Arthur turned and tried to follow, to use the magic to bring whatever it was into focus. He concentrated and tried to shut out the crushing emptiness, to ignore it.

He was a blind man on the edge of an abyss.

There!

He spun and reached out. Contact. Connection. Whatever it was radiated fear, was consumed by it, trembled with it. It tried to pull away, to run, to hide, but it had been running and moving ever since—images flashed, a different place, a dark night—ever since what?

The world spun and twisted, and Arthur hung on.

There was a man.

No. A boy.

Young.

A teenager perhaps?

Leather jacket and...what was that? A Guns N' Roses shirt.

Then the images came faster. A knife in a dark alley. A red handprint on a metal bin. A slumped body. A cry for a father. A man in black cleaning a blade and watching.

Darkness.

The sorrow and the pain of the images hit Arthur with full force, and he cried out. Whatever and wherever he was, he screamed in anguish. He cried at the pain of the blade riven into his gut. He cried for his own father. He cried for fear and for hope.

There should have been peace then, but there was none. Suddenly the weight was on him, and Arthur shuddered beneath the pressure of it all.

His greatest fear.

Darkness surrounded him again on all sides and crushed him, pushing into him from every direction. He was drowning in stone and soil, trapped in the earth, trapped in a coffin.

Then he was the one pushing, climbing and scrambling through the dirt, swimming through stone, and suddenly, there was light, but there was no relief from the pain and the torment.

He walked.

He walked through the woods and the trees and the streets and the city and finally stopped at the foot of a giant building. He knew this place.

He began to climb.

Arthur had no idea what he was seeing, but when the eyes he looked through rose over the top of the parapet, he instantly recognised the man who stood before him, standing on the roof of the Minster with the book at his feet.

Arthur could see it all now from both sets of eyes, the Shadowman and the man in the leather jacket. He saw everything. He saw the heart, the hand, the fire and flame, he saw the ash, he felt the pain, and he knew that this man—this poor innocent man— was trapped, trapped inside the Shadowman. Whatever it was that remained of him had retreated so far and so deep that it was all Arthur could do to hold on to the fragile threads. A swelling anger rose inside him, and he felt a searing contempt and disgust at the foul and black creature that had trapped this soul.

He couldn't let him get away with it.

He couldn't let this innocent man suffer this torment for eternity. He had no idea what the Shadowman had thought he was doing, but this was something that could not be ignored.

There were rules. There had to be rules.

Arthur focused, closed his eyes, and brought all his concentration to bear on the spirit of the dead man.

Dave. His name was Dave. Just like his dad.

He was slipping, scared and falling into the blackness. Arthur grasped and cried out, trying to hold on. He needed to hold on. To find something. Anything to give him enough leverage to close the gap.

And then he heard the singing.

A warm safe place... a child in hiding.

The music was there; it had always been there, at the core of the man. Arthur clung to it and felt the raw emotion, and the visions came again.

A handsome man sitting with his son on his knee, listening to vinyl records, a first guitar, tears in the eyes of a father as the first chords were struck, school assemblies, busking in the street, a stage, a door, an alley, a bin, a red right hand.

A grave.

R enae Ford stood at the very top of the west tower of York Minster as behind her, hidden in the shadows of the parapet, ignored and unnoticed by everyone, the burning flames on the severed hand of the Shadowman flickered their last breath, died, and went out.

The ravens fell from the sky in a great mass, finding their wings and swooping away over the rooftops with shrieking cries. The moon dropped below the centre of the sun, and the bright diamond that marks the beginning of the stage known as third contact flashed across the city. Shadow bands glowed around the edges as the thin crescent began to grow in the sky.

Birds rose from the trees as the ravens fell and they took up their song once again.

The cats perched on the rooftops stirred and stretched, and the Short Ones fled across the cobbles as they chased the retreating shadows.

The sky turned from grey to deep blue and began to lighten as sunlight once more bathed the red rooftops and golden stones of the Minster.

At the red-haired woman's feet, at the highest point in the city, the two men began to stir.

Nae stepped away and backed into the high stones of the tower. She shivered as the sun's warmth washed over her skin, raising goosebumps on her arms. She lifted her face to the sky for a moment, closing her eyes until the sharp cry of a descending raven made her jump and look up.

Two large birds settled on the tower on the opposite side of the stirring men. They sat still, watching.

Arthur was the first to lift his body to his knees and sit back. His face was drawn and peaked. She had no idea what had happened other than he cried, screamed, and wailed for his father while gripping the man in black's face.

But then came the silence, and that was worse.

The two men had sat locked together for a long time, their eyes moving rapidly behind closed lids, neither making a noise. It was then that the moon moved, and Nae noticed the howling winds drop. She thought she heard music filter up from the city far below, but it was unclear and indistinct. And then the two men fell to the stones and stayed that way.

But now Arthur was struggling to his feet, and she wanted to help him, but she couldn't bring herself to move. Her mind and her body hurt, and it was his fault, wasn't it?

Or was it the man beside him. How was that possible? How was anything that had happened today possible?

Nae looked down. She was standing on the west tower of the Minster, which as far as she knew, wasn't open to the public like the big one in the middle was, but she was definitely here—there was no doubt about that. She was in complete control.

Totally sober. Completely conscious.

And yet...and yet all of this was happening.

She imagined herself sitting in the *other* chair in her office trying to explain this to, well, herself.

I wouldn't believe me, she thought. *There's no way I'd believe all this.*

Her thoughts turned to Arthur. How long had he been living like this? What did he say, a year?

How hard would it be to live in a world where you knew with absolute certainty that there was life after death? But more than that, you could talk to the people trapped there; you could even touch them.

It would be enough to drive a man crazy.

Nae stepped toward Arthur and reached out her hand. He looked at her with exhausted eyes and a small smile, shakily gripping hold of her and staggering to his feet.

"Is every date with you going to be like this?" she asked.

Arthur laughed, coughed, and leaned heavily on the short woman who stumbled under his weight.

"Well, the view isn't bad," he said.

He was right.

As the moon drifted inexorably away from the sun's embrace, light spilled across the city, and all the colours of life stood out in dazzling array. The great number of bright green trees rose proudly among the red brick buildings and the blue sky above blazed down on it all.

Birds rose and swooped and sang, and far below, the city slowly stretched its legs and came back to life.

They heard laughter in the late evening air, and they both smiled at the glorious view, the Yorkshire Dales stretching endlessly away in the crisp evening as the sun itself sat heavy on the distant horizon. It would soon vanish but on this—the longest day of the year—the light would remain for another hour or so.

Arthur put his arm over Nae's shoulder more to steady himself than for any romantic inclination, and she braced him with her own arm around his waist.

In a moment such as this, it is easy to forget.

"Your...power," gasped the Shadowman, who as always, had absolutely no sense of occasion.

They both turned to face him.

He leaned heavily against the tower with something gripped tightly in his shaking hand. It was a withered black mess that looked to Arthur like biltong, but he knew from experience it wasn't. To hope otherwise would've been wishful thinking.

The Shadowman was old. His skin pulled tight against his skull, no longer sagging but dry and shrivelled. He raised his other hand, and the young couple gasped to see the stump there. Suddenly the thing he was holding made more sense, and Arthur grimaced at the sight.

"Your power is..." the Shadowman repeated, but there was no end to the sentence. He doubled over and coughed into the stump. Spittle flew over where a hand should have been.

"Thank you," he gasped when the coughing subsided.

Arthur hadn't expected that, and he also did not expect the wave of anger and revulsion that flowed through him hearing the words.

He stepped toward the man in black, shrugging Nae's arm away.

"You killed that kid!" Arthur said in a dangerous voice. "What had he ever done to you? Why did he deserve to die so you could... do whatever it is you've done!"

"Sacrifice," the old man gasped and coughed again. Arthur was revolted by the sight. So withered and decayed, barely able to move or speak. There were dark spots all over his sallow skin.

"Sacrifice!" he snapped. "A sacrifice to who? To what? Why did he have to die?"

"Not by day, nor by night," the old man intoned.

"What are you talking about?"

"Not by weapons of steel or flight."

"Stop talking in riddles and tell me what you did!"

"I cast a spell!" the Shadowman roared in a deep voice, and suddenly there was a glimmer of his old vigour. He stood up straight for a moment, and Arthur saw a flash of the handsome pale face, but then his body was wracked by another fit and he hunched over, straggly white hair dancing toward the ground as his body shook.

"Spells," he choked and spat, "require sacrifice!" The man sagged and convulsed violently, shaking his head from side to side.

"What did you do?" Arthur asked like he wasn't entirely looking forward to the answer.

"I took the gift you gave me, Arthur Crazy, and I became like you."

"What?" Arthur gasped and the Shadowman stood as straight as he could to face him, his mouth open in what was probably a smile, but the brown stumps of teeth ruined the effect.

"You showed me that a choice could be made. So, I made a choice. I became human. But in order to do that, I had to die, and believe me, boy, it is hard to kill *yr Angau*. I needed someone to kill me."

"But there was more to it, wasn't there?" Arthur said, the images flashing behind his eyes.

"Not in the sky nor on the earth, no death shall come from mortal birth," the man wheezed, and suddenly Arthur understood what he had witnessed. He saw how it all tied together, and a wave of revulsion washed through him. He remembered the moment of the Shadowman's death and how he had come back almost instantly to watch the two bodies collapse on the rooftop. The Shadowman was more than a physical body and somehow less.

"You needed a dead man to kill you," he said slowly. "And then you cut out his heart."

"To stop a revenant, you must destroy the heart."

"But you didn't just destroy it, you burned it, and you drank the ash!"

"It is the essence of man."

The ravens cawed loudly, a sharp sound that covered the noise of Nae's gasp at what she had just heard. One of them hopped along the stones, closer to the Shadowman, who ignored it.

"He was innocent!" Arthur shouted.

"Innocent of what?"

"Oh, fuck you! It was wrong and you know it. You killed a man. You murdered him!"

"He was going to die anyway," the man said with a sigh.

"Soon?"

"That same night. I took just a few minutes from him. He was going to be murdered. A horrific death. I spared him that. In the end, it was painless."

Arthur paused, his mind in turmoil. He was furious with the Shadowman, repulsed by him, and yet he knew the strange creature did not see the world the same as he did. How could he? The young musician was going to die anyway, later that night, just a few minutes later. Did that change anything? The man in black still killed an innocent. Did knowing that he was going to die regardless lessen his crime?

Arthur had felt the man's fear, somewhere deep and hidden inside the Shadowman. His death may have been painless, but there are many types of pain.

He looked at the man before him, and he knew.

It didn't change a goddamn thing.

"Arthur, I chose a man already about to die…because of you."

"Don't you fucking put this on me! This is not my fault!"

"No, but the reason I took this man is because I know how much value you place on life. I took his less than a minute before the book told me to. His murderer was already in the alley."

"So why didn't you just take *his* life…the murderer's!"

"It was not his time."

Arthur screamed in frustration and anger, punching the wall

of the stone tower and grimacing at the pain. Purple lightning rippled beneath his skin, and he felt every hair on his body standing on end.

"Arthur," Nae said in a scared voice, and he looked at her. She had backed away from him, and he saw the fear in her eyes. With an effort, he calmed himself and turned back to the Shadowman.

"So, what did I just do?" he asked through gritted teeth. "The essence of that man was inside you still. His...his soul. I thought I freed him. But there is more to it, isn't there?"

The Shadowman smiled but said nothing, still leaning heavily on the wall as the bird hopped closer.

"Fucking tell me!" Arthur shouted, tears streaming down his face.

"You set me free, Arthur," the man said. "I am, as you can see, human."

"This? This isn't human! Look at you! Is this what you wanted? You killed that man, you did all of this, and for what? So you could become a withered old fucker with one hand!"

"I am mortal. To be mortal is to be weak. It is a gift, ironically, that you do not understand."

"But you look like you're about to die!"

"No, I have died. I look like I am about to live!"

He dropped the gnarled remains of his hand to the rooftop, and his arm whipped out in a flash, grasping the startled raven by the head. There was a cry and a very brief attempt at a flap, but the Shadowman's grip was like iron.

He brought the animal to his mouth and sank his rotten brown teeth through the flesh of the neck.

Nae cried and turned away as the bird flapped and struggled, but Arthur was rooted to the spot.

Of all the things he had seen, this seemed to him the most ridiculous.

He laughed as the other raven rose into the sky in a panic, unable to help himself.

"You're not human! You have no idea what it means to be human. A human would never do that!"

"But I am hungry," the Shadowman said from between feathery mouthfuls, a line of red dripping down his chin. "When humans are hungry. We eat."

"Not like this," Arthur said, curling his nose at the crunch of bones. "We don't do this!"

"You eat chicken," the Shadowman said, chewing on the wing and spitting out feathers. "This is like chicken."

"It's not the same!"

"Why?"

It was a question asked with genuine interest, and something in the Shadowman's voice made Arthur pause. As he looked at the disgusting visage before him, the other memories of the Shadowman from long before filtered through. The constant near eternal obedience, the never-ending cycle of the dead, the witness to a million horrors and heartaches.

The loneliness.

We are all the heroes of our own story. He thought of the moment he freed this...man...from the torture and agonies of the witch. He remembered the gratitude, the relief, the spark of change.

This *was* his fault.

Perhaps not in the way he first thought, but the Shadowman started on this path because of Arthur. With great power comes great responsibility and all that.

Spiderman.

Steve loved Spiderman.

The thought arrived in Arthur's mind, and he groaned. Memories of sitting on the couch, absently stroking the head of the little terrier as they watched movies together. Poor Steve. Arthur was not good enough for him. He deserved better. All the little dog wanted was chase squirrels and watch Netflix with his best friend. And Arthur let him down. He had been self-obsessed and distracted, constantly playing with magic and looking for other people like himself, looking for company, when right in front of him, the whole time, he had all the company he could ever want.

The words of the fat duke came to his mind then—the temptation of power, the need to do something with it, to act selfishly, and Arthur realised the man was right. He had acted selfishly. From the moment the magic arose within him, he had used it for his own ends. He...

The Shadowman vomited all over the stones in a disgusting pyrotechnic interruption of Arthur's thoughts.

Feathers, bones, unidentifiable gristle, and a disturbingly identifiable eyeball—they all splattered onto the roof, and the old man heaved and heaved, retching and choking. He fell to his knees, and his back arched as he tried to clear his throat. Arthur stared in a mixture of dazed horror and wonder. It was like watching a cat trying to hack up a furball. The old man wheezed again, turning red, and lifted a hand to Arthur but he just stood there, wide-eyed with shock.

"Do something," Nae said. Her stomach churned at the sight, but she still pitied the suddenly aged Shadowman. The withered flesh and desperate eyes brought back memories she would have preferred remained hidden and not associated with such a bizarre and disgusting sight. It was the blue veins on the reaching hand that did it... and the crooked fingers. She had spent far too much of her youth holding a similar hand looking into eyes just as confused and desperate. Arthur was frozen in indecision and so, despite her disgust and revulsion, Nae took charge. Keeping her eyes firmly away from the mess on the floor she stepped forward and patted the Shadowman on the back, thumping him as he spat. She felt his bones under the black clothes, the narrow ribs and curved spine beneath her open hand just like any normal man's.

But then another eyeball shot from his mouth and, in a coincidence too ridiculous to believe, it rolled across the roof, and came to rest against the first. They rocked gently together and looked to the sky.

It was Nae's turn to throw up.

The Shadowman fell to his side and sighed, breathing easier and freer.

"Thank you," he gasped. "I had hoped for a few moments longer before shuffling off this mortal coil."

"You can't eat like that," Nae said, gagging and wiping her mouth. "It's not right."

"I did not know," the man said. "I am new to this."

He leaned his head against the stones, the dark shadows cast by the setting sun covering half of his body in darkness, but he already looked a little better. Some of the spots on his skin seemed to be fading away, and he looked less haggard than he had before. Nae blinked in numb amazement and turned to Arthur.

"What are we going to do?" she whispered.

Arthur knelt opposite her on the other side of the gasping man. He reached out a trembling hand to the shaking form and paused. The man in black closed his eyes and sighed, and it was as though the breath stripped away the last of the decay. His skin smoothed out before their eyes, no longer old and wrinkled, but healthy and clear, albeit a little pasty.

The Shadowman's eyes snapped open, and they too were bright and clear, the gaze strong and confident.

"We should leave this place," he said. His voice, like the look in his eyes, held no sign of the sickness or rot that had been there moments before.

"How did you do that?" Arthur asked.

The Shadowman ignored the question.

"We should leave," he repeated.

"Oh yeah, and how are we going to do that?" Arthur asked, irritated now by the changes and lack of answers. "And then wh..."

But there was no *and then*. The Shadowman gripped both of their wrists and rolled backward into the shadows, dragging Arthur and Nae with him.

The grotesque blinked in surprise as the three soft ones vanished. This had been the most fascinating day. He particularly enjoyed the part with the raven. He did not like birds. Ravens were admittedly better than pigeons but at the end of the day, but they all belonged to the same family. A family that liked to perch and shit in equal measure.

Speak of the devil and he shall appear.

A single black raven settled on the roof and hopped closer to the pile of feathers and gristle. It bowed its sleek head and regarded the mess with a serious expression (ravens are incapable of any other) before picking through the pile with its long beak. The complete lack of moisture was interesting. But so were the eyeballs. Another hop and a stab, and they were gone. Ravens never wasted a meal or failed to adhere to a stereotype.

CHAPTER 22

"...What? Shit!"

They were back in Marks and Spencer's, everything where they had left it not so long ago, but it was different now. They weren't alone.

Shoppers and employees moved among the shelves, and everything looked exactly as it should. Outside the long windows, the busy streets were bright and vibrant, full of meandering crowds and people sitting at the pop-up bars and restaurants lining the open expanse of Parliament.

"I did it," the Shadowman gasped, looking at his hand and turning it over. He touched his face with delicate fingers. The wrinkles were gone. His hair was black. He stood up straight and pulled the black cap into place. "I'm back."

"About time," came another voice. "Where the bloody hell did you go? One minute we're chatting, and the next you've vanished."

Arthur spun around to see the man in the well-cut grey suit standing a few feet away. It took a moment to place him without the dogs on his heels. "You're still here," he said.

"Of course, I'm here. Where else would I be?"

"Erm, excuse me," said Nae, "but who are you talking to?"

Arthur blinked in surprise and realisation slowly dawned. They were back in the real world, outside of the shadow realm, and so Nae could no longer see the ghosts. They could see her, of course, and Arthur could see them, but as far as Nae was concerned, he was having a conversation with some apples.

"It's the man in the grey suit," he explained.

Nae looked between Arthur and the apples, a myriad expressions vying for dominance on her beautiful face. It settled somewhere south of confusion and on an off-ramp to acceptance.

"You really can see ghosts, can't you," she said in a small voice.

Arthur stared at her.

"Well, you know what I mean," she replied to his silence with a smile. "It's still a bit hard to believe even with all the evidence."

"Easy to forget when the evidence goes away," Arthur said.

"Exactly. So, erm, hello," she said, waving to the apples.

"He's there," Arthur said, pointing to an identical looking blank spot a few feet to the left.

"What does he want?" Nae asked, still trying to wrap her head around the strangeness of the situation in the middle of the produce section.

"I don't know," Arthur said, turning to the man. "What do you want? Can I help?" But the man was staring at Nae, who had picked up an apple and taken a bite. She was hungry and the thought of paying for it didn't even cross her mind. In fact, she was eyeing off the alcohol on the shelves next to the Shadowman as well. A drink would go down a treat after everything they had been through. The man's eyes widened as a drop of juice glistened on Nae's lip and fell over her chin.

"What I want, no man can give me," he said.

"Bit dramatic," Arthur replied. Instantly kicking himself for it. That was the kind of banter he shared with Steve.

The man sighed.

"Sorry, I've been by myself for so long."

"Try me," Arthur replied. "I might actually be able to help."

"Ha! Well," he said, tearing his eyes away from Nae and turning to the front of the shop, "you see that church over there, on the other side of the street?"

He pointed out of Marks and Spencer's at the towering spire of

All Saints Church. Arthur nodded; he and Steve had walked past it earlier that day.

Steve.

He fought back the tears.

"Every day I try to get there, and every day I wake near the Minster and the dogs are always somewhere close by. They're always there. Chasing me."

"What is at the church?" Arthur asked.

"My funeral."

"Oh."

"And my wife."

"Right. And you, err, you can't run to the church?"

"Do you think I'd run in here if I could get there?"

"No, I guess not." Arthur said.

Behind them, Nae had opened a bottle of red wine and took a long drink before passing it to the Shadowman, who sniffed it with a wrinkled nose.

"Why here?" Arthur asked.

"It wasn't always a...market," the man said. "This is where I'm buried."

"Excuse me?"

"All of this, the whole shop, everything around it, was once a graveyard. This, my new friend, is my final resting place."

He laughed at the irony and then groaned as Nae opened a punnet of strawberries. Her lips were bright red, and he couldn't tear his eyes away as she ate and washed it down with more wine. Ghosts were always hungry, and many spent an embarrassingly large part of their days watching the living eat.

"What is he saying?" Nae asked, wiping her mouth with the back of her hand and handing the bottle to Arthur. He cast his eyes around and took a long swig when he saw that no one was looking.

"He's buried here," Arthur said.

"In Marks and Spencer's?"

"Kind of, yeah."

"That's some serious Scooby-Doo shit," she said, taking the

bottle back and having another drink. "Who'd have thought it, Marks and Spencer's built on an ancient burial ground."

"Not sure it's that ancient, to be honest."

"You know what I mean. So, what's the problem? Why don't we go over there?"

"The dogs."

"The dogs?"

"The ones that…got Steve. They stop him when he tries."

"Will they now?" the Shadowman asked. It was the first time he'd spoken in a while, and they all looked at him.

"What do you mean?"

"They have fed. They are probably satisfied."

Arthur was going to react. At least, he *thought* he was going to react. At the very least, he thought he *should* react. But he didn't. It was all too raw and the realisation that the Shadowman simply did not understand was slowly dawning on him. He stared at the man for a long time until Nae handed him an apple.

"Eat," she said. "You need to eat."

He took a bite without looking away from the black eyes of the man in front. He was a blank slate. An entirely new man. No, a child. He had all that experience. Had done all those things. And yet he had absolutely no idea how to act or how to speak. Arthur felt the weight of that responsibility, and instead of embracing the anger he felt rising at his words, he pushed it back down and sighed. He knew what Steve would do. Steve would see the best in everyone. He took another bite of the apple and tasted it this time. The sharp tang of the flesh and the sweetness at the back of his mouth. His stomach rumbled instantly.

"Let's try," he said.

"What do you mean?" asked the man in the grey suit.

"Let's see if we can get you to your wife. It could be as easy as walking across the street."

And it was.

They paid for the wine, the apples, and the strawberries, ignoring the look from the cashier as she clocked the half-empty bottle and the apple cores, and then the strange foursome walked through the sliding door of Marks and Spencer's onto Parliament and out into the dangerous, widely haunted city of York.

Where nothing happened.

Within moments they were standing at the entrance to All Saints Church. The crowds around them thronged and pushed, tightly packed even at this late hour, but of course, the ghost didn't notice, and both Arthur and Nae were used to it.

It was the Shadowman who had the hardest time. He had never experienced a crowd before—not one that could touch him at any rate—and a crowd in Parliament during a long summer day in York was a baptism of fire. He was pushed back and forth by the surging people and in the end opted to stand close to a cart on wheels and a tired man trying to sell roasted chestnuts on a hot day. It was a small patch of calm in the chaos.

The reunion between the man in the well-cut suit and his beautiful wife was something to behold, and Arthur found himself moving unconsciously closer to Nae as the two ghosts embraced on the front steps of the church.

The man's wife had been waiting, grasping flowers to her breast, her long blonde hair flowing loose over a lace dress.

Arthur asked if they wanted to be set free, but they were both so happy to be with each other after being so close for so long that they waved his offer away with heartfelt thanks. They couldn't be sure they would be together in the next life, but they were together now, and that was enough.

Arthur quietly narrated everything to Nae, and her hand found its way to his and held him tight. She looked at him with the eyes of a woman who had not seen what'd happened but understood it, nonetheless.

"This is what you do," she said. It was not a question. Her voice was filled with wonder and admiration.

"I try," Arthur said.

"You're a good man, Arthur," she said, and those words hit him somewhere deep and important. She reached up and kissed him, and it would have been a perfect moment if not for her next words.

"I don't even know your surname," she said. "Arthur who? I'm Renae Ford," she added.

"Oh, it, it doesn't matter," he said, a red flush creeping over his face. Of all the things to be embarrassed about on a day such as this.

"What? Of course, it does. What's your name?"

Arthur laughed and then sighed. "It's Crazy."

"That doesn't matter. I'm named after a car."

"No, I mean, my name is Crazy."

"Don't worry. You thought I was named after the noise a horse makes."

"No, I, I mean my name is Arthur Crazy. Arthur Benedict Crazy."

There was a pause.

A long pause.

It grew.

"It's true," the Shadowman said from his place of refuge near the cart. "That's his name."

"You're fucking kidding!" Nae laughed.

"Nope. I'm Crazy, my mum and dad are Crazy, and my grandparents on my dad's side are all Crazy."

"You've said that before, haven't you?"

"Once or twice," he admitted.

"It's really Crazy?"

"Yes, it is. A strong Yorkshire name. It comes from a little village called Gilling West out near Richmond...where I'm from," he added.

"Well, I knew I'd met a crazy man today, but I didn't quite realise..."

"Five generations at the last count," he said.

"Mr. Crazy." She smiled and kissed him.

Behind them, the beautiful ghosts held each other tightly on the steps of the church as the last light of the day vanished over the city.

This might, in fact, have been a great place for this story to end. We'd pan away, high above the crowd as they parted like the ocean around a lighthouse, and the couple who've been through hell and found each other on the other side would embrace in the setting sun as the sky blazed purple and the world turned.

But life doesn't work that way.

And neither does death.

PART II
THE SHORTEST NIGHT

CHAPTER 23

"What is happening?" the Shadowman asked. He had a bag of roast chestnuts in his hand and was standing very close to the young couple, peering intently at their faces. Nae turned red and pulled away from Arthur.

"Nothing," she said.

"Nothing now," Arthur mumbled.

"Why do you do that thing with your mouth? Is it for sustenance?"

Arthur and Nae looked at him.

"What happens next?" the man in black asked, unperturbed, sniffing the bag in his hand. Smells were new to him, and the scent of roast chestnuts was doing something to his insides that he did not understand. His mouth filled with saliva, and he dribbled, dabbing at his chin with his residual limb. He had tried to eat one of the chestnuts but instantly felt as though he was going to throw up. Which, to be fair, was entirely normal with roast chestnuts. So now he just stood there with the bag, not sure at all what to do with it.

Arthur shrugged. He looked at Nae, then at the Shadowman, and then across the street to the last place he had seen Steve. Happiness, anger, and sorrow. It was all there, simmering away just below the surface.

"I want to go home," Nae said, interrupting his scattered thoughts. "This has been a...strange day to say the least. I think it's about time it ended."

Arthur nodded.

"Can I walk you home?" he asked.

Nae smiled and linked her hand through his arm.

"You're a gentleman," she said.

They moved slowly through the city, both lost in their own thoughts. It had been a life-changing day for both of them, and there was a lot to unpack. How to even approach that conversation with a person who was essentially a stranger was hard to fathom, and so for a long time, neither spoke.

Behind them, the Shadowman followed along, clutching his bag of chestnuts.

They passed through Coppergate Walk and out onto Castlegate in silence, but it was Nae who broke first as they circled the foot of Clifford's Tower. The medieval fortress sat alone on top of a green hill on the outskirts of the city like a scene from a movie or a kids Lego set. The last remnant of York Castle.

Nae saw Arthur gazing up at the fort and she noticed once again that his eyes appeared to be focused on something only he could see.

"Who is there?" she asked.

"He's called Roger," Arthur replied, not taking his eyes away.

He was looking at a large metal cage fastened to the side of the fortress. It had long since been taken down and had rusted into nothingness, but for Arthur, it was still there, swinging gently in the summer breeze. A man sat inside with his legs dangling, whistling a jaunty tune as he watched a world he couldn't understand pass him by.

"What's his story?" Nae asked.

"He's Roger de Clifford. The tower is named after him. He was hung here and put in a cage. He's still there, like a canary."

"Where?"

"Just there," Arthur paused and pointed.

Nae looked, but of course, she could see nothing, just a few stars coming to life in the purple and grey sky, and so she never saw Roger de Clifford smile and wave happily, though she did see Arthur lift his hand and wave back.

"How many are there?" she asked, trying to wrap her head around the fact that she believed Arthur's story, believed that there was indeed someone there. It flew in the face of everything she knew, everything she had spent her professional life studying. Sure, she viewed all her patients with the understanding that their reality was true to them...but that was in a clinical setting, the boundary between patient and practitioner firmly drawn. This, however, was different; Arthur was genuine, but to the rest of the world, he was indeed crazy.

"What, ghosts?"

"Yeah."

"Not as many as you might think. Tonight was the most I've seen in one place, but I think that was because of the solstice. They could, well, move freely."

"And they can't normally?"

"No. At least I don't think so. Usually, they stick to the same places. Some are different than others, but most stay put. Like Roger, he doesn't leave his cage."

"Wait a minute," she said, putting her hand on his chest and stopping beneath the looming shadow of the tower. "He's a ghost, so how is he trapped?"

Arthur smiled. He had asked Roger the very same question the first time he spoke to the dangling man. "Ghost cage," was the simple answer, and Arthur repeated it now. Nae just shrugged.

"Stands to reason, I guess," she said. "I mean, you hear stories about ghost ships and phantom stagecoaches, so I guess it makes sense. I wonder why it's all old stuff though?"

"What do you mean?"

"Well, are there any ghost speedboats or, or ghost motorbikes?"

Arthur laughed.

"Not that I know of," he said.

It felt great to be talking about this sort of thing with another person, but then he thought of all the similar conversations he'd had with Steve, and the feeling vanished. He choked back the tears that threatened to spill and looked away.

"It must be awful, though," Nae was saying when he dragged himself back, "to be trapped forever in a cage."

"It is for some," he said, keeping the shake from his voice with an effort, "but Roger seems to like it. I offered to set him free, but he says it's his tower, and he doesn't want to leave."

"So, that's what you do? You're a...Ghostbuster?"

"Ha! Not really. Good movie, though."

"Better cartoon."

"True. I can—I don't know how to explain it—I can release ghosts. Set them free from where they are trapped. Stop them being ghosts."

"Oh, like that *Ghost Whisperer* show with the girl with the big boobs!"

"Kind of, just without the boobs."

"Where do they go?"

"I've got no idea," Arthur said. "And neither do they. That's why many of them choose to stay."

They walked on in silence, heading toward Skeldergate Bridge. They left Clifford's Tower and the swinging Roger behind them, each lost in their own thoughts, the man in black an all-but-forgotten shadow at their backs.

"I live on the other side," Nae said when they got to the road before the bridge. The river moved gently below, twinkling with the reflected lights of the town, and the grass of Tower Gardens shone in the muted glow of the orange lamp posts beside them. The world appeared peaceful and serene, an endless night of potential. They both looked over the river but neither moved. "Let's walk a bit further," Nae suggested, handing Arthur the bottle of wine. "It all seems so, I don't know, normal now. Almost like it didn't happen."

"I know what you mean," Arthur said, taking a quick drink. He glanced behind them out of habit, half-expecting to see Steve trotting alongside or pissing on a tree. The momentary glimmer of hopeful memory teased him with the idea that the little dog was still there, still alive.

And then it passed.

There was nothing there but the shadows and the Shadowman.

Arthur turned away, and they walked along the banks of the river, away from the city as the streetlights lit the path in a soft orange glow. They passed through the pools of light with the Shadowman trailing behind. Nae was right, Arthur knew. These ridiculous things kept happening, and yet the world plodded along as normal. It always did.

It'll be reet, as they say. It's the Yorkshire way.

A couple walked toward them, the young woman laughing at something the man had said. A group of teenagers sat on a patch of grass sharing a joint, the thick scent sharp and sweet in the air. Cars trundled over the bridge behind, and the stars moved above. Tired birds sang in the treetops as the light faded, and it did indeed seem like the end to a perfectly normal day.

"Favourite movie?" Nae asked suddenly.

"Pardon?"

"What's your favourite movie?"

"Right." Arthur smiled and stopped, trying to gather his thoughts. "I, um, I'm not sure. It changes every day. What about you? You go first." They were on the blue bridge that crossed the narrow channel where the Foss meets the Ouse and Arthur was very conscious of it being a romantic spot—especially by lamplight. Luckily for him, so was Nae.

"Okay, I'll give you a clue," she said and stepped closer. The two rivers joined beneath them in a slow dance as she looked up. "I hear relationships that start in intense circumstances never last," she whispered.

Arthur's cheeks burned red, and his heart pounded in his chest as he wondered whether he had the courage to say the next line rather than the title of the film. He knew it. Of course he knew it. And he guessed Nae knew that he knew, but still, he hesitated.

Steve would have called him a dickhead by now.

Arthur swallowed and hoped his voice wouldn't tremble.

"I guess we'll have to base this one on sex then," he said. His voice did indeed tremble, but Nae laughed.

"*Speed*! Got it in one," she said. "But then, I do have a massive crush on Keanu Reeves, so I'll take any movie he's in."

"I think everyone has a massive crush on Keanu Reeves," Arthur said. "He's one of the few nice guys left in the world."

"I hope not," Nae said and stood on her tiptoes to kiss him on the lips. They walked on.

"What was Steve's favourite movie?" Nae asked, taking Arthur's hand in hers.

Arthur blinked at the use of the past tense, and his mouth curled into a smile that did not reach his eyes. As polite conversations go, asking what movie your dead dog liked was odd by anyone's standards, but he guessed Nae was trying to get him to talk. A maelstrom of emotions washed through him, though, and he fought hard to keep them in check. Nae pulled him over to a patch of grass beside the still waters of the river. They sat side by side, Nae's shoulder resting lightly against Arthur's.

"Steve loved *The Italian Job*," Arthur said with a sigh.

"The original Michael Caine one I hope," she said.

"Definitely," Arthur said. "He loved the ending more than anything."

"Really? That bit where they're hanging off the edge of the cliff and he says...what does he say?"

"'Hang on a minute, lads. I've got a great idea.'"

"That's it! The camera just pans away, doesn't it? And leaves the bus teetering on the edge. The ultimate cliff-hanger." She laughed.

"Yeah, Steve loves it."

Arthur paused and stared out over the water. Nae squeezed his arm and he shook his head, clearing the image of snapping jaws and grasping claws. He drank a mouthful of wine and went on. "He always said it was the fact that you don't know what happens next that makes the movie so great. Knowing what comes next isn't all it's cracked up to be."

He fell silent again, and Nae rested her head against his shoulder. They let the noises of the restful evening wash over them for a while, and then Nae spoke again.

"Okay, then, the ultimate question. Favourite book?"

Arthur leaned back and laughed. There was a glimmer in his eye now.

"Oh, this could take some time," he said.

And it did.

They finished the bottle of wine on the banks of the river while the night turned black, and the Shadowman wandered, almost forgotten, among the trees.

CHAPTER 24

All over the world and throughout any multiverse worthy of a glance, there had always existed the issue of the third wheel, the candleholder, the awkward man in a Weezer shirt. The companion destined to lag behind the cute couple and wait for one of them to bugger off.

The Shadowman waited now on the city walls and watched Arthur walk Nae to her front door, a feeling he couldn't understand gnawing and building inside him. It was a little like the anger he felt at the man on the bench, though this tasted different.

He watched as the young couple walked hand in hand across the road and approached a house with a bright yellow door. It sat nestled in a line of identical stone houses parallel to the high walls of the city. A swath of green grass ran from the wall to the road filled with patches of swaying daffodils that glimmered in the dim light of the streetlamps.

On the doorstep of the house, Arthur and Nae kissed, and Nae went inside. The door closed, and Arthur thrust his hands in his pockets and walked slowly across the road, turning halfway to look back.

The young man hopped a small wall and pushed his way through the daffodils toward the waiting man at the top of the slope. He clambered onto the footpath and stood in front of the Shadowman with a strange look on his face.

"I could do with a cigarette," he said, patting his pockets and coming up empty. The man in the black suit nodded and walked away without a word, heading into the shadows.

A dark copse grew around a small hill that marked the end of the city wall. Arthur looked in shock as the man stepped off the path and pushed his way through.

"Hey, what's going on?"

There was no reply.

Arthur jogged along the wall and followed the man in black. He ducked under low branches and emerged in a small clearing on the top of the hill.

It was empty.

The Shadowman had gone.

"What the fuck?"

Arthur climbed back onto the path and looked up and down the wall. There was nothing there but a ribbon of moonlight stretching away on the cobbles. He walked to the top of the steps and peered into the small gatehouse, but the Shadowman was nowhere to be seen.

Arthur leaned against the wall and groaned.

His heart was light with the memory of the kiss, but it felt like a lie. Such happiness so close to the sorrow of losing Steve. He felt like a traitor to the wee dog.

"Here."

The Shadowman stepped from the trees, and Arthur let out a cry of shock. The man in black held out a pack of smokes.

"What the fuck!" Arthur repeated.

"You said you wanted cigarettes. I got cigarettes."

Arthur looked at the strange man who smiled and offered the packet again. At least his smiles were getting better. Arthur took the pack and opened it. He placed a cigarette in his mouth and clicked his thumb, the flame flashing across the pale face of the newly minted man before him.

Arthur took a long drag and then blew out the smoke, offering the packet to the Shadowman.

"Do you smoke?" he asked.

"I do not know."

Arthur stared. "So, what are you going to do now?"

"What do you mean?"

"Well, you got what you wanted, right? You're a man now. So, what are you going to do?"

"I'm going to live."

Arthur sighed. "Come with me," he said and pushed past the Shadowman into the trees.

Baile Hill was a small hillock that most people walked past or had no idea existed just off the footpath on the wall. It was one of the old remains of a motte-and-bailey castle that marked this side of the river. Now it was a small round hill with a tiny clearing at the top between a circle of thick, heavy trees. Arthur sat down on the grass and smiled as he saw the yellow door of Nae's house through a gap in the foliage. The Shadowman hesitated, then sat with him, carefully copying the way Arthur tucked his legs beneath his body.

Unknown to either of them, a small green figure watched from the branches.

"I don't even know what to call you," Arthur said. "Do you have a name?"

"I do," the man nodded, thinking of the carved pottery that had allowed all of this to happen.

"What is it?"

The Shadowman made a noise that had more in common with someone coughing into a bagpipe than any discernible language.

"Bless you," Arthur said, but the joke was lost on the man. Arthur sighed. "You need a name. That's the place to start. A name is important. And it needs to be something people can actually say. And spell."

"Arthur."

"That's my name."

"Can it not also be mine?"

"That's a bit weird."

"Arthur?"

"No, choosing the same name as me."

"Steve."

"No!"

They sat in silence for a time while Arthur smoked and thought. He didn't like this man. He didn't like being so close to him. He felt uncomfortable around the Shadowmen at the best of times, but there was something especially unnerving about this one. The spell, the magic, the eclipse—whatever it was—had changed everything. The Shadowmen were supposed to fix things, to put things right, but this one had done the exact opposite. And people had died. Steve had died. Arthur didn't know what to do and just wanted the man to go away, to slink back into the shadows. He just wanted to be left alone.

"What have other people called you?" Arthur asked. "You must have had names. Pick one of those and go...live your life."

The Shadowman looked into the branches of the trees above. Arthur tapped the cigarette packet impatiently.

"I was once called Meagre Hein," the Shadowman said after a time. "But I did not like it very much."

"Hein?" Arthur repeated, trying the word. "Hein. Well, what about Heinrich?" he suggested. "It'll give you an interesting foreign flavour, which, you know, will probably help with a few things."

"Heinrich?" The Shadowman tasted the name. "*Lord* Heinrich."

"Excuse me?"

"Someone called me Lord. I liked it."

"How about we start with Heinrich?"

"Yes."

Arthur stood up, and the Shadowman rose with him. He held out his hand.

"I am Heinrich," he said. He had seen humans do this.

Arthur nodded and took the hand in a quick grip.

"Nice to meet you—"

There was a short flash between the two men as their hands connected, and Arthur blinked in shock. There wasn't much there. Not a lot at all. Almost as though there wasn't much to see. A nearly blank slate but there were some experiences. New ones. It was enough. More than enough. Arthur pulled his hand away and chose his words carefully, trying not to react to the visions he had seen. "So, what's next?" he asked. "Do you have a plan?" He finished the cigarette and lit another one. The shaking flame bathed the little clearing in a purple glow, and the shadows around them danced, as did some of the leaves in the tree above. Heinrich didn't speak for a moment, and Arthur waited, not actually smoking at all but thinking quickly.

"I had a plan," Heinrich said after a while. "But now, I do not."

"You haven't thought about what you're going to do?"

"*Do*?"

"You know, how you're going to live, where, how you're going to earn money for food—" He paused, picking the right moment, flicking ash to the ground, the image from their handshake fresh in his mind. "Heinrich?"

The man smiled at the use of his new name. "Yes, Arthur?"

"How did you pay for the cigarettes?"

"Pay?"

"How did you get them?" Arthur said, his voice carefully measured and level.

"I took them."

"Without paying?"

"Why would I pay?"

"Because that's what you're supposed to do," Arthur said slowly.

"Why?"

"It's just what happens. It's the way things are done." He dropped the cigarette and ground it beneath his heel into the grass, trying to think.

"I do not understand," Heinrich said, and Arthur closed his eyes. The image flashed in his mind again. A figure slumped over newspapers and chocolates. A stain growing around him.

"Did you kill a man to get these?" he asked, holding the cigarettes between them.

This was dangerous.

"He is not dead."

"What did you do?"

"I got cigarettes."

"I mean what did you do to the man!" Arthur demanded, growing frustrated.

"I moved him out of the way."

The infuriating, uncomprehending calm of the man in black was difficult to deal with. "Why did you do that?" Arthur asked, his fists clenched by his side.

"He would not move."

"Because you have to fucking pay!" Arthur said, the mask slipping. "You can't just take things. You can't just hurt people. You can't just move them out the way if you want something—"

"Yes, I can," Heinrich said, and his voice was so calm that it cut through Arthur's anger like the blade of the Shadowman.

He meant it, Arthur realised. He meant the words literally and he did not understand the complexity. He could do it and so he did. He never stopped to ask whether he *should* because that was not a question that ever occurred to him. He was a blank slate. There were no morals. No learned experiences. No sense of right and wrong. He was a child born with selfishness and power.

He was dangerous.

Stop him before it goes any further.

The thought was there. Fully formed. It didn't feel like something Arthur would think, but there it was, and he felt the truth of it. Part of him stood away from the rest, looked at the thought, and nodded assent. His whole body prickled with the heat of his magic, and he felt it surge within him, a depthless source of power. He could finish it now. Before it got worse.

You should.

He could put a stop to all of this.

It is the right thing to do.

Arthur looked into the eyes of the man in front of him, and the childlike innocence there suddenly made him think of Steve.

Steve, who saw the best in everyone.

With a considerable effort, Arthur relaxed his shoulders and unclenched his fists. The uncomprehending black eyes of the man bore into him the whole time. Who was he to judge if a person lived or died? That made him just as bad, didn't it?

"This," Arthur sighed heavily, trying to find the words to make the man see. "This isn't what it means to be alive. There is more to being human than skin and bones. Much more."

"I do not understand."

"I know you don't, I know. And I guess it's not your fault, but you can't...you shouldn't," he corrected. "You shouldn't go around hurting people and taking things that are not yours. There are rules. Humans have rules. I mean, you've watched us, right? You've spent ages watching us."

"Of course."

"Then you've seen that we have laws. Good things, bad things, right and wrong. People...society...there are things you do and things you don't do. It's how all this works. It's how we function as a...as a species."

"But the strongest do what they wish, do they not?"

Arthur paused. Heinrich wasn't wrong, not really, but how did you get across thousands of years of civilisation and philosophy over a pack of stolen cigarettes?

"We act in certain ways because it is the right thing to do," he said, but even as he finished he knew it wasn't the right approach.

"Agreed. It was the right thing for me to do," Heinrich said. "You expressed a desire for cigarettes, and I provided cigarettes. This was a good thing."

"But that's not..." Arthur started again and hesitated. "Look, how would you feel if someone just took something from you that you didn't want them to take?"

"I would not let them."

The blunt truth of the sentence stopped Arthur in his tracks. He looked into the eyes of the Shadowman and saw no arrogance there. There was no guile, no cunning, no malice. He was a truly blank slate, and the implications made Arthur shiver. He really should put a stop to this before it got worse, but then he thought of Nae, and her patients, and their lived realities. It wasn't the Shadowman's fault he didn't know better. If anything, it might be Arthur's. It was all tied back to him after all. He banished one Shadowman here in the city, he spared the life of this one in Richmond Castle. Even if that was a mistake, he couldn't just 'erase' it. That sort of thinking was what he was trying to get Heinrich to understand was wrong in the first place.

"It's just wrong to take things like that," he said, infuriated that he couldn't find the words.

"That does not make sense to me," Heinrich said. "If I want something, why should I not have that thing? Unless," he added, one perfect eyebrow raised in thought, "unless it is another deal, no? Such as our deal earlier tonight. Do you now owe me for the cigarettes?" He held out his hand for Arthur to shake.

"That's not how it works!" Arthur snapped, pushing the Shadowman's hand away. "We don't just take things. We don't just act without considering the consequences. That's not what humans do. It's not what people are."

"I have watched humans for thousands of years," Heinrich said. "That is exactly what you do and what you are. You take and you are selfish. You have choices and you make them. It is a wondrous gift."

"Maybe," Arthur said, kicking the ground. "We shouldn't be like that though. Most of us try not to be. That's the point. We learn."

"I can learn."

"Can you?" Arthur said under his breath. He looked up into that curious gaze. "Can you learn? Can you tell me why killing that young man, the one who climbed the Minster—even just a few minutes before his time—was wrong? Can you tell me why taking the cigarettes was wrong? Can you tell me why hurting someone to get them was wrong?"

The two men stared at each other, the only sound was that of

Arthur's heavy breathing and a small rustling from the trees above. Heinrich looked thoughtful, and Arthur thought he might actually be getting through to him, but then the black-clad hand reached up suddenly and snatched a struggling creature from the low branches.

Arthur saw a kick of a small green leg gripped in Heinrich's fist before he raised it to his mouth and ate it.

"What the fuck?" he gasped in a small voice. "What the actual fuck did you just do?"

"I ate. I was hungry, so I ate."

"You don't get it, do you?" Arthur said. "That's not normal! That's not right! It's not fucking human! You aren't fucking human!"

"I am."

"No! You're not!"

Kill him.

The thought was there again, and Arthur closed his eyes against it. How could he convince the Shadowman of right and wrong if he couldn't even convince himself? He felt that strange energy crackling through his arms, raising the hairs, rippling over his flesh to his hands. He clenched his fists and opened his eyes, staring deep into those of Heinrich. They were black like oil, and Arthur saw his own reflection in the deep pools.

"Being human isn't about selfishly doing what you want," he said. "It isn't about taking something and eating something because you feel like it, or being more powerful than others, or using that power to push people down. It's about using power to lift people up. You don't get that? Even if someone uses power for wrong, the point is we *know* it's wrong. Even after centuries of watching us, you don't see?"

Heinrich said nothing, and Arthur stared at himself in the man's eyes, then looked away. "You aren't human," he said quietly.

A heavy hand rested on his shoulder. Heinrich had moved closer without a sound.

"You mean I am not you, Arthur. Don't you?" he said. Arthur

tried to move away, but the grip was too strong. "In this, you are right. I am not Arthur. I am my own man. I am Heinrich."

"You didn't listen to anything I said," Arthur said, sadly, shaking his head, but the truth of the Shadowman's words had cut him and the voice telling him to destroy the creature faded to a whisper. How could you teach someone to be a man if you barely even knew what it meant yourself? His own dad had spent a life-time being a role model to young men, not just his own son. People back home regularly told Arthur what a good man his dad was. He always nodded and smiled. He knew and he was forever grateful. The Shadowman—Heinrich—didn't have that. He wondered what his dad would say now.

"Being a man is about doing the best you can without being a dick to other people," he said softly. "It's about more than satiating appetites, and taking what you want. Otherwise, we're just animals, right? You can talk, and think, and feel, and that's great. But being a man is about using those things to better yourself and other people. It's about building relationships. It's about finding moments of joy with people you care about." He glanced through the trees to the yellow door. "It's about finding happiness and maybe even love."

Heinrich let go. "I do not know love," he said.

The words were simple but cutting. Arthur thought he had been lonely, but he realised now it was nothing compared to that of the Shadowman. Here was a being surrounded by people but completely alone, for thousands of years, and now, suddenly, he wasn't.

It was certainly going to take more than a five-minute chat and a pat on the back.

"Some things take time," Arthur said. And then, because the night wasn't strange enough, the Shadowman turned and vomited into the bushes behind him.

The smell was appalling. He hacked and he heaved, and Arthur grimaced at the sight, patting him on the back.

"This isn't right," Arthur said, softly. "This isn't good. You're lost and the world is too big to make sense of in one night."

"I have much to consider," Heinrich said, turning and wiping his mouth. "I have...I do not know how to describe them...I have urges, this body wants things that I do not fully understand and the"—he tapped his head with his finger—"voice inside?"

"Thoughts?" Arthur said.

"The thoughts do not always seem to match what the body wants. Is this normal?"

"I guess so," Arthur said.

"It seems like a poor design."

"Maybe it is, I don't know, but part of being human is learning how to live with the thoughts and knowing which ones to pay attention to, and which ones to ignore."

"Even the ones that go against the urges of the body?"

"Especially those," Arthur said. "Well, sometimes. Just because you're hungry doesn't mean you have the right to eat whatever you want. And people can be judgemental, hey," he added, trying to lighten the mood. "If you do things that freak them out, like eating wild birds, they'll treat you like an outcast...like you're crazy. It's better sometimes to just do what everyone else is doing."

"I will think on this," Heinrich said.

He faced Arthur for a moment, his face expressionless, then he strode into the shadows of the trees.

Arthur knew instantly that he was gone, off somewhere down the dark paths, the clearing on the top of the hill suddenly empty.

"That's not bloody human," he said, but then he lit a cigarette with the magic from his hand and paused. Self-reflection is a wonderful bitch sometimes.

Arthur shook his head to clear it and sighed loudly, gripping his hands into tight fists and crying out with frustration. "Fuck this. I need a drink," he said. "Fancy some pork scra—"

Arthur stopped mid-sentence and stared at the empty patch of grass by his feet.

Then he cried.

The black cat in the shadows of the city walls watched the man walk away. It noticed the way his shoulders were slumped, and his head was bowed, and it wondered if there was something wrong.

And then it licked itself.
Because it didn't care.

CHAPTER 25

Arthur walked away from the city walls in a daze, crossing Skeldergate Bridge and descending the steps to Tower Gardens and the river with no real conscious thought of direction. He just walked, absentmindedly retracing his steps from earlier in the day.

With Steve.

He'd peed on that lamppost just a few hours ago. He chased seagulls right there. He begged for a chip from a cute girl on that corner.

"Hello, boy!"

The familiar voice cut through Arthur's thoughts. He looked up and groaned. The fat duke from the Cock and Bottle grinned at him. He was naked, leaning against a table with his arms folded over his enormous belly, which, mercifully, covered everything else.

Arthur looked around and noticed the absence of people for the first time. It was usually bustling around here at this time of night, but police tape fluttered in the breeze outside the King's Arms, and he guessed the duke had something to do with it.

Kings Staith lay empty in the moonlight.

Just him and the duke beside the river.

"Georgie," Arthur said with a sneer. He was done with manners.

The reaction was instant, as deep-down Arthur hoped it would be. The duke snarled and lunged at him, but he stepped smartly to the side and stuck out his leg. The graceless duke went tumbling to the floor and rolled. He got up quick, much quicker than expected, and roared a challenge at the dark-haired young man.

"Villain!" he screamed, and Arthur laughed, his brooding thoughts vanishing as the man charged at him. He didn't step aside this time. He stepped forward and punched the ghost square in the face. All his anger, all his pain and frustration came roaring to the surface, and he grinned as his fist connected, sending the duke tumbling once more. Arthur stepped forward and loomed over the panting man.

Kick him.

The thought was there, so bright and clear in his mind that it almost drove his foot to action, but the words of Arthur's father broke through and quelled the almost overbearing compulsion.

Never kick a man when he's down.

It wasn't just a figurative lesson, and Arthur knew he was teetering on the edge of losing all sense of control, all sense of who he was. If he gave in now, he'd be lost.

"Feels good, doesn't it, boy?" the duke spat from the ground. "Doing what you want simply because you can."

He rose to his feet and behind him, behind them both, the dark waters of the river churned and frothed.

"When you have power and you don't use it, what are you? Are you even a man? This is the way of the world, boy! There are those with power and those without." Arthur glanced across the river in the direction of Baile Hill, thinking of the words Heinrich had said, of the argument, the conversation, the debate on what it meant to be a man and have power, but the duke wasn't done. "We are the same, you and I!" he said with a preening sneer.

"I am nothing like you!" Arthur shouted, stepping forward and driving his fist into the man's soft belly. All the rage, all the contempt and frustration and anger and temptation were in that punch, but it still wasn't hard enough. The duke doubled over but remained standing, staggering back a small step toward the edge of the river. The infuriating man grinned at Arthur, who hit him again and again, screaming with rage, but the duke just took the hits and laughed.

"Oh, aren't you like me, boy? You're enjoying this. I know you are. You've been taught your whole life to follow the rules and be a good boy, but it feels good to let oneself go, does it not! Especially," he added, stepping closer to Arthur, "when you know you are stronger than the rest. *That* is the true joy of power, boy! What can the peasants and the paupers do against nobles and royals?"

"*Georgie Porgie, puddin and pie,*" Arthur sang, but the duke just smiled, and Arthur stopped. He shook his head and closed his eyes for a moment, shutting out the duke, shutting out the world, shutting out his own thoughts. Just moments ago, he had been lecturing the Shadowman on restraint. No, not lecturing, *judging*. And here he was using whatever means he had to bring someone down, not lift them up. Arthur felt his father's gaze on him more strongly than ever before and shame washed through his soul, quenching the fire.

"You're not worth my time," he said at last and turned to walk away.

"Where's your dog?" the duke asked.

There was no malice in his words, not really, it was just a question—but Arthur spun, a fireball leaving his hands before he even had a chance to think. It hit the duke high in the chest and threw him backward, over the edge of the riverbank, and down to the dark waters below. Arthur ran forward in time to see the mocking expression on the duke's face turn to horror as he was dragged below the surface by a long, grey form.

CHAPTER 26

An hour or so later, Arthur nursed a second pint of Adnams Broadside with a double Laphroaig on ice for dessert. They were the strongest drinks in the pub, and he was making short work of them. An unopened pack of pork scratchings sat on the windowsill as he stared through the glass at the painfully familiar steps of Marks and Spencer's across the road.

His mind was in turmoil, his thoughts scattered and dark, and so he was going to do his best to drown them.

The image of the duke's horror-stricken face, the thrill of the punches and the power leaving his hands, Heinrich, Steve, Nae. They were all there. Tears for his lost friend sat heavy in his eyes, but the memory of Nae's lips and the smell of vanilla in her hair elicited an entirely different reaction.

He hated himself for thinking of Nae when Steve was dead.

He hated the fact he had pretty much carried on as normal after the death of his best friend, even laughed and joked and shared a passionate snog on the doormat of Nae's home.

'If you bring beer, you're welcome here,' the mat said.

Well, when in York. The Golden Fleece just so happened to be on the walk home, and the gilded sheep hanging over the doorway had lured him in.

Admittedly, it didn't take a lot of effort.

Arthur knew the Fleece well because of its reputation as one of the most haunted pubs in the city, and though the story of the Canadian Airman was true, the poor guy wandered around the bar completely on his own, occasionally hanging out the top window and shouting into the street below.

The pub only had one ghost, and he pretty much kept to himself.

In an effort to draw in more tourists, the manager had placed a skeleton on a bar stool, but now, as it was nearing time, there were only one or two people left in the dark, low-ceilinged pub. That suited Arthur perfectly, and he'd managed to find a seat at the front window overlooking the road outside and the entrance to Shambles.

It did not seem right to him that just a few hours earlier he had raced out of that street with Steve and Nae and fled for cover in Marks and Spencer's.

He laughed to himself and hiccupped. What a ridiculous sentence. He raised his glass to the steps, to Steve's last stand, and finished his drink.

"All right, stranger, fancy another?"

Arthur turned on his seat and it took him a while to focus on the man standing in front of him.

"Si?"

"Haven't seen you in a long time, mate. How are you keeping?"

Arthur thought about lying, but what was the point when the person asking had seen you at your worst and your best for years? Si was the manager of Arthur's favourite pub. One he hadn't been in for nearly a year due to making a total tit of himself when all of this began.

"I've been better," he managed.

Si smiled and nodded to Arthur's nearly empty glass.

"You're not drinking your usual?" he said.

"Fancied something a bit stronger."

"I've got just the thing," Si grinned.

"I think they called time."

"Come on, mate. You know the managers look after each other in this town."

Si walked to the bar and was soon back with a tray of drinks. Two pints and two extra glasses. Arthur watched as Si poured half of a pint of Adnams in each glass and then topped it up with Guinness. He made two drinks and placed Arthur's on the windowsill next to the pork scratchings.

"Cheers."

"Cheers."

The two men touched glasses.

"That's good, what's it called?"

Si grinned.

"That, my friend, is an Oprah."

"Oprah?"

"Don't ask."

Arthur laughed, and there was genuine humour there, a light relief. They relaxed back into silence and took another drink.

"It's been a long time since you've been at my place," Si said after a while. "I think the ass-groove has worked its way out of your stool."

"Ah, that's a shame. I'd been working on that for years."

The silence stretched on again as the two men watched the world go by outside the window.

"I made a bit of a twat of myself though, didn't I," Arthur said.

"Is that why you haven't been back?"

"Yeah, I guess so."

"Mate, I don't know the details, but I know you lost someone close to you. Any kind of drunken behaviour is acceptable there. Except pissing," he added with a smile, trying to break the mood. "You know I don't accept pissing on the floor in my bar."

Arthur chuckled. "Yeah, I remember that lad you threw out when you just opened the place. I swear you nearly got him to the other side of the street!"

"Shouldn't have pissed in my bar then, should he!" Si laughed, taking another drink. "So, what's troubling you, mate? You look like you've seen a ghost. In fact, look like you've seen a few of them."

Arthur glanced around the bar. The only people left were him and Si, the two bar staff, and the ghost of the Canadian Airman who had wandered downstairs. He smiled, but it didn't reach his eyes. There was so much more to that question than he was prepared to answer. He opted for what felt real.

"My dog died," he said, and as he did, he felt a heave in his chest. Tears rolled down his cheeks, and he took a big swallow, then choked on it and finished the whole act with the very definition of an ugly cry.

There was no judgement from Si. He let Arthur cry.

"I'm sorry, mate," he said. "That really sucks."

"You know what the shit part is, though?" Arthur went on. "I met a girl today as well, and she's awesome, but my dog died and I don't know what to feel, you know. I'm really happy and really fucking sad at the same time. And I...I did some things I regret."

"Ah, life." Si grinned at him, raising his glass. "Never fucking simple. I'm sorry about your dog mate, but the best thing about dogs is they always want their humans to be happy you know. So, tell me about this girl. What does she do? What does she look like? When are you going to bring her to the pub? Arthur?"

But Arthur wasn't listening. He was watching a familiar redheaded figure jog across the street toward Shambles.

"That's her!" he said, getting to his feet and knocking over the stool in the process. "Sorry, Si! Great to see you, but I've got to go."

Si, who had been looking out the window trying to catch a glimpse of the girl, turned to see Arthur dance around the Canadian Airman with an apology and dart out of the door. Of course, Si couldn't see the baffled ghost, so it looked to him as though Arthur did a happy little twirl on his way out. That made him smile.

He went back to the window just in time to see the dark-haired young man dodge a taxi, but the mysterious new girl must have already vanished into the shadows of Shambles.

Shame, he thought, but he was sure he'd see her before long.

An unopened packet of pork scratchings caught his eye, and he reached for the half-finished Oprah.

"Don't mind if I do," he said and sat back to watch the world go by.

 ⁓

Arthur caught Nae just inside the entrance to the old street. She turned as he called her name loudly, scaring a group of photo-taking tourists who laughed nervously and moved away. She looked confused for a second, then her face split into a wide grin.

"There you are!"

"What are you doing her? I mean here?" Arthur stammered, trying to catch his breath, instantly regretting the scotch. The world swam at the small effort it took to run across the street, and Nae drifted in and out of focus.

Get a grip man, he told himself. *Not now. Fuck.*

"I came to find you. I didn't really know where I was going, though."

"Why didn't you call?"

"I didn't think."

She seemed nervous, jumpy, looking around the street and over Arthur's shoulder. He turned to see where she was looking.

"Has something happened?" he asked. "Are you okay?"

"Yeah, I mean. Yeah, I think so. I just got a little scared. Can we go somewhere?"

"Where?"

"Just...inside somewhere?"

"Come on." Arthur took her by the hand, his heart racing in a combination of the thrill of seeing her again so soon and concern over what might have happened. A part of his mind immediately filled with an image on the Shadowman, and a wave of anger simmered just below the surface. He knew instinctively the man in black had something to do with whatever had happened.

You should have done something.

The couple walked down the street a small way, Arthur checking all the windows and dark places for things that shouldn't be there, but at this time of night and with the amount of alcohol he'd downed, the world was full of them. He closed his eyes for a moment and took a deep breath to gather some control before leading Nae into the sanctuary of St. Margaret Clitherow's chapel.

Two candles still flickered in the darkness near the small altar, and the dim lights attached to the wooden beams in the ceiling filled the room with a peaceful glow. They sat on two chairs with faded upholstery at the back, and Arthur noticed how Nae was trying to catch her breath.

"What happened?" he asked, taking her hand. "Are you okay?"

The pretty woman smiled, and Arthur grinned to see her dimples again. She was so beautiful. She ran a hand through her bright red hair and then rubbed her neck as she closed her eyes.

"That man," she began, and Arthur felt a lead weight drop into his gut and push the anger higher.

Told you.

His skin pricked in anticipation of what she might say.

"He came to see me," she said.

"What did he do?" Arthur's voice was low and dangerous, his skin on fire, the magic within him boiling.

You should have stopped him.

"Did he hurt you?"

"No, no. Not at all. He...he just turned up at my house with a bottle. I-I don't really remember. He was just a bit creepy, and I got scared. Silly really." She laughed. "I think I drank too much wine too fast."

"Not silly at all," Arthur said, grasping his hands tightly in his lap. "Tell me what happened."

"I don't really know," she replied. "He just knocked on the door and stood there for a bit. I didn't open it, but he didn't go away for ages. I think there's something not quite right about him, and so I came to find you. I didn't feel safe, and I didn't want to go to any of my girlfriends, and my brother and his husband are out of town. Can I—" she paused and bit her lower lip in embarrassment, and

Arthur nearly died. "Can I stay with you, please? Just for tonight, I'll sleep on the couch or in a spare room or something. I'm sorry, it's so weird. We've only just met."

"Of course you can! It's fine, it's fine," Arthur said softly. She was getting herself worked up, and though he was thrilled to see her, he was also furious at what the Shadowman—what fucking Heinrich—might have done to upset her so much. What had he said that made her run out into the night looking for a guy she'd only just met? She didn't even know where he lived! He must have really put the wind up her for her to leave home without really knowing where to go.

"Of course, you can stay with me," he said. "As long as you need. I'll sleep on the couch."

"You're a good man, Arthur," a voice said, but it wasn't Nae.

The young couple turned to see the smiling face of Margaret Clitherow standing in the doorway with William close behind her, holding on to her skirts. The couple stood up awkwardly, as though they were intruding on her space, but she just smiled at them. "I didn't think you would visit so soon," she said, "but you are most welcome."

"You're not in your house," Arthur said, always a champion at stating the obvious when drunk.

"No," Margaret replied. "I found that even after the eclipse, I could wander further afield, and there are certain ties to this place that make it less uncomfortable than it might otherwise be."

She glanced at Nae and smiled softly. Then she looked back at Arthur.

"Will you stay awhile?" she asked.

"Thank you, but I don't think so," Arthur said. He had a sudden urge for a large glass of water and perhaps a Berocca to try to stop the world from spinning.

"It's been a really long day, and I think it's time we all got some sleep." He held out his hand to Nae, and she took it, squeezing her fingers around his. "I don't live too far away," he said to her. "And you'll be able to call whoever you want or use the Wi-Fi. Let people know you're safe so they don't worry. I don't even know if you have a flatmate."

"I do," she said. "Well, I live with my brother and Dan, but they're out of town. It's their anniversary," she added.

"Okay, well, let's go. I'll make us a cup of tea, or we can have a drink."

"I just want to sleep," she said, and there was something in her voice that got through to Arthur. There was exhaustion there. Fear, perhaps. A pleading. Arthur turned to face her.

"Did he hurt you?" he asked again, his own anger rising to the surface and flushing across his cheek and neck in a vivid red that Margaret Clitherow marvelled at.

Kill him.

"No, no." Nae shook her head. "It's just, he, I don't know."

She cried then, and Arthur reached out for her and held her tight.

They stood together, holding each other in the shrine of Saint Margaret Clitherow, and Arthur stroked her hair and kissed the top of her head. Vanilla. But he was drunk and swaying. He could barely focus. His mind raced with disconnected thoughts and images. His vision blurred at the edges, and his head spun.

"Bloody Oprah," he said.

"Pardon?"

"Nothing. It's okay," he soothed. "He won't hurt you. I've got you."

He stared at the flickering candles as Nae sobbed quietly in his arms, and the meagre flame flashed in his eyes like fire.

Margaret Clitherow shivered when she saw him. The young man was full of goodness, but there was a rage deep within that the fires of the candles magnified in his eyes.

"Peace be with you, Arthur," she said, reaching out to place a delicate hand on the side of his face. She could feel the fury radiating from him. "Be at peace. What is done is done. You do not see it now. But your anger will not help."

Arthur could barely control himself. The raw emotions and the alcohol flowing through him made the world tumble and spin.

He could feel Nae's fear; it was visceral and real, but as Margaret Clitherow touched him, his focus shifted, and through the magic, he saw her again. He saw the moment of her arrest this time and the terrified, tear-soaked face of a young boy who pointed to the priest hole as the authorities ransacked the house. Through Margaret's eyes, he watched as William, full of fear, gave away the location of his mother's secret that would ultimately condemn her to death. He gasped and looked into the deep black eyes of the beautiful saint. She smiled.

"He knew no better," she said softly. "And so, the fault lies not with him but with me."

She held William's hand in her own and walked to the chapel door. "Take this young lady home and get some rest," she said, watching as Arthur nodded and walked with Nae up Shambles toward home. The young redhead leaning heavily on the tall, dark-haired man.

"I fear you are going to need it," the saint said softly to herself and returned to the chapel to pray.

CHAPTER 27

Arthur and Nae arrived at his apartment without incident, though Arthur barely blinked the whole walk home. He had watched the shadows carefully for any sign of the unusual, straining his eyes against the darkness and the drink. The cats were out in force, and a few ghosts crossed their path, but nothing bothered them. The occasional flap of silken wings set his teeth on edge and sent shivers down his spine, but other than that, the streets were empty. There was a definite tension though, an underlying nervousness in the lamplit streets of the city.

They passed through pools of soft orange light, and Arthur wished that Steve was with them. Steve always made him feel safe. Even with all his power and all his experience, there was something wonderfully comforting about having the little dog running at his feet, peeing on the lampposts without a care in the world.

Opening the door to the empty flat was worse than he expected, up there with the first time he'd arrived home to find that Wendy, his ex, had moved all her stuff out.

It wasn't that Steve was gone. It was that it felt like he was still there.

His bowls lay near the door, his ball abandoned in the middle of the floor where he had left it. The remote control, with the extra-large buttons designed for the elderly but perfect for a dog with little paws, sat on Steve's side of the couch. But Arthur would have to process all that later.

Nae hadn't spoken and she blinked in the sharp light as Arthur flicked the switch on in the living room. He left her near the door for a moment and dashed over to turn a reading lamp on, then returned to turn off the main light. The brightness in the room settled, and he guided Nae to the couch.

"I'll make us a cup of tea," he said and walked into the kitchen to fill the kettle. He pulled two mugs out of the cupboard and gave one a quick clean with a dishcloth. He gripped the sink with both hands while he waited for the kettle to boil and fought for control over the spinning room.

The drinks were definitely a mistake.

When will you learn?

He glanced to the pretty redhead on his couch as the kettle bubbled and steam filled the small kitchen, and he thought about what *she* had been through in the last few hours.

It was too much.

Even for the most logical and rational person, it was too much. In fact, being logical and rational made it so much worse, and he should know.

He remembered his first night with all this kind of chaos and how he'd got a train the next day and gone back to his parents...for months. The poor woman needed him. He understood. He could help.

Arthur reached up to the top cupboard and pulled down the box of Nurofen, popping two of the little tablets from their foil and swallowing them dry. He put a Berocca in a glass of cold water and let it sit and fizz while he made two cups of tea.

"How do you take your tea?" he asked.

Nae turned to him and smiled. The dimples were back—a good sign.

"Milk and two sugars, please...and leave the bag in."

"A woman after my own heart." Arthur grinned.

He brought the steaming mugs into the front room and placed

them on the small table in front of the couch, sitting beside Nae, who smiled shyly.

"Thank you," she said.

"Pleasure. Look, I'm so sorry about today. I can't imagine what you must be thinking."

"It was...a lot." She nodded, her eyes downcast.

"It sure was, but I totally understand. I get it. I was where you are now a year ago."

"It's not every day you find out ghosts are real," she said.

Arthur nodded and took a careful sip of his tea. Nae left hers on the table and clasped her hands in her lap.

"I'm really sorry," she said. "This is so silly, but I didn't know where else to go."

"I told you, it's fine. Look, I promise I'm not a creep, okay. I'll sleep on the couch, and you can have my bed. There might be a bit of dog hair on there, but it's clean," he said.

"Steve," Nae said, her eyes brimming with tears. "I'm so sorry."

It was Arthur's turn to stare into nothingness. "Yeah," he said, "it's a bit shit. I'll see if I can find him tomorrow, if he's...in this world."

"Jesus," Nae said.

"I know. I'll—" Arthur's voice caught, and he swallowed before continuing. "If I can get him, I'll bury him in Museum Gardens. He'd like that. Lots of squirrels." Tears rolled down his face, and he jumped a little as Nae wiped them away with her finger.

"Let's go to bed." She took him by the hand, and Arthur didn't argue.

The young couple lay in each other's arms. Fully clothed. Their shoes on the floor beside the bed. Arthur's hand rested on her shoulder, and Nae rested her head on his chest, rising and falling with his steady breathing. Both were wide awake, staring at the ceiling and deep in thought. Sleep was not coming easy, and the clock on the wall had both hands straight up, two softly glowing lightsabres pointing to midnight. It had been a very long day.

"Have you ever been in love?" Nae asked in a voice barely more than a whisper. She could hear Arthur's heart through his chest, and she smiled at the strong and steady rhythm.

"Yes," he replied, just as quiet.

The silence settled like an invitation, and so he told her about Wendy, about how they were university sweethearts, how he thought they'd last forever, but she left him suddenly a few years ago. How she never looked back as she walked alongside the long GNER that would take her out of the city, and his life. How that was the last time he ever saw her.

A woman he shared years of his life with, gone in a moment.

"Do you miss her?"

"No," he said, "not anymore." And he knew that he truly meant it. It was amazing how life could change. "It was coming," he admitted. "She was a woman, and I was just a bairn. I see that now."

"Has there been anyone else?" Nae whispered, and she smiled again as Arthur's chest rose sharply.

"Kind of," he said.

"What do you mean, kind of?"

"Well, we only knew each other for two days, but I thought there was something there and...I know she felt the same," he said.

"What happened?"

"She died."

"Oh, I'm so sorry," Nae placed her hand flat on his chest.

"Thanks, but it's okay. It's all a bit weird."

"How?"

"Well..." he paused. How the hell was he going to explain this? But she'd seen his world now, hadn't she? He closed his eyes. In for a penny, in for a pound. "Promise you won't freak out?"

She raised herself onto her elbow and looked at him with wide eyes. They were so close to each other. Her hair fell over her face, and she brushed it away. The smell of vanilla filled the air. She didn't speak. She just looked.

"She was a ghost," Arthur said quietly. "I didn't know. I met her when all this started, and I had no idea. She seemed completely real to me."

Again, Nae didn't speak. She just kept looking at him, and Arthur had to look away. Slowly, she rested her head on his chest, and the silence spread between them.

Arthur's heart was racing. He'd ruined it. He knew he'd ruined it, but Nae drummed her fingers on his chest and then rested them gently.

"Two days," she said.

It was so quiet, he barely heard her.

"I've never been in love. I spent so long travelling and working I just didn't stop."

"Well," Arthur said, "there's always hope." He was pretty sure he could feel her smile through his T-shirt.

With the press of Nae's body against his own, Arthur Crazy fell asleep.

CHAPTER 28

Arthur woke with a start, gasping for breath and fighting against dark dreams that seemed all too real. Faces and images flashed before him and he struggled and cried out, panting and kicking. It took him a long time to tear himself awake, and when he did, he sat on the bed and panted to catch his breath. His body rippled with electric charge, and his pulse roared in his ears. It was still dark outside, and the lightsabres on the wall hung like a drooping moustache in the dim light as he looked at the time.

Twenty to four.

Fucksake.

Arthur realised Nae was no longer in the bed. He swung his legs over and groaned as he sat up. His mouth felt clammy with the taste of beer and toothpaste, and he staggered into the living room, gripping hold of the wall to steady himself.

"Nae?" he said to the dark, but there was no answer. He hadn't felt her leave, but it must have been recently. It was probably her moving that had woken him up. With that in mind, he crashed back into the bedroom to grab his shoes, hopping into the kitchen on one foot as he pulled the black Vans on without socks. He grabbed the forgotten Berocca and drained it in one, dropping the glass into the sink and moving away. He heard a smash but didn't care.

"Steve!" he shouted and then shook his head, not ready to process that just yet. One thing at a time.

He grabbed his phone and blinked in the light. No messages. He turned all the lights on and looked quickly around the small home.

No note. Bollocks. He *had* scared her off, hadn't he!

What do I do? He was wracked with indecision. Should he go out to find her? Would she want him to? Why did she leave if she did? Where did she go?

He gathered his keys from the small table near the door, stood on Steve's squeaky toy, and closed his eyes against the sharp noise. He yanked the door open and stopped.

The Shadowman.

Heinrich.

"You!"

"Me."

"What are you doing here?" Arthur demanded. Heinrich looked young and fresh, and there was a glimmer in his eye that Arthur didn't like. It was a sneer. A dark shadow began to crawl through his mind, and he knew instinctively that he had something to do with Nae leaving.

"Where is she?" he demanded.

"The woman?"

"Yes, the woman!" Arthur shouted. "Nae! Where is she? I know you know. Did you take her?"

The man was infuriatingly calm, his face expressionless except for what Arthur took to be a small smirk tugging at the corner of his mouth.

"I have not been in your home, Arthur Crazy," he said.

"That's not what I asked!"

Heinrich looked down at Arthur's hands. They were gripping his shirt, the two men standing on the doorstep. Arthur had stepped through the door and grabbed him. The light from inside washed onto the stone steps and cast long shadows into the street.

"Let go," Heinrich said simply.

"Fuck you! I know you did something, and you're going to tell me!" Arthur tightened his grip and dragged the Shadowman into the apartment, but something strange happened. Although the man in black moved toward the door, he stopped dead as though he had hit a wall. Arthur lost his grip, fell into his house, and tumbled to the floor.

He looked up at the dark figure, silhouetted in his doorway, the light unable to penetrate the pure black of his clothes, the hat pulled so low it hid his eyes and nose. The only thing visible was the man's sharp chin and the curled lips of his smiling mouth.

"You have much to learn, Arthur," he said. "I thought it was I who would learn from you, but I think you have shown me all that you are capable of. But I thank you. You provided wise counsel. Though your use is not at an end."

"Where is she!" Arthur shouted, rising to his feet and firing a blast of purple magic at the man standing in his door.

He didn't hesitate. He didn't warn him. He just attacked.

The magic hit Heinrich in the face and snapped his head backward, the cap flying into the night as the Shadowman stumbled and fell down the steps. It was much more powerful than Arthur had expected, and the savagery of it shocked him, but he barely paused. Instead, he strode through the door and leaped from the steps as the man in black crashed to the ground. Images of Georgie Porgie flashed in his mind.

Peasants and paupers. Nobles and kings.

The true joy of power.

Lights flicked on in the surrounding flats, but Arthur didn't care. He stood over Heinrich, grabbed him by the collar with one hand, and punched down again and again with the other, screaming and shouting.

"Tell me where she is!"

Purple light flickered and sparked as the skin on his knuckles split and bled. It cast dancing shadows on the Shadowman and on the walls of the houses around them, but Arthur was blind to the pain and the warning.

"I do not know," the man gasped, turning his bloodied face away from Arthur. "I never know what happens after."

"After?"

Arthur dropped the Shadowman and ran.

He took shortcuts no other person could, sprinting along the narrow streets, ignoring his fears and racing through walls, crossing alleys and buildings in the blink of an eye.

Out of one wall, through another.

Arthur ran for all he was worth, chasing after a sudden and intense premonition. His hands began to shake as he crossed Shambles Market and burst through the shops to fly across Parliament. The sound of barking filled the night, and he put his head down, keeping as straight a line as he could, heading like an arrow toward Skeldergate Bridge and the river. Above him, sleek black shapes traced his path in the sky on near-silent wings. Cats, grotesques, and one remaining green figure watched him go. Roger de Clifford smiled and then began to rattle his cage in excitement as Arthur skirted the green hill of Clifford's Tower. The echoes of the dogs faded behind. His whole body burned and ached by the time he hit the bridge and crossed the river. He was halfway over when he saw the lights flashing in the trees and on the rooftops of the houses on the other side. Blue and red. The unusual but horrifyingly recognisable colours danced like muted fireworks in the night. Arthur slowed and gasped for air as he leaned against the city walls on Skeldergate, fighting the panic that surged within.

And the Shadowman took him.

He emerged from the darkness of the walls and dragged the stunned man to the ground by his collar. He heaved him backward up the steps and through the locked metal gate. There was a moment where he let go, just a moment as he flashed through the dark paths while Arthur's power let him fall through the gate, but then the gloved hand was back, dragging him through the dark by his collar.

Arthur struggled to stand, choking and kicking as he tried to get purchase on the stones, his own hands gripped around the wrist of the Shadowman, but there was no give. The man was too strong.

Heinrich flung Arthur against the city wall, and his head smashed into the stones, once, twice, again, the Shadowman's grip like iron as he pulled Arthur further along the path. The lights bouncing on the walls and trees spun in Arthur's eyes as the world blurred and tumbled with savage flashes of pain. He felt a momentary weightlessness as the man in black threw him, and he hit a tree, crashing through sharp branches and falling to the ground in a heap. Terror and anger drove him to his feet, and he thrust his hand out, feeling the burn of his magic as it rippled up his arm, but the Shadowman was already there, insanely fast in the darkness, gripping Arthur's fist in his own hand, forcing it up. The fire burst and burned, but the man just roared and gripped tighter. Arthur cried out as the bones in his hand ground together and his knuckles cracked and broke. The magic died. The last errant sparks fizzed away into the canopy above like weak fireworks.

The two men were face to face, inches apart in the darkness. The Shadowman held Arthur in a macabre dance. The look on his face was one of pure delight as his dark features creased in savage pleasure.

"This is what it means to be alive," he said.

Then he smiled and let go.

Arthur dropped to the ground, panting and gasping, clutching at his shattered hand. "Why?" he managed to spit. He could taste the bile and blood in his mouth, and a burning on the side of his face. His vision swam, and his body felt far away.

"Because I can," the man said, kneeling in front of Arthur and lifting his chin with a sharp finger. "Peasants and paupers. Nobles and kings. I heard. I know. I understand."

Arthur coughed and spat blood onto the grass. It glistened by the light of the emergency vehicles flashing through the small gaps in the trees.

"You feel the same," Heinrich said. "I know you do. You all do. Rules and laws, do this and don't do that. You are ants! Now that I have one of your bodies, I see it more clearly than ever. No, no! Don't pass out. Not yet."

He gripped Arthur's face tightly in his hand and then punched him with his other arm. Arthur's nose broke, sending flashes of crackling electricity across his vision. The Shadowman swam in the dark places between the lightning bolts. Smiling. Always smiling. Visions of Arthur's dreams came back to him in the flashes. The Shadowman had been there. Standing at a door. Holding a bottle. Now inside. Smiling. But he hadn't been smiling at Arthur. Warm blood poured from Arthur's face and soaked the hand of the man in black.

"I so desperately wanted to be human that I didn't even stop to think about that fact that *you* barely even want to be human. You cling to these fictions of nobility and ethics when you should be revelling in your place at the very top of the food chain!"

He pulled his hand away from Arthur's face and ran his tongue over his palm and up his fingers, gathering the warm blood into his mouth. He smiled the whole time, and Arthur saw his teeth were stained red.

"I have been a man for a few hours, and already I know far more than you. Though you are interesting, Arthur," he added, getting to his feet and stretching in the small circle of trees. Arthur slumped and tried to breathe, tried to gather himself, but his body was beaten and broken. The movies never got that right. Arthur had been smashed against a wall, thrown against a tree, had his hand crushed, and his face beaten. He was barely hanging on. There were patches of light in the small gaps, but Arthur couldn't tell if it was the sky behind the trees, the flashing lights on the road nearby, or his own vision playing tricks on him.

He closed his eyes and descended into darkness.

There was no peace.

His eyes opened again, and he had no idea how much time had passed. It could have been seconds. It could have been hours. The grinning face of Heinrich was inches away, holding Arthur by the hair. He was barely conscious, the world a blur—soft around the edges and sharp in the middle—the Shadowman's smiling face at the centre of it all. There was nothing Arthur could do. He was lost, broken, defeated.

He closed his eyes again.

Angry barks and howls filled the world, and the trees danced in the early morning light.

Something crashed through the branches, and Arthur's eyes snapped open as the Shadowman dropped him and spun away with a shout. He fell face first to the floor and scrambled in the dirt, unable to see what was happening. There was a roar and a cry, a wet thud, and angry shouts. Arthur could feel his body being pushed and shoved by clambering figures, but there was nothing he could do about it. He was barely holding on.

His head fell to the side, and he scraped some of the blood away from his eyes, blinking and trying to focus. The Shadowman was on the ground, fighting desperately against a snarling mass of animals.

It was the pack of dead dogs.

Somehow, bizarrely, in *this* world.

A Doberman with half a face tore at Heinrich's arm, and a large Alsatian ripped into his stomach with teeth and claws. There were ragged bodies everywhere, ribs showing, skulls shining in the darkness, blood splashing onto the grass. Heinrich made a desperate lunge for the throat of the Doberman and managed to catch it, crushing the neck and breaking it with a sickening snap. The body dropped onto Arthur, and all went black.

"Arthur."

His name in the dark.

"Arthur, it's me."

So, this was what awaited on the other side. He sobbed. It wasn't fair. He knew the voice so well. Tears fell down his cheeks.

Tears.

He could feel them.

The warmth.

"Arthur."

Pain ravaged his body, and his eyes blinked open. Piercing light stabbed him, and he closed them tight again.

"Arthur, get up, you dickhead!"

He groaned and cried out, a wave of nausea ripping through him, and he tried to move.

"Arthur, you need to move. You need to go!"

Arthur's eyes flickered open, and he saw the shape of the speaker, indistinct but recognisable, nonetheless. Always recognisable.

"Steve?" he croaked.

"It's me, mate, yeah!"

Steve licked Arthur's face tenderly and nudged him with his nose.

"You need to go," he begged. "You need to go now. I don't know what the fuck happened, but you need to run."

"I..."

"The police are here."

"I haven't..."

"Arthur!"

The urgency in Steve's voice cut through the layers of pain and grogginess, and Arthur rolled and pushed himself up, crying out as fresh agony coursed up his shattered hand. He opened his eyes and looked directly into the remains of the Shadowman, his body barely recognisable, utterly savaged by wild animals who were nowhere to be seen. One dark eye hung on a grisly stalk. The other was gone.

Arthur vomited onto the grass, and his body felt as though it was on fire. A crashing through the trees and torchlight in the dim morning light drew his attention. The leaves above shifted and moved with the flapping of wings. Shouts and whistles in the distance.

"Run!" Steve shouted, and Arthur staggered to his knees and scrambled forward, clambering over the remains of the dead man. He aimed for the wall but knew he wouldn't make it, could never make it onto the path. The footsteps were louder now. Running.

Sharp beams of light flashed through the trees. There was no way he could get away.

"Hey!"

"There's someone there!"

"Stop! Police!"

Arthur cried out and surged forward. With a gargantuan effort, he pushed himself around a thick tree trunk and did the only thing he could. Instead of climbing onto the path and trying to make a getaway with a body that could barely move, he pushed his way *through* the wall and collapsed inside a sarcophagus of stone.

It was a stillness like death, though the pain remained.

Arthur was inside the wall, crushed on all sides by heavy, centuries-old stone, a blackness so complete, it pushed at him from every angle, but he had no choice. There was nowhere else for him to go.

He forced his way through, focussing all his willpower on keeping the magic flowing. If he lost concentration for one moment, he...he had no idea what would happen. He always imagined it was like the islanders who walked across hot coals; if you put your mind somewhere else, the body could do anything. But he didn't want to think of that now. He couldn't.

Arthur crawled through the dark on his hands and knees, trying to keep a straight line within the wall. He knew he was heading away from home, but that didn't matter. He just had to get away. There was no time to think of anything else. Just keep moving.

His head broke through the wall suddenly, and Arthur gasped in the open air, half in and half out of the wall. He had only gone a few metres and veered off course, but the tableau in front of him blazed into his vision, and he paused.

The familiar row of stone houses glowed by the light of the rising sun and the blue and red of the emergency vehicles.

Ambulances, a fire engine, police everywhere. Car, vans, and trucks. High-vis vests lined the street. Police with guns. You never saw guns in England, but that wasn't the worst of it.

Over the heads of the golden daffodils, Arthur saw Nae's house.

Police tape fluttered in the morning breeze, marking a yellow door open to the world.

A door with a welcome mat.

Arthur cried out and rolled back into the stone, back into black.

CHAPTER 29

"Officer Boardman? Officer Mark Boardman?"

"Yes. Can I help you?"

Officer Boardman looked over his newspaper, but when he saw the speaker, he folded it and put it down next to his coffee. The clothes said off-duty, but the expression on the stern face was all business.

"I understand you were covering the area of Museum Gardens and surrounds yesterday afternoon into the early evening, is that correct?"

"Yes, it is. Can I ask who wants to know?"

"I do."

"And you are?"

The man presented him with an ID, and Officer Boardman nodded. "How can I help you, sir?"

A photograph was placed on the newspaper. Officer Boardman picked it up and looked at it. His heart sank and he closed his eyes. Fifteen years in the job, and he never got used to this sort of thing.

"You recognise the girl?" the man said, sitting opposite and leaning on the table. His arms were thick with muscle and the kind of tattoos men usually got when serving overseas in dangerous places. The sleeves were rolled up to the elbows. He did not wear a tie.

Officer Boardman looked at the image of the smiling, beautiful young woman, dimples in her cheeks as she laughed at someone off-camera. It was a photograph probably taken from a social media profile as they all seemed to be these days. Nothing horrible about it in its own right, but the policeman's instincts were good. Men like this did not show photographs like this if the news was good.

He nodded.

"I saw her leaving the gardens yesterday as they were closing the gates."

"Time?"

"A little before eight p.m."

"You're certain?"

"Yes sir. It was the end of my shift."

The other man smiled, though it did not reach his eyes. Beat cops could always be counted on to get the time right at shift's end.

"And you're certain it was her? We have unconfirmed reports she was seen in the gardens in the company of a man. We would very much like to speak to him, but we need a positive ID."

"I'm certain. I remember the hair." He tilted the photograph and sighed. "She was with a young IC1 male, dark hair, about six two, black shirt, blue jeans, black Yorkshire Terrier dog. They headed down Lendal, laughing and joking. They made a cute couple."

He sat back with a sigh.

"What happened to her?"

The man across the table looked him in the eyes and shook his head, taking the photograph back and placing it into a manila envelope.

"You don't want to know," he said.

He pulled another photograph out of the folder and placed it on the paper. It was black and white, taken from CCTV somewhere in the city.

"Is this the man?" he asked.

Boardman didn't pick it up this time, but instead he leaned over the image and nodded.

"That's him. Do you have a name?"

"Not yet. We're working on it."

He snatched up the photograph and stood, nodding at the policeman and turning away.

"Wait!" Officer Boardman said, getting to his feet. "Is she? Did he? Is she dead?"

The man paused and looked back, the hard eyes appeared to soften for a moment, but it was quickly controlled, and he nodded again. "Are you on duty today?"

"I am."

"Be careful. This man is an animal. He tore her apart."

The news spread around the station quickly, and there was an unusual silence in the locker room as stab vests were secured and last checks made before heading out. The feel of the city had changed. The police were on edge. Appalled and heartbroken. A spate of murders of such disgusting violence in their beautiful town. Death wasn't uncommon, but not like this.

Never like this.

This was different.

They were briefed heavily about any interactions with the media. They all knew the official lines, the pale story to tell, but the horror of the previous night was locked in all their minds.

The first responders to the house on Baile Hill Terrace were nowhere to be seen—locked down, debriefed, and counselled.

The scene in the house was bad enough, but the grisly discovery of a second body on Baile Hill had rocked them.

It wasn't just the savagery of it; it was the fact that it had happened while the police were just metres away.

They chased the suspect from the scene—he moved like an animal, they said—but somehow, he got away.

And the man had been alive.

For a while.

There were other reports, whispers and comments passed from ear to ear—the kind of stuff that would be ignored as fantasy in any other workplace, but coppers don't exaggerate.

They don't need to.

One officer said she'd chased away a great black bird as it pulled at the tattered eyeball of the horrifically injured man. He had cried out some indecipherable words and then collapsed. She tried to save him but didn't know where to start. When backup arrived, she was covered in his blood and sobbing against a tree.

And those weren't the only deaths in the once peaceful city.

A homeless man was found decapitated on a park bench by a student out for an early morning run. There were unsubstantiated rumours of a murder in a traveller camp, and a much-loved shopkeeper was discovered by his teenage daughter slumped over the newspapers on the counter of his shop.

In the space of twenty-four hours, all their lives had changed. They could *feel* it. They already feared the city would never be the same again.

But there was a name now.

A name to match the face.

A chief suspect.

They all knew his picture, and they held it in their mind's eye as they climbed into the vans that would take them to his flat.

The home of Arthur Benedict Crazy.

A name to match a monster.

CHAPTER 30

Arthur didn't know how he got home, but the sun was high in the sky when he finally made it to the stone steps that led to his front door. He dragged himself up them on his last legs, barely able to move. The door was open, but he didn't care. He was past caring. He hadn't even bothered to hide in the last few streets before his house. He was too tired. Too raw. Too overcome with agony of the mind, body, and soul. There could be anyone waiting for him in the house, and he didn't care. He pushed the door with his shoe, and it swung inwards.

Steve sat on the carpet, growling with bared teeth, his hackles raised, but the growl soon turned to a whine when he saw his best friend.

Arthur collapsed and pushed the door shut with his foot. Steve was there instantly, licking him all over, bombarding him with questions.

"How did you get back? What happened? How did you get away?"

"Shh, buddy," he croaked. "It's okay."

"No, it isn't!" the dog yelped, jumping around in an anxious circle. "How is it okay?"

"You saved me, mate!" Arthur coughed, and blood splashed

onto the green carpet. "You're alive. We're both alive. I'd be dead if it weren't for you. I thought you were dead. How did you…?"

"I became the alpha," Steve said quickly, sitting down and scratching his ear. He was nervous and jumpy and didn't stay still for long. "We've got to go; we can't stay here!"

"Alpha?" Arthur groaned.

"Why are you focused on this? We've got bigger problems!"

"But…"

"I can talk, okay! Becoming alpha is easy when you can tell them all to sit! Now come on! We've got to go!"

"Why?" Arthur said, falling to the floor and looking up at the ceiling. He sobbed. Everything hurt. "What's the point?"

"The cops! The cops will come looking for you, and if they do, we're screwed. You need to get away, rest, have time to think!"

"He killed her!" Arthur cried. "Just because! Just because he fucking could. That's what he said." Arthur screamed in anguish and punched the wall, then the floor, then threw Steve's dog bowl across the room where it shattered somewhere in the kitchen. He cried out at the agony of his broken hand and then punched the wall again, relishing the pain. He fired magic from his hands blindly into the world, scorching the walls, setting fire to the Millenium Falcon, exploding the TV. Steve darted away in panic and hid under the kitchen table. "I could've stopped him!" Arthur roared. "I should've stopped him, but I was trying to be a good man and fucking look where that got me! Aaargh!" Arthur turned the fire on himself, bunching his fists into his chest and summoning everything he had left. He vanished in an incandescent explosion of flame, but when it faded, he was still there, not a mark on him, impervious to his own destructive power. Arthur broke down and curled into a ball, holding his head in his bleeding hands and rocking back and forth. "It's not fucking about me," he sobbed. "It was her. All her. She was innocent. She was fucking…amazing. Amazing! What did she do to deserve this? Nothing. Just met the wrong fucking guy on the wrong fucking day. It should have been me! I should've fucking died when the Fetch got me. When I was supposed to!"

Arthur cried for a long time and Steve crept across the floor to lick his tears and nuzzle his face while behind him the apartment started to burn.

"I know, mate," the dog said. "I know. I'm so sorry. She was unreal. But you're not going to be able to help her from a prison cell."

"What do you mean, help her? She's dead! She's dead because of me! Because of that fucking animal!"

"Since when has that stopped you from helping people!" Steve said, and then, fed up with talking to Arthur's backside...he bit it. "Get up!" he growled with his mouth full as Arthur cried out and turned over to shake him off. "We'll mourn her later. We'll mourn *with* her. You know as well as I do that death isn't the end. Don't give up now." He let go and sat back, panting heavily. "But she still needs your help, Arthur. She's out there in the city. Lost and alone."

"That bastard!" Arthur moaned, rubbing his hands over his face...and then his arse.

"Is dead!" Steve said. "And there's nothing you can do about it. But if you stay here, they'll pin it on you, and it's not like you can tell them what really happened! You can turn yourself in later when we've had time to figure out a plan. You've got alibis, but right now, the cops are on a witch hunt."

In the distance, the sound of fast, powerful engines grew louder. Tyres screeched to a halt in nearby streets and Steve's ears twitched at the sound of heavy boots.

"Get up, you prick!" he shouted. "I didn't run through the night with a pack of devil dogs just to see you give in! Get up!"

Arthur rolled to his knees and pushed himself up, crying out and clasping his broken hand to his chest. There was blood everywhere. Steve jumped and spun on the spot. Barking loudly.

"What do we do?" Arthur said to himself, swaying a little as he stooped to pick up the little puppy and gather him under his one good arm. He headed to the door and stood on the edge of the steps, looking down into the street. Nae was out there somewhere. He wasn't going to leave her. He couldn't.

The sound of running boots drew nearer. Blue and red lights reflected from the windows and joined the sun as it bathed the red bricks of the city in golden light.

Arthur looked at the city walls and closed his eyes for a moment, gathering his thoughts.

"Hang on a minute, lad," he said, patting Steve on the head. "I've got a great idea."

ABOUT THE AUTHOR

In 2025, Alex became a librarian, fulfilling a life-long dream since he hid Stephen King novels in Asterix comics at his local library when he was a kid. Now, like his childhood librarian heroes, he gets to pretend he didn't see anything while accidentally leaving cool books on the tables.

(Honestly, I'm not sure I need to write anything else because being a librarian is the coolest thing that's ever happened to me. Um, sorry to my wife, kids, family, and friends).

WWW.ABFINLAYSON.COM

facebook.com/abfinlaysonauthor

x.com/ABFinlayson1

instagram.com/a.b.finlayson

www.ingramcontent.com/pod-product-compliance
Lightning Source LLC
Chambersburg PA
CBHW061656190726
48289CB00006B/1895